In a future built on the motto "Fences and bars make men free to rebel," fences and bars—and even chains—are in abundance. Humanity, guided by an Artificial Intelligence system called the Evolutionary Quantum Leap (EQL), fences itself in 12 communities, completely shutting out the International Wilderness. Men and women cast off all responsibility and live for themselves.

Utopia? Well, the EQL and its mouthpiece, Our Benevolent Liberator, make it sound that way. But one regular citizen, Berdin Dwate, isn't so sure.

His suspicions are confirmed by a barefoot stranger who claims to be from the International Wilderness and whose first words to Berdin are, "Follow me." In spite of himself, Berdin follows—and freedom takes on a whole new meaning . . .

ian

HARVESTING AFTER THE FALL

Ben —
Christ calls us His friend.

J.F Baldwin Jr.
John 15:13

J.F. Baldwin

FISHERmen
press

© 1994 by J.F. Baldwin and Fishermen Press
P.O. Box 104, Manitou Springs, CO 80829
(719) 685-5269

First Printing 1994
Library of Congress Catalog Card Number: 93-090941
ISBN 0-936163-18-6

Cover Design by Jeff Stoddard

To Linda:
My ever-graceful partner for the One True Dance.

PREFACE

The world described in this book parallels our own world in many ways. It should. This is a book about our world—only not exactly. More accurately, it's a book about what "might have been"—an alternate reality. For this reason, there are two things this book is *not*.

This book is *not* an effort to predict future events. I can't even tell you who'll win the Series next year.

This book is *not* a new translation or summation of the Bible. Christ died and rose again about 2,000 years ago, and when He returns He will usher in the Day of Judgment. I believe this is the central truth of all reality.

This book is a story—a reminder, like a note stuck on the refrigerator that says, "read your Bible." Just in case you forgot, the Creator of the universe wants to be your best friend. Even if you're as impulsive and crotchety as a certain apostle (or a certain author), this friend is calling you. And he's calling you not just to receive friendship, but to live the same kind of love and loyalty He exudes every minute.

This book is just a story—with a little truth snuck in.

CHAPTER ONE

"[T]he whole world once very nearly died of broad-mindedness and the brotherhood of all religions."
—G.K. Chesterton, *The Everlasting Man*

"Our Benevolent Liberator's got the longest canine teeth I've ever seen," Berdin thought distractedly. He lay on his greyish-white couch, hands behind his head, vaguely paying attention to the Conventional Wisdom Output (CWO) monitor in front of him. A yellow street light shone through the bars of his cell door. Outside, fugitive footsteps echoed through the night.

The rhetoric poured forth from the monitor, bouncing off the cement walls and rattling in Berdin's subconscious. " . . . more tolerance necessary . . . must be open to other lifestyles . . . preference for human flesh no different than vegetarians . . . narrow-minded bigots . . . ." Our Benevolent Liberator, Global President Arthur Aphek, was at it again. He addressed the public every evening at 6:00, and then repeated his speech at 10:00. It made one wonder when he found time to run the world—but then, he had a lot of help. Every person in the world was a state employee in one sense or another.

Berdin groaned and flicked off the CWO monitor. He picked up the latest issue of *Nudes Illustrated* and leafed through it absent-mindedly. He couldn't wait for morning to arrive, for work to begin again. Was he crazy? He liked his job. Everyone else said their jobs were awful: tedious or unfulfilling or just plain too much work. But most of them had never worked in The Field. In The Field a man could take off his shirt and feel the sun on his back and the sweat brimming on his brow. Wind moved through the green rows of crops, gently exulting in the vibrant life growing richer every day. No harsh yellow lights glared, no shoes clattered on metal grating, and no voice chattered cliches in your ear. Life seemed valuable somehow, out in The Field.

Most of Berdin's acquaintances also found life valuable, but in a less esoteric sense. Life was valuable because their son just earned a promotion to Third Assistant Secretary to the Senate (which meant 750 extra lottery tickets per salary cycle), or because Happy Hour at the Palace had draft beer for just six lottery tickets, or because the Era of Mindless Censors was a thing of the past and NBC now showed Topless Dancing every night from 7 till 9. Working, for most people, only detracted from enjoying the fullest fruits of life, and to that degree infringed upon the truly important. Fortunately for these citizens, the Student Leaders Organizing Time for Humanity (SLOTH) had been successful in lobbying for a 30-hour work week and were beginning to demonstrate the need for further cut-backs. Every sensible person on the block was sending their tax-deductible donations to help SLOTH fight the tyranny of the time clock.

Berdin felt anger boiling in his stomach whenever he thought about it. Work was all that kept him here, in Block A12 of Coastal Community Twelve. If it wasn't for The Field . . . those crazy kids in SLOTH! He cocked his leg to kick his synthetic marble coffee table, and then checked himself. Guilt rushed through his mind. He was being intolerant—he was so often intolerant—he had to stop. Berdin reached for a much-used CD, #6 in the series on values clarification, and inserted it in his CD player. A soothing female voice reminded him that every man must choose the path he will walk, and no man may judge another's choice. The intolerance of the Close-Minded Age stifled man's natural urges, thereby creating guilty, un-actualized men and women. Only through cooperation grounded in tolerance can humankind achieve a perfect society. Berdin lay back on his couch, closed his eyes, and let the patient, innocuous voice lull him to sleep. When he awoke it was morning, his CD player's batteries were dead, and he had an idea.

Chapter Two

"The worst solitude is to be destitute of sincere friendship."
—Sir Francis Bacon, *De Dignitate et Augmentis Scientiarum*

A short, wiry redhead dressed in red and blue community clothes stepped out of his second-floor unit in Block A12 and rolled the barred gate closed. He turned his key in the lock, rattled the door to test it, descended the dilapidated black metal stairs, and then moved westward down the cement avenue. His footsteps echoed in time with the tune he was humming, gently breaking the stillness of early morning.

Berdin was the type of man people noticed. At a party, on the street, in a meeting, he stuck out—not because he was particularly tall or handsome or flashy or loud (perhaps a little loud)—but because he was painfully self-aware. His nervous attention to the image he presented was a kind of electricity.

People were attentive to his presence just because he was so eager not to stand out—all his efforts to appear normal conspired to reveal him. This self-consciousness haunted him, and fed on itself, and redoubled his anxiety. He was like a painting that, due to its artist's express intent to portray neutrality, excited controversy.

His jaw was square and tan, and usually dabbled with stubble. (He couldn't always be bothered with shaving.) His hair was thick and tousled—not unkempt but often troubled. Bags showed darkly under his eyes—a result of restless nights wrestling in his mind—but these were seldom noticed. His eyes were too striking. Slate grey circled his pupils, intersected uniformly by tiny black rays. Once he held your gaze, it was difficult to look away. Many women remarked on his intensity, not with distaste, but neither with admiration.

Berdin was always one of the first workers awake each morning. His early emergence from his unit was as constant and neutral as the morning itself. Each day at 5:30 a.m., a fuzzy humming would signal the dawn, and the yellow street lights would flicker and die. Rain never fell, and snowflakes never drifted. The cold wind never blew. The SHELL— Specialized Housing Engineered to License Liberty—enclosed the community in a dome and protected it from all inconveniences of weather. Six hundred feet above, on the ceiling of the SHELL, intensely bright fluorescent lights cast a white glow that mirrored dawn and eventually stark daylight. Evening fell in the same unchanging mood: the low humming clicked off, and the ceiling lights cooled to darkness and were replaced by the higher-pitched humming of the yellow street lamps. Citizens of Coastal Community Twelve spent their lives in-between, insulated from the nasty whims of nature.

Except for The Field Engineers. As a government representative assigned to The Field, Berdin walked to the Westbound Monorail, boarded a train, and then rode to the end of the line, where he flashed a pass and was ushered through a gate into the real light of the sun. From the gate (Checkpoint M74), Berdin faced a two-mile walk along an unused asphalt road through The Field. This was the highlight of his commute: the dim warmth of the low sun, an occasional rabbit bounding across the road (Berdin hadn't told anyone about the rabbits; the Environmental Watchpeople would close down The Field if they knew man was infringing on his fellow animals' boundary rights), the rows and rows of green and gold stalks on either side of the road. The asphalt road was disintegrating pleasantly, conceding to the tireless forces of rain and sun. The road was even the old type of asphalt, with different-colored pebbles and a white, broken line intersecting it. It provided a much-needed contrast to the unfailing newness of life in the community, where everyone got new furniture every six months, and the avenues were resurfaced continuously. Berdin savored every aspect of this walk: the road, the rich brown furrows, the rabbits, the sky, the crops, and the knowledge that six hours of hard work lay ahead of him.

The road ended at Bureau of Agricultural Engineering (BAE) building #4, a small complex situated in the middle of a square of barbed wire. A yellow sign on the gate declared: "Maximum Security. First Class Field Engineers Only." Berdin unlatched the gate and moved inside. He turned the handle on the main door, which was unlocked, and squinted in the artificial light. The BAE building was really nothing more than a glorified locker room. Shower stalls filled the center of the building, and individual changing rooms were neatly arranged across the hallway from the showers.

Berdin usually hustled through this part of his day, since the building served only to keep him from the sights and smells of The Field. But today he dawdled. He sauntered toward the computer monitor on the north wall and typed in his security code to check his personal messages file. As usual, he had none. In fact, no one ever received personal messages via the Compsystem—it was deemed conspiratory to share with one person what you would not share with your community. Next Berdin checked his Job Specifications File. Naturally, nothing was new there, either—but he read the paragraph that flashed on the screen as carefully as if he had never seen it before.

"Berdin Dwate, Field Engineer, First Class: As Field Engineer, you are one of the most integral members of Coastal Community Twelve. Your unflagging attention to your government service ensures the rest of the community the security that is the right of every living being. As such, your reward is not only monetary; it is a sense of fulfillment that is beyond measure. Go forth and realize your potential for good."

The green words on the screen blazed in his eyes, mirroring the words he had memorized years ago, mirroring the words that appeared on every job description of every member of Coastal Community Twelve. He let the paragraph blur and run together, staring blankly at the monitor as he searched his mind for flaws in his plan. Time passed slowly. It was a full seven minutes before the front door opened.

Berdin looked up from the monitor, feigning distraction. He allowed for a dramatic pause, and said, "Hello, Willis."

"Hello yourself," said the tired-looking blond man in

the doorway. "I haven't seen you since the Planting Time, Berdin. Seems like you're always here before me and still in The Field when I leave."

"Yeah, it has been a while. I . . . guess we must schedule ourselves a little differently."

Willis, carrying his 180-pound frame like a sack of rocks, moved toward the computer. "Might as well punch in and get things over with as fast as possible."

"Yeah, I'm doing that now. Listen . . . do you, well, are you enjoying working in The Field?"

"Ha. Like I enjoy listening to Our Benevolent Liberator every night. What's to enjoy about . . . what kind of a question is that, anyway?"

Berdin tried to look innocent. "Well, it's not, I mean, obviously no one's thrilled with all this work but it's just . . . it's just that you've been lookin' awfully tired lately, I mean, since I last saw you and I was wondering if this is worse on you or if . . . you know, you *really* needed a break or something."

"Of course I need a break! Actually, that's awfully perceptive of you to say that—see, Liz, that's one of my girls, has been taking up all my time (and my cash) lately—you know, claiming I don't take her out enough (Bytes! Like we do anything else), and keeping me out till all hours dining and dancing and now Graham is saying he's going to subtract the hours I've slept through work from my vacation time, which Liz expects me to use to take her to the Gaming Commission, don't ask me when she expects me to sleep . . . yeah, I could use a break, things are rough for me right now. But so what? The Field is one of those lousy jobs where they can actually measure your work output. You know?"

"I know, and I feel bad for ya," Berdin drew a breath. "And that's why I'm offerin' to do yer work for you for a while—punch in and punch out for you at the right times and just stay after to do yer work. What do you say?"

Suspicion flamed in Willis's eyes. "Yeah, right. And this is all out of the goodness of your heart, right? Just because you like The Field so much you'd like to bust your back an extra six hours a day?"

"Yes, yes," Berdin said eagerly. "Yeah. What do you think?"

"I think nobody gives something for nothing. I think you've got something up your sleeve, Citizen. And I don't like the favor system." He punched in and turned away.

Desperately, impetuously, Berdin grabbed his arm. "It's true, I tell you. I mean, you *are* givin' me somethin'—you're giving me the chance to work more, but it's perfect 'cause I like The Field and you don't and I'd rather be here and you wouldn't." Willis glared at him until he sheepishly dropped his arm. "I mean, why not?" Berdin mumbled.

"You must think I just came in out of the International Wilderness or something—like I haven't got a brain in my head. You like The Field? Sure, and I like monogamous relationships. C'mon, Dwate, I'm not a fool. Nobody wants to work more and not get more. What's your angle?"

Berdin felt sweaty. His plan, which seemed to have so much promise, was caving in. All he wanted was more time in The Field, yet such desires were so foreign to Willis he wouldn't capitalize on the offer of his dreams. How to salvage six more hours in The Field? How to save himself from mindless afternoons and anaesthetized twilights? He stared, speechless, at Willis.

"This is going nowhere," Willis growled, "and it's not getting my weeds picked. See you." His footsteps sounded hollow as he walked toward his changing room.

"All right, I'll tell you!" The words came tumbling from Berdin's mouth, surprising him. But when Willis paused, he recognized the wisdom of his exclamation and grasped at the new hope. Struggling to look ashamed, he said, "I'll tell you . . . I . . . I need more, uh . . . I need more lott'ry tickets."

Willis turned around and strode back to face Berdin. "Aha! Not enough gambling action for you, eh, Dwate? I should've known; I should've known you'd be a Lotto man . . . So what, you want to do all my work and collect all my lottery tickets too? Some favor! All that does is make me unemployed—and how far do you suppose that would get me? I'm already scraping by now."

Berdin was waving his hands and making emphatic denials, but Willis seemed not to notice—he was staring over his co-worker's shoulder and cultivating a greedy gleam in his eye. "Say," he said, "I know you're not trying to boot me into unemployment. You just want a cut, right?" He slipped his arm around Berdin's shoulder. "Yeah, you just want a cut. Alright, here it is: 500 lottery tickets a week for doing all my work. That's fair enough, isn't it? I mean, you don't want me to starve, right?"

Plenty fair, thought Berdin. But in order to stay true to form he exclaimed, "Fair?! Fair? I won't do it for a ticket less than 600!"

"Just like everyone else, huh, Dwate? Out for the bigger piece of the pie? Well, I can respect that. And frankly, I'd say you're still doing me a favor." He grinned widely (really quite a pleasant grin), tossed a key to Berdin, and then disappeared out the front door of the BAE building.

Berdin slumped against a counter, allowing a worried frown to grow slowly into a triumphant smile. He had swung it: twelve hours in The Field, with no one to disturb him. A five minute conversation had effectively doubled his daily intake of happiness. He allowed himself roughly half a minute to gloat, and then hurried to his changing room.

Once inside, he changed from his polyester community clothes to his "uniform": an old grey sweatshirt, denim coveralls, and leather workboots. These old-fashioned, proletariat clothes were yet another aspect of Field work which offended men like Willis and thrilled Berdin. He loved the rumpled, comfortable clothes that smelled of fresh earth despite the best efforts of the Overnight Laundering Corps. He loved knowing that both knees of the coveralls would turn a rich, damp brown through the course of the day, and that the sweatshirt would be too warm by 10:00 in the morning. He savored these feelings as he left the BAE building and turned toward Section V5, the most carefully-tended section in The Field.

Section V5, as with every other section, covered precisely four acres. This, in fact, was one of the most well-documented measurements in the world, because Field Officials had checked and re-checked this statistic forty-five times. The reason for their diligence lay partially in the fact that they had nothing better to do; but it also stemmed from the remarkable discrepancy between the production of Section V5 and the output of every other section. The "magical" soil of good old V5 produced nearly two and a half times more than any other plot at harvest-time, and a full five times more than Section X5, responsibility of Field Engineer Willis Irsay. Field

Officials had run soil content tests from the topsoil to the bed-rock, and found nothing unique about Section V5. And yet every harvest, Berdin walked in rows of corn or wheat that waved a full head above the produce of other sections. It was enough to make one believe, as so many of the Close-Minded Age believed, that factors existed that could not be observed and quantified by science. Such mysteries drove more than one Field Official to the Pharmaceutical Counseling Center.

The theory most Field Officials eventually chose to cling to was necessarily vague in its cause and effect relations. Modified to specific tastes, the theory went something like this: Since Section V5 was on the part of The Field that bordered the International Wilderness, it received unique benefits—namely, the dense forest growth in the Wilderness protected it from unseasonable winds and also generated a more humid (and therefore more desirable) environment for crops near the trees. Further, the complex root systems in the Wilderness may add nutrients to nearby soil which are not yet detectable by modern science. All of these factors combined to increase the fertility of Section V5.

Of course, this theory failed to explain the relative infertility of all the other sections which bordered the International Wilderness. The Field surrounded the rectangular metropolitan area where Berdin and three million others lived (Coastal Community Twelve), and was in turn enclosed on all four sides by International Wilderness. Thus, each section of The Field with suffix "5"—twenty-six in all—lay next to pristine forestland. If Section V5 benefitted from its location, why didn't Sections A5, B5, etc.? No one knew. Berdin didn't even try to figure it out—he just thanked his lucky stars he'd been assigned the best section in The Field.

And now he'd assigned himself the worst section in The Field. By telling Willis he'd work his plot, Section X5, he'd taken on the most barren stretch of land—but what else could he have done? He needed more time in The Field—as crazy as that was—and in order to work more, he had to "trade" for a section that was inconspicuous and near his own. Sections U5 and T5 were on one of the main asphalt roads, and Section W5 was worked by Paul Eskis, a man so loyal to Our Benevolent Liberator he recorded the Global President's nightly speeches and listened to them while working. That left Section X5, which lay in a corner of The Field, bordered on the North and East sides by International Wilderness. Few Inspectors visited it, and when they did it was in the morning before the Engineers arrived. No one need ever know that Berdin was farming Willis's section.

And so it came about that at 1:00 in the afternoon, Berdin placed his hoe in the Section V5 toolshed, locked it, and turned east on a small roadway till he reached Section X5. He was dismayed by what he found there. Everywhere he looked, large dillweeds and fireweed were overpowering thin shoots of corn stalks. Where neat, freshly tilled rows should be, a quilt of wild-looking vegetation spread out. Even Willis's tools were disheartening. Berdin found that he would have to spend his first day in X5 doing nothing but mending hoes and cleaning spades. He would have felt overwhelmed, but he remembered his alternative—lying on a dull couch scratching off hundreds of Lotto tickets—and found himself whistling instead.

The sun was at the level of the highest pine trees when Berdin finished repairing the tools. His back ached from hunching over, and his eyes stung with sweat. He rose slowly, placed both hands on his back, and gradually straightened himself. On the horizon, the big sun dazzled his eyes, and he blinked. A man stood before him.

No, it was just the light. Berdin rubbed his eyes. No, it wasn't. There the man was again, moving toward him out of the sunlight. Berdin's heart sank. He looked for the badge of Inspector on the man's clothes, but they shone too brightly for him to make it out. The man's face also got lost in the glow, but Berdin knew his expression was stern. He held his breath, watching the stranger glide barefoot across his pirated section of The Field.

Barefoot? *Inspectors don't go barefoot,* Berdin thought—*they're so hygienical they probably don't take their shoes off to shower.* He breathed a sigh, but found he still couldn't relax—couldn't take his eyes off the stranger. He moved four paces to the right, so the sun wouldn't be directly behind the man's head, but it didn't help. Four more paces produced equal results—Berdin's eyes were too dazzled to make out anything more than light and bare feet.

"Who are you?" Berdin demanded. His words seemed to break the spell: the sun dipped below the tree-tops and a bracing wind blew across The Field. The man's features came into focus—strong jaw, ragged cheekbones, curly brown hair cut short, eyes!! The eyes, the spell started all over again with the eyes: They seemed—it was hard to say—actually four-dimensional; not just a height and width and bulge, but with a depth—an internal depth—that made you feel as though you could be drawn into the eyes and beyond the eyes to see down into the heart . . . the heart of everything, of all existence. Berdin looked away quickly, before he tumbled in. As he did so, he amended a previous thought: the face was not exactly stern—"determined" was a better word. Set in an unshakable determination.

Berdin felt the eyes patiently bore into him and reluctantly turned back to meet the gaze. With a feeling of helplessness, he began to fall—into the eyes. "Follow me." The stranger moved on to the simple asphalt road and began walking.

An immense feeling of relief swept over Berdin. The stranger was gone, those haunting eyes were gone. He could go home to his new dull couch and watch "The Sex Boat" on CWO and forget all his troubles. He could forget he ever saw the stranger. He . . . he turned and hurried after the barefoot man.

CHAPTER THREE

"The promised land always lies on the other
side of a wilderness."
—Havelock Ellis, *The Dance of Life*

When Berdin caught up with the stranger, he matched
his stride and began asking questions.

"Who are you? Where'd you come from? What makes
you think you can tell me what to do? It's a free Community,
ya know. 'No man is above another,' that's our motto here,
and we don't like anyone tellin' us what to do." The stranger's
silence, for some reason, prodded Berdin to new heights of
indignation. "I don't think you know who's boss 'round here!
I think you have an idea that you might be better, that you
might be boss! Well, let me tell you . . ."

The stranger turned on him and spoke sharply, in a
low voice: "Who is your boss, then?"

"Me! That's who! And your boss is you! And don't

be gettin' the two mixed up, as they say. We've got another motto, and it says, 'one boss per person, and one person per boss.' Now what's wrong with that I ask you?" The Field Engineer was starting to calm down, and feeling a little embarrassed by his tirade. He spoke the last sentence in a deferential tone.

The stranger stopped, and looked away toward the still-light horizon. In the dusk he seemed larger, and a little frightening. He thrust out his jaw and said quietly, "How, then, do you explain the Benevolent Liberator's position in your society?"

"He could be gone tomorrow," Berdin said confidently. "He's just a figurehead, a leader in the abstract ta voice the will of the people."

"And he never tells you to do something you don't want to, or voices an opinion you disagree with?"

Berdin hesitated. The stranger spoke again: "And what about the EQL—the Evolutionary Quantum Leap? It exerts authority over others."

"It has that right."

"Why?"

"Who is mankind to stand in the way of evolution?"

"That's just a slogan. You don't believe that." The stranger spoke the last sentence very carefully, measuring Berdin while he said it.

The rage jumped in Berdin's breast again. "Don't tell me what I believe! Don't . . ."

"Why not?" the stranger snapped. "The EQL does."

The words hung in the air, suspended in the warmth radiating from the asphalt road. The first star, the evening star, gently shone in the East. Berdin looked into the stranger's eyes again and grappled with his gaze. Once more, slowly, he asked, "Who are you?"

"I am Ian," the stranger replied. He began to walk again, slowly. "I come from the International Wilderness. You have been taught all your life that no one can exist outside the Community. I tell you no one can live within the Community."

"Listen, Ian (if that's really your name). The fact is, you've been spending a little too much time at the Pharmaceutical Counseling Center, and we just need to find you your shoes and tuck you into your little Unit for three or four weeks and then everything'll be fine. Either that or treat you to a little Advanced Electro Shock therapy. Then you'll realize yer not from the International Wilderness, and yer not God's gift to the Community."

Ian looked at him sideways. "If you really believe that, how come you're still following me?"

Berdin sputtered. "W-w-what? As it happens, I'm just concerned about you, and happen to be goin' the same direction."

"That's not true. To reach block A12, you should have turned left at the last intersection."

A blush stung Berdin's cheeks. He didn't know how to answer and his pulse was racing. He would have turned and fled, but he was not easily cowed—-and so he stood in the middle of the road, dumb, shifting his weight on his feet.

"You can leave me if you choose," Ian said gently. "But you know I have spoken the truth. Can you walk away from that?"

"Truth is relative," Berdin said distractedly.

"Another slogan. Can't you think on your own terms?"

"I can. I'll follow you. For now," Berdin made up his mind impulsively. When Ian moved on, he followed.

As he walked silently by the taller man's side, he tried to quiet the questions in his mind. *Am I crazy? I'm still in The Field, the gates to the Community close any minute now, and I'm with a nutcase who thinks he lives in the Wilderness. How does he know where I live? Why is he interested in me? Am I crazy?*

"We'll sleep here tonight." Ian gestured toward the toolshed in Section R3.

Berdin felt himself begin to sweat on his back, just below his shoulders. His stomach felt the same way it had the day he leaned forward to kiss Marcia Thomas, the first girl he ever kissed. Sleep in The Field? Outrageous! To get caught would be to single oneself out as a freedom-hater, a Nazi. Our Benevolent Liberator would hold them up as an example to the whole world, and then commit them to a life of Chemical Rehabilitation. And yet—the idea of a night in The Field— a whole night—with the stars shining overhead and the smell of the earth, perhaps even the sounds of nocturnal animals in the International Wilderness, was an idea so sweet he marveled he had not thought of it before. Waves of anticipation battled with his self-preservation instinct, and the only words he could find were, "Are you kidding?"

"Why not? Wouldn't you like to?"

"Well, well of course. I'd like to, but Our Benevolent Liberator . . ."

"Oh, is he your boss?" Ian tried to look as though he asked the question innocently, but had to grin.

The grin irked Berdin, but he shrugged and said, "No, it's just that such actions defeat the purpose of the Community. As the EQL said (and it's a wise saying, in my opinion), 'Fences and chains make men free to rebel.' Without protective devices a man might, in pursuing his own impulses, infringe on another man's rights, but with proper external protection no such infringement can occur."

"You sound like a textbook."

"What, I use a few big words and ya think I'm parroting a book?"

"Are you?"

"What I'm tryin' to say is, by sleeping in The Field we're abandoning the protection of our society. We're jeopardizing other people's rights to act however they please by placing ourselves in a position to be hurt by their actions."

Ian studied the anxious Field Engineer, as one might study a man who claimed he was a lizard. "Let me tell you a story," he said. "A wealthy man owned a large house (you remember what a house is, right? Okay). In his home, the man kept many treasures—fine paintings, plates of silver, many beautiful things. But when he left the house, he always barred the door on the outside. And every time he returned to his home, he found some evil done—money missing, a statue broken, his valuables stolen and mistreated. He cursed the days he had to leave the house, for he knew he'd find it wronged when he returned. But he never thought to place locks inside his door. And he died a man in a battered home, broken by the ravages of evil."

"Well, any fool knows ya don't lock a door on the outside."

"My point exactly." Ian had led them to the north side of the toolshed, and was kicking a hole in the ground with his heel. Berdin was staring at the night sky, relishing the starlight and the fidgety state of his nerves and wondering if he had always had such a capacity for criminal activity.

"I'll be back in a minute," Ian said. "Would you mind expanding this hole, at the same depth, to a circle with approximately a three foot diameter? Thanks."

He disappeared into the night, leaving Berdin kicking at the hole. *Went to notify the proper authorities*, Berdin thought. *Well, too late to run now.* He knew he was in over his head, but he had a stubbornness that caused him to stick to his charted course long after it seemed unwise. He'd found this trait usually served him well, although it did occasionally lead to run-ins with society—like the time in tenth grade he stubbornly refused to concede to his teacher that the area of any rectangle equaled seven meters plus width. He'd disrupted the class, and the instructor had sent him to the Educational Corroborator (whom he also flatly contradicted), who sent him to the District Executive Superintendent. The Superintendent explained to him that he was acting as a "cancerous" force on society and also that he was sadly mistaken because the EQL had only yesterday informed the world that the proper formula for the area of a rectangle was 7m+w. Berdin countered with the claim that every child since the age of ten knew very well the formula was length multiplied by width, but the Superintendent was unimpressed. He informed Berdin that that was merely "the truth of a generation" and that further insubordination would not be tolerated. Berdin had been indignant, but he recognized the fire in the Superintendent's eyes as the same light in his Growth and Development Supervisor's eyes when he was preparing to assign Berdin more peer counselling, and he retreated in bitter silence. Berdin had taken some solace in the following days by watching the new formula play havoc with the Strategic Planning and Design Commission's projects, but this small measure of consolation was short-lived; in two weeks, Our Benevolent Liberator's Science Cabinet had arrived at the corollary to the new area formula [always add (l-7m) and (lw-w-l)], and soon society was functioning flawlessly again (although math became even less popular with the students). Berdin, in time, pushed the whole ugly affair into the back of his mind, but his part in it always remained on the cover sheet of his Personal Academic and Career Report.

Berdin's reverie was broken by the sounds of Ian's return. The barefoot man stepped back into Berdin's eyesight carrying a load of wood, mostly tinder but with some larger sticks as well.

"Where did you get *that*?" Berdin asked, startled, still rankling with his memories.

"Where do you think?" Ian said quietly.

"What I think," said Berdin (after a pause), "is from the International Wilderness. But I know that can't be true 'cause the Wilderness is held out on all sides by a fence 14 feet high, consisting of electrified barbed wires spaced only a quarter of an inch apart. Even if you tried to tunnel under, you'd find concrete as thick as a bunker extendin' 30 feet below the surface."

"Well, 'fences make men free to rebel,'" Ian said, and he grinned.

"Sorry, I thought . . ." muttered Berdin.

"Don't be. I wish you'd do it more often." Ian began arranging the smaller pieces of wood in a teepee shaped pile in the middle of the hole.

Berdin watched gloomily. *He's not building a fire*, he

thought. *Surely even he's not that stupid and bold.* He watched Ian crouch over the firepit and saw a tiny light illuminate his hands and face. He groaned, "Oh, great, great. Hang on a second. You want me to get a bullhorn and start shoutin', 'We're over here, in section R3, doin' everything we can to undermine society!'? You want that?"

Ian looked at him patiently.

"Do you know what you're doing?" Berdin continued, looking hysterical (although, to be honest, hysterical wasn't exactly how he felt). "Do you realize that that little fire will be the first fire these fields—The Field—has seen since the Close-Minded Age? Don't you think that maybe, just maybe, people will see that fire and ask themselves WHO THE PIXEL is out in The Field?"

"No one will see it," Ian reassured him. "No one remains in The Field but you and me. Your precious Community is shut off from their breadbasket by their SHELL."

Berdin sat down abruptly, and assumed alternating expressions of gloominess and hysteria. Ian looked at him. "By the way," he said, "I don't think you *need* a bullhorn."

Berdin blinked, and sheepishly moved closer to the fire. He watched Ian throw bigger sticks on the struggling blaze, and noted (with some pleasure) the crackling noise the wood made as it burned.

The men sat on their haunches and stared at the fire for a time in silence. Every once in awhile Ian would feed the fire from his small woodpile, which, oddly, never got any smaller. The fluid motions of Ian's big hands reminded Berdin of a magician he had watched on the CWO. Each movement Ian made looked deceptively easy, so that the most intricate machinations seemed somehow contrived. The size of Ian's large-veined hands caused the "tricks" to appear even more unlikely; Berdin had the impression he was watching a skilled carpenter who had adapted his skills to prestidigitation.

Eventually, Ian turned to Berdin and said, "Tell me more about this EQL."

Berdin snorted. "I thought you knew it all already," he said. But he continued anyway: "The EQL is, as far as I can tell, exactly what it's called: an Evolutionary Quantum Leap. See, even in the Close-Minded Age, men had computers, and some of the most enlightened—" ("That's not your word," Ian muttered) "men recognized in these computers the rudimentary foundations of AI (Artificial Intelligence). Um, in other words, these men realized that mankind would some-day be able to produce computers that could *think like men*, only faster and more competently, without the hindrances of emotion and negative envir'nmental influence."

"Negative environmental influence?"

Berdin looked impatient. "You know, like inadequate parents (something we've, thankfully, replaced with Growth and Development Supervisors) or," he paused meaningfully, "unsavory acquaintances." Ian smiled, so Berdin continued: "Anyways, mankind worked for a long time developing these AI machines, and even a longer time perfectin' them. Many of the AI fore-runners, I've heard, went—uh—more or less berserk and began spouting nonsense—stuff like, 'pepperoni moderates peace,' and other ridiculous garbage. Some men gave up hope that real, meaningful Artificial Intelligence could ever be created. Some men—you know, the real reactionar-ies, the ones that propagated closed-mindedness in that Age, even said that AI was fund'mentally impossible because—geez, I feel funny even sayin' it—men's intellects were not strictly physical; men have something . . . something *ethereal* in them that couldn't be duplicated. Luckily, of course, the dogmas of these reactionaries were ignored by modern science, and the real visionaries of that time pressed on with the job of creatin' the perfect mechanical brain. And finally, not but seven years ago, they succeeded. They named it the EQL for obvious reasons: a being that could think like a man, only perfectly, and was more or less eternal—you just replace its parts when they wear out—and that could withstand all kinds of, uh, envir'nmental disasters and possibly even the eventual implosion of the sun, well, it's obviously a step above man on the evolution'ry ladder. See, it's just like the real visionaries predicted: man would sometime reach a point where he wasn't just subject to the whims of the evolution'ry process, but where he could harness evolution and channel it—mankind gained control of the evolution'ry process. And now we've 'created' a higher being, and can reap the fruits of our labor by following the advice of that being, thereby allowing us to, um, to . . . further evolve ourselves. In other words, mankind can now develop toward perfection by looking to the perfect being for means to achieve that goal. Get it? Did I explain that clearly?"

"Quite. So this EQL now—shall we say—lays down the law for the human race?"

Berdin thought. "No, that's the wrong way of lookin' at it. Let's see . . . remember how people used ta own pets?" Ian nodded. "Well, it's more along that line: dogs should listen to humans because humans are more highly evolved. When a human told a dog to 'stay', see, it was for the dog's good—the man may want the dog to stay so it doesn't run in the street and get hit by a car (you know what a car is, right?).

Well, it's the same way with the EQL. It doesn't 'lay down the law,' but it tells us things for our own good. We can listen or not listen, but if we choose to ignore it we'll be makin' a mistake. That way, everyone's their own boss, but everyone knows enough to take the advice of a more highly-evolved being."

"But sometimes this advice is a death sentence."

"What? Oh, you're talkin' about the EQL's LiST— Life Span Termination? I see . . . you think the EQL is over-stepping some boundary by determining what human beings are violating the Species Equal Opportunity Act? But, there, again, you're forgetting the context—men often choose the times when animals should die; why, they used to shoot horses just because they broke their legs. This is simply the same thing on another level: the EQL calculates the proper envir'nmental balance according to the SEOA (you know, two billion groundhogs, seven billion sheep; perhaps half a billion humans), and then determines which humans are least-suited to take up space in our ecosystem. By choosing the humans which are contributing the least to the evolution'ry progress of mankind, the EQL is furthering our eventual development. That is . . ."

"But suppose a man or woman doesn't want to die? Suppose they still perceive themselves as valuable?"

"Oh, we've accepted the ramifications of the system quite easily. Man isn't as troubled by the concept of death as they were in the Close-Minded Age, 'cause the EQL provides us with a measure of immortality. Sorry I forgot that, it's an important point—see, when a man or woman is terminated nowadays, all their specifics (that is, their consciousness) is inputted into the EQL by the Science Cabinet. Every spec—

from their brain weight to their job description, from their diet preferences to their day-to-day habits—is added to the Artificial Intelligence of the EQL. Granted, we haven't yet discovered the way to synthesize this information so that these consciousnesses possess their own identity within the greater context of the EQL's intelligence, but bein' merged into a powerful collective consciousness still is a satisfactory piece of immortality (immeasur'bly more than any man could hope for in the past), and as I've said, there's a very real possibility that these inputs can someday be synthesized to re-create the identity of every individual. All in all, a very promising scenario, and comforting to everyone, I'm sure, whose name has appeared on the LiST."

Berdin sighed and assumed a more relaxed position by the fire, pleased with his articulate explanation. Ian studied him for awhile, and then said, "So, you believe that if *your* name, the name 'Berdin Dwate,' was spit out by the EQL tomorrow, you could go happily to your grave knowing your brain weight was a part of the collective consciousness?"

"Haven't you been listening?" Berdin sputtered. "It's . . . it's so much more than my brain weight—it's everything about me that matters: every specification that goes inta my make-up, everything that makes me *me*. The EQL gets it all—and I become part of the next evolution'ry step."

"Every part of you? You talk about specifications— but can the Science Cabinet input the things that really make you unique? Can they, for example, design a formula or create a piece of software that conveys to the EQL the fact that Berdin Dwate loves to work in The Field? That Berdin Dwate, unlike every other Field Engineer in the whole of Coastal Community Twelve, actually relishes the sunshine, the soil on his hands, and the knots in his back? Can they?" Ian leaned forward, impassioned, his eyes glowing in the firelight.

Berdin blinked. He looked away, up at the stars. He moved his lips, started to speak—stopped—started again, and said, "This is going no—"

"*Can* they?"

"No!" Berdin shot back. "No, they can't. And it don't matter. This crazy attitude I have toward work is just that—crazy. And it doesn't mean a whit about who I am. The fact that I like . . . that I love, The Field is just some lingering negative environmental influence I probably picked up from some, some maladjusted classmate or under-qualified G & D supervisor—it's an imperfect part of me that'll be burned away in my merger with the EQL—it's, it's insignificant beyond mentioning. The parts of me that matter—those are the parts that will become one with the collective consciousness."

"And those parts that matter are your brain weight and the fact that you find broccoli largely indigestible?"

"Yes!" Berdin glared at him.

"So you would willingly die tomorrow?"

"Yes! With a smile on my lips!"

"Brave . . ." Ian muttered.

"What?"

"Have you ever thought there might be more?"

"Like what?" he drawled the words, a challenge.

"Like a life outside this tiny world you've bound yourself up in? Like more than your precious little block in your precious little Community? More than 'The Sex Boat' at night and blathering speeches by the Benevolent Liberator and winning the Lotto and randomly-generated electronic music? Have you ever thought," Ian said, standing up abruptly and waving his hands in a broad circle, "that there might be more to all this than what you see? That something, someone, else is out there—just out there in the International Wilderness—very close at hand—which makes your reality seem small and shabby? That the life you've thought is all there is is really just a dim reflection, a dress rehearsal, and that the real meaning lies just beyond your reach? Have you ever thought . . ." he sat down again, and lowered his voice, "that life, real living, is outside the Community, in unlikely places, like beside a small campfire in Section R3? Have you?"

Berdin was awed. The fire in Ian's eyes blazed high, brighter than a mere reflection of the campfire. The eyes broke him, without apology, and looked inside him with a dignity founded completely on their clarity—their magnificent vision unimpaired.

Berdin had already been through a myriad of emotions today—shock, hysteria, curiosity, anger—and now another welled inside him: fear. Not the feeble fear about undermining the Community or of being caught, but unbridled fear that caused him to mentally shrink back at what lay before him. He was a hard-nosed man, not often prone to fear, and what he felt now he had never known before. It scared him more than it would an average man, the way angry emotions further enrage a generally placid person. He felt not only the starkness of indisputable terror, but also the odd sensation of fearing the very emotion coursing through him. He was scared of being scared. He hadn't really thought such emotion possible.

He reacted in a most peculiar way. His eyes were wide, it's true, and his pulse quickened, but other than that he gave no sign. He didn't bolt; he didn't grab the stranger (in some ways, the embodiment of his fear) and shake him and cry for mercy. Instead, he sat stock-still for a moment, and then slumped to a casual, half-reclining position by the campfire. His face assumed an expression of stunned resignation, and he concentrated his gaze on the burning red coals. Perhaps all the emotions had somehow over-ridden his natural reflexes. Whatever the case, he accepted his fate with a Sphinx-like stoicness.

Ian did not begrudge him his time of reflection. He, too, sat very quietly, looking into the fire. His attitude was that of a man hearing distant noises. He listened attentively, full of concentration, unwilling to speak or otherwise scare away the noisy thoughts. Gradually, Berdin emerged from his cocooned analysis, slowly awakening to his surroundings. Crickets chirped impatiently, and a breeze blew softly over the wheat stalks in R3. Far away, in the International Wilderness, he heard the call of what he assumed must be an owl—a deep, majestic cry: "Who." The campfire burned low, still clicking and popping occasionally, glowing alternately bright and dim.

Berdin looked up at the stars, those lights he had seen so often on CWO, and was awed by their faint testimony to the overwhelming size of the universe outside Coastal Community Twelve. He felt his mind switch off, abandoning its usual course of cluttered thoughts strung together, and felt himself as just a part of a bigger, more coherent continuity. The campfire had brought it out, but it was always there: a stream heard only in quiet moments. Involuntarily, his mouth hung open.

"Not really a bad way to spend an evening, is it?" Ian spoke very softly, his words no louder than the faint hiss of the campfire. Berdin shook his head.

"Hungry?" Ian asked. Before Berdin could get out, "Now that you mention it . . ." Ian had produced a loaf of bread and two large, wet objects from under his cloak. He broke the loaf, gave half to Berdin, and then selected a stick from his woodpile.

"These are rainbow trout," he said, as he slipped the stick along the spine of one of the wet forms. "Have you ever eaten one before?"

Berdin shuddered. "Bytes, no. I mean, I've seen trout before, at the aquarium, but we don't . . . society, our society doesn't allow the eating of endangered species—in fact, we don't eat any meat except for beef and even that only 'cause the Agriculture Cabinet figured out that when the EQL said 'man should not eat cows' it only meant wild cows, not domestic ones . . . I don't think I'll like trout."

"There are plenty of trout in the International Wilderness."

"Well, there's not enough by the EQL's optimal envir'nmental balance standards. You know, I told you, it figures exactly how many of everything there should be—like seven billion groundhogs and all—maybe it figured there should be two billion trout and there's only one-point-five billion."

"Well, I have decided there should be two less trout," Ian said, as he calmly roasted the dark fish over the coals of the fire.

"Shoot, we've broken every other rule . . ." Berdin muttered. He *was* hungry.

And the fish *did* taste good. He only nodded when Ian asked him if he liked it, but he savored every smoky, delicate bite and licked his fingers when he was done. *Probably my last meal*, he thought, *I'd better enjoy it.*

Aloud, he said, "So, Ian, tell me—if the International Wilderness is so terrific, why'd you bother to leave it to come here? Just wanted to cause some trouble for an honest Field Engineer?"

Ian concentrated on the second trout, which he was turning slowly over the fire. "I had to tell you about it. And to make it accessible to your Community."

"Oh, I see. That's how you got in—you've found a way around The Fence?"

A cloud passed over Ian's face. "Yes." He sat silent for a time, lost in thought. "Listen," he said. "A servant worked a piece of land, raising wheat for his master. The land was uneven, dusty, and thick with sage and many deep-rooted plants which choked back the wheat. Each year at harvest-time, the master sent for the servant's crops, allowing first for the servant to hold back what he needed for himself and his family. The servant's harvest was consistently poor; some years he could send his master very little; many years he had to keep all for himself. So the master sent a man to the servant to tell him of another plot of land—an even field with rich soil that lay on the master's own property. The servant was invited to till that field, so that he might produce more for himself, and truly serve the master. Tell me, shouldn't the servant obey the call?"

"You're not much for simple answers, are you?"

"Yours was not a simple question. It wasn't easy for me to leave the International Wilderness."

"Well, let's go back, then, tonight." Berdin surprised himself with this statement, but he stuck out his jaw to show he was willing to back it up.

Anger flashed in Ian's eyes, and he spoke sharply: "You tempt me. Do not do so again."

The authority and passion in Ian's voice shocked Berdin. *Tempt you?* he thought. *Isn't it you who's led me into all sorts of trouble today?* But he dared not articulate these thoughts. Ian had rebuked him more harshly than he'd ever experienced, and he intuitively felt such a passionate rebuke must be justified. Much to his dismay, Berdin felt his cheeks burn with a blush, as if he were a child scolded by his G & D Supervisor. He looked away.

A minute passed before Ian spoke again. "Can you really be so selfish as to believe I came to save only you? Don't you care anything for your fellow citizens?"

"I care," Berdin mumbled. "I . . . I guess I was just testing you."

"And that is something you must never do again. I told you you could walk away from me. It's your choice to receive me or shun me. You have already decided, and you may rest assured you've made the right decision. But now that you have chosen, follow. Trust. Test me no more, but instead have faith."

"It's . . . it's just all so odd . . ." Berdin said weakly.

Ian ignored this statement, concentrating instead on eating his trout. Once finished, he pulled a silver flask from his cloak, drank, and handed it to Berdin. The water in the flask was icy cold; so cold it stung Berdin's throat. It tasted, he thought, exactly like the word "brisk," if words could taste. He handed the flask back to Ian and said, "Don't tell me, it's from the International Wilderness, right?"

Ian nodded. He stood and began kicking dirt on the

red coals of the fire. After he had buried the firepit, he spoke. "Berdin Dwate," he said—and his words sounded strangely distant in the sudden darkness—"you are a brave man. You're headstrong, it's true, and too often make decisions dictated by passion, but you have the courage of your convictions and the guts to follow through. You are capable of great things. But you'll soon find that those capable of greatness are also capable of great misdeeds. The choice, I'm afraid, is yours. Before it's all over, I suspect you'll wish it weren't—a strange emotion for you. The world is not the simple place you think it is. Discovering this, depending on the timing, is man's greatest joy or greatest sorrow. Tonight, you have taken the first step on the proper path, the path to joy."

"I, uh, well, I enjoyed it." Berdin didn't know what to say.

"You won't always. There will be weeks when you hate it. Sleep now—tomorrow will be full." Ian lay on his back, gazing up at the stars.

Berdin watched the stars, too, and wondered at his broken plans. From everything he had seen today, he felt he should bolt in terror, but in his stomach he had the vague sensation that his fear was the very thing that kept him from running. He lay quietly, wallowing in the strange chemistry of fear wedded with anticipation—an anticipation so severe it rendered every other hope he'd ever had drab and somehow perverted. The waves of emotion ebbed in and out, lulling him to sleep. When he awoke, it was light and Ian was gone.

CHAPTER FOUR

"Liberty consists in doing what one desires."
—John Stuart Mill, *On Liberty*

"But now that you have been set free from sin
and have become slaves to God, the benefit
you reap leads to holiness, and the result is
eternal life."
—The Apostle Paul, Romans 6:22

Berdin lay with his head propped up on the back of
the toolshed and thought. His first thought was not of Ian's
desertion, but rather of the unguessed beauty of sunrise. The
incredible promise bursting from the new orange sun over the
pine trees warmed him from the inside out, while the birds
hunting in the undergrowth chirruped pretty "good mornings."
It's a shame Ian's missing this, Berdin thought. Ian's possible
desertion never entered his mind—he felt no sense of aban-

donment, no outrage.

This strange confidence would have bewildered Berdin, given the time to identify the emotion. But his sleep-drugged mind was still bushy with dreams and specters when Ian reappeared, walking south on the nearest road.

As the barefoot man drew nearer, Berdin noticed that he was smiling and humming. Berdin started to shout a greeting, checked himself, and sat still, absorbed in the other man's music. Ian continued to hum until he reached him, and then spoke softly: "Good morning, Berdin. I'm surprised to see your snoring didn't shake the toolshed down last night."

Berdin brushed the comment aside. "What were you humming just now?"

"Oh, an old song. A forbidden song, actually, for you— it comes from the Close-Minded Age. Back then, people believed songs should have harmony and rhythm. But today, you know such standards are 'reactionary dogma,' right?"

"What do *you* say?"

"What do I say? What do I look like, the EQL?" Ian offered him his hand and helped him up. Berdin opened his mouth to speak, but Ian waved the words aside and said, "You're right, I shouldn't tease you. You are wise in asking. My answer, I think, is obvious—at least, it will become obvious. Now," he looked around, "should we head indoors?"

"Back to the Community?" Berdin swallowed hard.

"Well, we can't stand in another man's section all day, can we?" Ian started down the road.

Berdin followed, completely at a loss. He had known he'd have to go back to the Community, and yet . . . he'd never really believed it. He paced alongside Ian, frantically weighing options.

"The Arrival/Departure Monitor must report us, you know," he said.

"Actions have consequences," Ian answered.

"Am I s'posed to take comfort in that?"

"Yes. You were designed to admire truth." Ian said the words matter-of-factly, in a way that did not invite comment. Berdin slipped into a desperate silence, walking mechanically and searching for an excuse which would at least protect him from the direct ire of the Justice Cabinet. By the time they reached checkpoint M74 of the SHELL, he'd conceived just one threadbare alibi: temporary insanity.

Ian walked directly toward the gate, but Berdin turned aside and spoke into the microphone to the left. "Hi, I'm Elvis," he said.

The gate swung open. *Great, the Law Enforcement Agents are already waiting for us*, Berdin thought. But when he could see inside, all he saw was Mary Paxton, one of the quietest Field Engineers, waiting to get outside. Berdin dove past Mary, muttering "Forgot something," and turned breathlessly to Ian when they were both safely past the checkpoint. "Boy, that was close. We were lucky old Mary was right there at just the right time, weren't we? I didn't know what we would do."

"You," Ian said (with a hint of a twinkle in his eye), "were apparently going to make a complete fool of yourself. For my part, I was going to ignore you. And, by the way, I don't believe in luck. You shouldn't either by now." In an attempt to hide his amusement, Ian looked away from his friend, apparently absorbed in the interior of Coastal Community Twelve.

The Community was impressive. Great grey cement

thoroughfares, twenty feet across, stretched out at right angles, delineating "blocks"—cement buildings more than one hundred yards long and four stories high. Each block had wrought iron railings around the edges of its flat roof, signaling the border of the patios on top of each building. Statues, fountains, and various artificial plants decorating the patios were visible from the street-level. Still other patios, Berdin told Ian, had synthetic putting greens and billiard tables and roulette wheels. Such amenities could be left in the open, of course, because the entire Community was enclosed, cut off from the elements.

The blocks themselves greatly resembled cell blocks from the penitentiaries of the Close-Minded Age (a fact about which the present residents of these blocks were blissfully unaware, having never seen a penitentiary, nor heard that criminals were at one time "punished" rather than assigned to Pharmaceutical Counseling sessions). Each unit was distinguished by a heavily-barred sliding door, with its number emblazoned on it in excessively bright colors ranging from hot pink to a rich phosphorescent blue. Outside stairways, much like fire escapes, provided access to the second, third, and fourth floors, with narrow walkways jutting out at each level.

Vandalism seemed to have flourished everywhere. Graffiti sprouted up on the sides of the blocks and the cement thoroughfares at a rate faster than the Visual Pollution Managers could paint over it, and anything breakable (which wasn't much) had been broken. Many of the statues were decapitated or worse, the artificial plants were jumbled, and sections of railing were battered and dangling uselessly.

"Why all this destruction?" Ian asked.

"Well," Berdin responded hesitantly, knowing his answer would meet with disapproval— "in a society where everyone is free to really get in touch with himself or herself, some people take advantage of that freedom. But in the end, these people will understand that their destructive tendencies are really only negative responses to an imperfect envir'nment, and they'll focus instead on contributin' to society in a way that improves the envir'nment."

"How come, when I ask you a tough question, your answers always sound like one of the Benevolent Liberator's nightly monologues?"

"I didn't figure you'd like that answer."

"Well, does it make sense? Are only young people acting irresponsibly, and then as they grow older are they mending their ways and becoming productive members of society? Or are older people, who should have recognized the so-called motivations for their destructive actions, still destroying? Are most people maturing, and growing more perfect, or are they deteriorating and becoming less perfect? And where, may I ask, did you obtain this objective standard for perfection?"

"How am I s'posed to know?" Berdin grumbled.

"You know."

They walked on in silence. As they passed further in, toward the center of the Community, the blocks and thoroughfares became more shabby, the patios more sparsely decorated. The wealthy segment of the population, as has always been the case, gravitated toward the "suburbs," while the poorer citizens stayed in the inner city. Countless incentive programs had attempted to lure the wealthy deeper into the Community, and countless programs had failed. Something in the wealthy kept them on the fringes—in the shallow part of society, where the hard questions, the sharp realities of life, could not overwhelm them.

Occasionally, Community Transport Systems (in the form of monorails) would thunder high overhead like low-flying jets. These monorails provided transportation for people strictly to and from their jobs, and each person's commute was monitored by various Transport Engineers, who knew the work schedule of their designated passengers as well as they knew their lucky Lotto numbers. This accomplished two desirable results: the use of pollution-creating transportation was kept to a bare minimum (the small amount of pollution created was simply filtered from the enclosed atmosphere), and public transportation was rendered remarkably safe, since it is generally unwise to mug a person you must commute with every day.

The unfortunate flip-side of the Community's transportation policy was that every person not in commute and not performing job-related activities must walk—and walking was a hazardous undertaking. Persons unbalanced by their imperfect environment and a little low on cash understood perfectly the significance of a solitary figure hurrying down a lonely thoroughfare: that person was seeking a form of entertainment not found in his or her own home, and was carrying enough money to subsidize that entertainment when they reached their destination. It was a simple matter for the former to overpower the latter and make the victim's environment a little less perfect through a simple cash transaction. It seemed that lately more and more people showed themselves willing to do so. Some didn't even bother to look for cash; their concern was violence. These people caused the streets of Coastal Community Twelve to be lonelier every day, and inspired the slogan, "Fences and bars make men free to rebel."

Not coincidentally, children under 18 years of age never walked the streets alone. The only time most of the community ever saw children was in a huddled herd shepherded by two or three Growth and Development Supervisors. These Supervisors superseded the traditional role of parents—another strange institution foisted on society by the Close-Minded Age—and oversaw the physical and social maturation of their charges. In the streets, G and D Supervisors looked grim and carried stunguns.

The Psychological Cabinet assured Our Benevolent Liberator (and the EQL concurred) that men acting according to their true individuality, in touch with their real self, would eventually achieve harmony with their inherent goodness and thus act in ways beneficial to themselves and mankind in general. So Our Benevolent Liberator ignored the street crime statistics, and concentrated on the ideal, using slogans.

The community was rich with slogans. Some blocks were so papered with flyers proclaiming the latest truth, the whole building seemed to flutter in the breeze created by the passing monorails. Bold letters declared, "Truth is what we make it!" and "I'm my boss, you're your boss: if you forget, it's your loss" and "Walls make good neighbors." Sometimes the words stood alone; sometimes they were accompanied by the images of pop heroes: electronic music programmers, CWO starlets, political leaders.

Ian stopped in front of a sign which proclaimed, "Safety first! (safe sex, safe drugs, safe abortion, safe infanticide). Ask your Physician for guidance." He reached out to it, contemplatively traced its letters, and then said simply, "This is trash." He crumpled up the flyer and threw it in a nearby garbage incineration chute.

"You can't do that!" Berdin gasped. He looked around quickly, checking up and down the avenue for witnesses.

"Why not? It isn't true. One can never obey one's own rebellious will and not suffer the consequences. A man cannot 'safely' flaunt the very order of the universe by disobeying the moral fabric of reality."

"Listen—" Berdin started.

"What the pixel's goin' on out there?" a harsh female voice echoed out of a nearby cell.

Berdin froze. The owner of the voice stuck her small, narrow face between the bars of her unit and looked sideways at the two men. "I want to know what you two are doin' here and who you thi'y'are, interruptin' my soaps. I got my rights! Ya want me t' call the LEA, is that what ya want?"

"Ah, stick to bein' your own boss," Berdin said, "and I'll stick to bein' mine." He stared the woman back into her unit, and then guided Ian by the elbow down a side street.

"Listen," he said, "What you just did you can call upholding truth or whatever you want, but the Ethics Cabinet calls it censorship, and considers it a crime against society. They'll definitely put you through Intensive Electro-shock Therapy if they catch you at that, and they might just decide you need a Cerebral Restructuring as well. It ain't worth it, truth or no truth."

In answer, Ian walked across the street to another block and tore down another "Safety First" flyer. He turned to Berdin. "The truth is precious—a thing without price. The truth is the only reason for getting out of bed in the morning, for toiling another day at a menial job, for making a courageous stand. Courage is but a tool, and can only properly be wielded for truth. Without truth, no situation or occurrence is better or worse than another—the world slips into a dismal grey, without distinctions of line or color. Without truth, distinctions become meaningless, and with them man's capacity to distinguish (his mind). Man becomes an animal, only less than an animal—for even animals live by the simple truths that are the laws of nature. The bird in flight testifies to the truth of aerodynamics, but the man without truth stands only as a testimony to futility. Man becomes infinitely pitiable, a creature with courage and no reason to be courageous—a bird with wings and no desire to fly. Truth, only truth, can take a man and shake him and cause him to rise up and be as noble as he feels in his heart he can be when he awakens and understands the promise of a new day. Truth, Berdin, matters. And I tell you the truth, you must obey a higher will than your own or society's."

"Oh, very good, very nice. Pretty—a very pretty speech," a loud voice called out from the nearest unit, "only it's interfering with my hacking rights, keeping me from my program! Can't you shut up so's I can hear the seer tell my fortune by the stars? I . . . oh, oh NOW I've missed the daily Capricorn predictions, NOW I've missed it! Just who," a large sweaty man appeared at the unit door, "Who do ya think you are? Just let me—"

"Quiet!" Ian spoke sharply. The man clapped his mouth shut and stared. "Go and turn those lies off now. Think on those things no more—their time is over. Think instead on the time at hand—a time, finally, to live."

The burly man turned and disappeared. With a "click," the seer was quieted, in the midst of sage financial advice for Cancers. A female voice shrieked, "George! Turn that back on this instant! Have you lost your mind?"

"There's someone you need to see," George said. But by the time he guided his wife to the door, Ian and Berdin were disappearing around the corner.

"You've got to understand," Berdin was saying as he walked briskly alongside his friend, "You're in civilization now. It's all well and good to think and act the way you do in the International Wilderness, but you can't do that here. You'll cause trouble." He absently cracked his knuckles.

"You're right, I will cause trouble. We will both have trouble, and deep down you're prepared for that. But it's a trouble that your race has brought upon itself, and I must act as both the catalyst and the solution. I've accepted that."

"Then I must accept it too?"

"If you care for the truth. And you do."

Berdin and Ian walked on, talking animatedly and eliciting stares from the citizens who could tear themselves away from their CWO monitors. The tall, robed man swept his arms in expansive gestures, and was rebuffed by Berdin's curt and surly body language. The blocks dragged on in monotonous rows and columns of fluttering grey facelessness, splashed obscenely with neon colors of green and pink and orange and blue. Monorails rattled in the distance, and monitors screamed and moaned and droned in echoes. The avenues were completely deserted—enforcing an odd sensation of walking in a ghost town haunted by grotesque automatons. In spite of himself, Ian felt cold. Only the increased shabbiness of the occasional patio decorations and the numbers flashing on electronic street signs at regular intervals betrayed the progress of the travelers, so that eventually the oppressive changelessness weighed so heavily on the men they fixed their eyes straight ahead and lapsed into silence, like soldiers patrolling a gutted city.

When they reached an electric sign that read "Westside 10NW," Berdin stopped. "Here's our street," he said.

"Oh, we're not going back to your unit yet," Ian said. "We've got a lot to do before we call it a day." He started walking south down the same avenue.

Berdin hesitated. "Well . . . uh, I thought I'd go back home and wash up and try 'n squeeze in a little work today. I could still put in a half-day at The Field, and . . ."

Ian stopped and turned around. "You're not going back to The Field, my friend. You've concentrated long enough on causing wheat to grow. Now it's time for you to cause men's hunger for the truth to grow."

Berdin still hesitated. "I can't do that."

"Do what? Give up working in The Field? Or propagate truth?"

"Well—" Berdin walked toward Ian, so their conversation would be quieter. "Well, actually neither. See, if I stop working in The Field, my contribution to society is severely diminished, and they'll put me on WELFARE—Wealth is Everyone's Legal and Fiscal Assured Right on Earth—and I got a hunch that WELFARE recipients always find their way to the top of the EQL's life span termination output. So, really, quitting The Field would be a little like signin' my death warrant (and besides, you know, I like working The Field for some crazy reason) . . . But, yeah, also, I mean, I can't, uh, propagate truth, 'cause I'm not that good of a talker anyway and besides I don't really know what the truth is."

"I am the Truth."

"I was afraid you were going to say somethin' like

that."

"Afraid? That's not the right word. You'd rush in where angels fear to tread."

Berdin looked puzzled. "Angels?"

Ian laughed. "I'd forgotten . . . 'angels' for you is just another word for pretty girls. Never mind. What I'm saying is, you know the truth now, and to know the truth and ignore it is the deadliest of mistakes. So, I'm afraid you are stuck with me. Come on."

Uncertainly, Berdin began walking next to Ian again. "I just don't like not having any choice in the matter . . . I mean I like you and of course you need me with you, but it doesn't seem . . . *fair* that I don't have any say in the matter."

"Oh, you have a choice," Ian said. "You may choose your way, or you may choose the right way." He looked at Berdin with a twinkling in his ferocious eyes.

"That wasn't a very nice way to put it."

"I'm sorry, Berdin. I'm less interested in 'nice' than I am in the truth. Now hurry. We've got a lot to do today, and I'd like to reach the Central Planning Agency when it opens."

"The CPA?" Berdin asked, even as he quickened his pace. "What do you want with that beehive of bureaucrats?"

"I must tell them why I'm here."

"They're not going to like that, you know. Not a bit."

Ian sighed. "Yes, I know that. Probably better than you think. Still, I must try. It would be wrong for me to ignore them."

"No, you don't understand. They won't just 'not like it.' They'll have you committed! If you tell them you're from the International Wilderness and everyone should listen to you and not themselves and the EQL, they'll fry their circuits! Not to mention me—oh, they'll be glad to see me—playin' hooky fr'm my job to bring them some guy in a robe that probably isn't even *registered* with the EQL. Oh, I can hear them now: 'Welcome, Berdin, we're so glad you took time off your busy schedule to tell us WE'RE COMPLETELY WRONG and you're not going to COOPERATE WITH SOCIETY ANY-MORE!! Thank you SO MUCH for your time! Now, would you mind kindly stepping into the CEREBRAL RESTRUC-TURING DEPARTMENT for just a moment or two? Oh, yes, very nice, I can see it all now. I'm, I . . .'" Berdin spluttered to a stop, a little surprised he hadn't been interrupted.

"Finished?" Ian said calmly.

Berdin glared. "I suppose so." They walked on. "I don't suppose I changed your mind?"

"Nope."

"I can't believe you! And sticking with you—for actually sticking with you—I must be a complete fool. This is *absolutely* the worst decision I could ever make."

"The worst or the best. Either decision excites one to the same level of emotional intensity."

"Unnngh!" Berdin made a grinding, growling noise of frustration. He walked on in silence, in a distracted marching gait. He cursed himself again and again for spending the night in The Field with this headstrong character. *Just let him go,* he thought. *Walk away. He doesn't need you, that's clear. Why risk your own neck?*

The answer, unfortunately, kept popping into Berdin's mind: *Because he wouldn't desert you.* He tried repeating the old slogan "Loyalty forgets who's boss," but it sounded hollow; footsteps on an empty avenue. Grudgingly, he conceded to himself that loyalty was a gift best rewarded with loyalty.

Besides, the two men were rapidly approaching the worst part of Coastal Community Twelve—home of WELFARE recipients, Electroshock Therapy patients, and men and women who visited the Pharmaceutical Counseling Center too often; Berdin wouldn't have made his worst enemy run that gauntlet alone. He turned to Ian. "Hope those bare feet can move fast."

"Pardon me?"

"I'm sayin' I hope yer ready to hustle, 'cause we're almost in the Societally Impinged Zone, and the only way to make it through (other than the monorail) is to run so fast you don't get caught."

"Run? I've no intention of running."

"Well, you'd better cultivate one. This place has every freak and killer ever crippled by society crawlin' through it, and I don't care to become another statistic."

Berdin's caution was indeed well-founded. The blocks the men were approaching made the rest of the Community seem festive and warm by comparison. Each block was completely covered by flyers, which in turn were obliterated by graffiti. The avenue was flooded with black spray-painted skulls and death threats, and the patios were surrounded by chain-link fence. Already, randomly-generated electronic music blasted an assault on the travelers' ears.

"See?" Berdin said. "Now are you ready to kick it inta high gear?"

Ian looked around sadly. "Such pain . . ." he muttered. He turned to Berdin. "These people won't hurt us. Besides, running only advertises the fact that you're a target."

The truth of Ian's statement did not assuage Berdin's fears. He had seen too many people on the 11:00 news that had gambled in the Zone and lost. But he knew, too, that there was no arguing with his companion, so he summoned his courage and set his jaw.

Eight paces into the Zone, a light bulb flew just over Ian and crashed into the block to his right. Soon a flurry of light bulbs, eggs, ashtrays and bottles was unleashed in their direction, along with a host of profanities (barely audible above the noise of the music). Berdin concentrated on dodging the various projectiles and wondered at his friend's composure and unchanging gait. They reached the end of the first block unscathed, only to find their path blocked by an enormous man with stringy black hair and muscles encased in chains and spikes.

"Here's a lotto ticket, leave us alone," Berdin offered.

The man slapped the ticket out of Berdin's hand and grabbed him by the shirt. "Not good enough, citizen," he growled, spitting out the last word sarcastically.

"Stop!" Ian commanded in a voice as loud as the monorails' roar.

The ogre looked at Ian in disbelief. "What?"

The barefoot man turned aside and said firmly, "Be quiet!" The random music died out instantly, in sync.

Ian turned back to the man and stared at him. "Stop, I said . . ."

Berdin felt the giant's grip relax, and he stepped away from him with as much dignity as he could muster. "Lucky for you you made the right choice, bub . . ." Ian silenced him with a wave of his hand.

"Your anger is misdirected," Ian said, "as well as your sense of responsibility. You, who have lived your life mired in a world steeped in lies, should welcome the truth with hosannas instead of hatred. You, Larry Garnot, have blindly lashed out against untruths you couldn't understand. The time for understanding has come."

Larry stood, open-mouthed, looking hard at Ian's eyes. He struggled to speak three times before he finally said (weakly), "Teach me."

Ian began walking. "You are right to feel cheated by society." The two men fell in step with him. "But you are wrong to blame this world for everything you do. If, indeed, the lies were true and you were your own boss, then why have you trapped yourself in a prison of drug use and whoremongering? But of course you are not your own boss. Nor should you be. Nor should society be. Who, then, should you trust in? Who can break your chains?"

Larry and Berdin walked quietly, awaiting the answer. As they did so, Berdin became dimly aware that the barrage of light bulbs had stopped, and that (stranger still) the loud, eerie strains of music died away in every block they approached. Many men and women, bleary-eyed and disheveled, stared from the windows of their units and spoke in hushed tones to one another. Long-unspoken words drifted in the air.

High above, a monorail rumbled. When it had passed, Ian looked at Larry and demanded, "Who?"

"You." The word popped out of the huge man's mouth and seemed to scare him. "You," he said—gaining conviction with every word, "can . . . break . . . my chains."

Stopping suddenly, Ian faced Larry and placed his right hand on the big man's head. "You have chosen. Let no trial drive this decision from your mind. Go now and never return to your angry ways."

"But," Larry blurted, "I want . . . I want to stay with you. I want to learn from you." Berdin wondered at the odd sound of pleading in such a gruff voice.

"It cannot be. Listen," Ian said. "A man awaking from a terrifying nightmare finds great comfort (as well he should) in the sight of sunrise. The rays of the sun—"

"Wait a minute," Berdin interrupted. "Is this going to be one of those stories again? Your stories never make sense to me, you know. Why don't you just—"

"Stop whining." Ian looked at Berdin until Berdin lowered his head and mumbled something about "understanding." Ian resumed:

"The rays of the sun warm the man, all the way to his heart, and assure him that reality is far better than the awful images and ideas he believed were reality. And at that moment the man wishes the sun was always with him, burning bright and true. But such direct, powerful exposure—untempered by experience—can be taken for granted; indeed, after weeks and weeks of sunshine the man may even become callous toward it, unappreciative of its brilliance. Only cold nights and cloudy days can remind the man of the precious nature of sunshine, and only in this understanding can the man learn enthusiasm for helping his neighbors to see and love the light. The sun always shines, but men must first taste the awful void of darkness before they cherish seeing the sun. Do you see?"

"I'll have to ponder it," Larry said gruffly.

"Fine. 'Ponder' it and then, when you understand, live it. Now we must go. But I promise, you'll see us again."

The two men turned and continued their trek toward the center of the Community. When they were out of earshot,

Berdin said in a confidential tone, "Nice trick, getting the gorilla-man to be our escort through the Zone—you definitely saved our butts . . . I do think, however, that you needn't have turned on me so harshly when I commented on your stories. It's not like I ruined the effect or anything."

"I reprimanded you because you spoke before you thought, a mistake you have an unfortunate tendency toward. In fact, you did it again just now." He looked at Berdin. "'Nice trick'? What an absurd thing to say—you know very well I'm not some shyster. If I thought you really believed most of what you say—well, that's when I'd offer up a really 'harsh' reprimand. But, of course, you do not. So I do not."

"So I'm a liar?" Berdin's eyes flashed.

"No, only a fool. And a rash one at that."

Berdin actually hopped a couple inches off the ground, he was so angry. "*That* does it! That's the end of the pixel! I've taken more than any sane man should take, and then I've taken a little more. But that"—here he poked Ian's chest to accentuate his words— "THAT's all I'm going to take!" He turned north and began storming down the avenue.

Ian let him storm 50 yards before he spoke. "Well, if that's the way you feel," his voice boomed down the concrete corridor, "have a nice time in the Zone . . . Elvis!" He smiled as he spoke the last word.

The wiry redhead took just two more steps before stopping. With his back still turned to Ian he cursed mightily. Then he took a deep breath, expanded his chest, and turned around. Without a word, and with as much dignity as he could muster, he marched back to Ian.

"Change of heart?" Ian looked innocent.

"Yes," Berdin growled. he walked right past his barefoot tormentor, and Ian fell in step with him.

"There's no cause to be jealous, you know. I can be friend to both Larry and you. In fact, I can be friend to every person in Coastal Community Twelve and still be true to Berdin Dwate. You needn't worry." Berdin just looked angrier, so Ian continued. "Further, Larry is not a gorilla-man. Yes, he is the size of a full-grown male gorilla, but he is every bit as human as you. Such an inaccurate description is unnecessary."

The men were now passing through the industrial part of the Community, which looked just like the Zone except it had less graffiti and fewer flyers, and each block had only two doors and one giant neon sign which brightly proclaimed the name of the business. They passed the Agricultural Processing building, the Publications Development building, the CWO Manufacturing Plant, the Furnishing and Decor Engineering facility, the Electronic Innovations building (its sign was unlit), and the Fashion Accessories and Clothier factory.

Soon, a block unlike any other they had passed loomed on their right. Its sign proclaimed "Transportation Unlimited," and two enormous glass elevators protruded upward from its center. The tops of the elevator shafts ended 200 feet up beside the monorail track, which hung gingerly in the air like a single strand of a spider's web. A small platform jutted out from just below the top of the shafts, almost connecting with the delicate strand. As the men looked on, a few harried people emerged from one of the doors of the building, looked around hastily, and moved in a group down a side avenue to their place of employment, the Architectural Design building. Immediately, another group of men and women emerged from Architectural Design, looked around, and rushed to the transportation depot.

Ian slowed his pace, watching the events closely. Berdin took no notice, but unconsciously slowed his gait to accommodate his companion. After a few more blocks he pulled up and muttered unhappily, "Here we are."

The two men's path was impeded by a large dull yellow wall, over 60 feet high and marked in new black letters (that even now were being repainted by a man on a scaffolding) proclaiming "CPA." The wall stretched out of sight in both directions. Beneath the letters a gate was cut into the wall, and an odd little tollbooth stood directly to its left. "Derive Authorization Here," read a small sign on top of the booth.

"You up to your insanity routine again?" Ian looked sideways at Berdin. The redhead jammed his fists in the pockets of his overalls and clenched his teeth. "No, I didn't think so. Well, let's try a more direct approach." With a sullen Field Engineer in tow, Ian moved toward the gate.

CHAPTER FIVE

"The wicked man flees though no one pursues,
but the righteous are as bold as lions."
—Proverbs 28:1

The intentionally bored-looking young man that sat in the booth didn't blink when Ian and Berdin approached his gate. He absently ran his hand through his already tousled hair and looked down again at the copy of *Nudes Illustrated* in his lap. He let Ian rap the glass three times before he looked up.

"Yeah?"

"We need to derive some authorization," Ian said. Berdin thought he noticed a trace of sarcasm in his companion's voice.

"Well, who the bitmap are you? I can't just authorize every yukface that comes in off the street." He mustered a bored sigh.

"I am Ian. This is Berdin Dwate."

"So?"

"So . . . we must speak with members of the CPA. Preferably various Cabinet members and possibly your Lieutenant Liberator, George Beaker."

"Is that so?"

"Yes, it is so."

"Well," the young man said as he defiantly pressed a red button beneath his desk, "may I ask where you work and why you think you're so neat you can waltz your problems straight into the CPA without going through the proper channels, like your department supervisor?"

"Neither of us are employed by your Community"— here Berdin's eyes widened considerably— "I am from the International Wilderness and my friend recently resigned from his position as a Field Engineer. As to why I think I'm 'neat,' I don't; I am simply right. And right need not explain itself to wrong."

The youth dropped his bored expression and stared unabashed. "Mister, you two need some Counseling. We don't talk that way around here."

"That's what I've been tryin' to tell him," Berdin muttered. He was wondering where he could run to when the kid decided to call the Law Enforcement Agents.

Ian put both palms on the glass front of the booth and leaned in close. Despite himself, the young man leaned back. "You don't talk that way around here," Ian said, "because you don't think around here. Now please, stop being difficult and open the gate."

"Uhh," the gatekeeper glanced at the red button, which was flashing. "Okay. You asked for it." He pulled a lever.

The gate rolled back. Berdin cringed. Ten men in

body armor, carrying stunguns, stepped through the opening. "You have forfeited your right to act as your own boss," said the Captain of Law Enforcement Battalion Eight, "by demonstrating yourselves to be uncooperative with society. One right remains: the right to be cured. It is our duty to escort you to the Justice Cabinet, which will oversee your rehabilitation, guaranteeing that right. Resistance will only prolong the cure."

Ian quietly studied the battalion. Slowly, he said, "The Justice Cabinet? Well, it's a start." And he walked toward the armored gang.

Inexplicably, Berdin did not flee. He wanted to—in fact, he decided to, but his legs refused. The horror of his plight washed over him, but it couldn't move him. He stood firmly, legs apart, and let Battalion Eight take him into custody. As they guided him back toward the entryway where Ian stood, he walked with his head held high, glaring at his captors.

"Brave . . ." Ian mumbled. Then he and Berdin were guided through the gate.

The inside of the CPA was warm and cheerful compared to the rest of the community. It consisted of a broad cement avenue which ran next to the outer wall, and a perfectly octagonal building which was encircled by the avenue. The building was six stories high and carved from a rough granite-colored stone. Clearly, it was meant to be a triumph of modern architectural design—but it tenaciously resembled an enormous paperweight. Still, the simple fact that it was a mute speckled color made the building seem lovely to citizens constantly faced with neon and grey.

Berdin and Ian were escorted around the building until they reached a door labelled "Justice." Berdin was sulking, so he was silent. Ian had attempted to share his wisdom with the guards, but the largest agent—the Captain—drowned him out with explanations of more ethereal rights. When Ian told him he considered rights granted by the state "transitory and therefore meaningless," the Captain recommended he "tell that to the Head J.C." Before Ian could reply, they were jostled through the door, through a crowded lobby, and into an elevator. There Law Enforcement Battalion Eight held a hurried conference in which it was decided that Agent KB75 would stay with the M.I.'s (Mentally Impinged), and the rest would adjourn to the Patrol room for extended mission execution debrief. Agent KB75 did not look thrilled by the decision.

In fact, as soon as the other agents had retreated and the elevator door had closed, the Agent backed into the corner, fixed his eyes on the two men, and drew his stungun. "Look, you crazies," he said—looking just a little crazy himself— "I don't want any trouble. I don't care ya lost your marbles . . . I don't care if yer Our Benevolent Liberator himself in yer own minds. Just stay back, stay quiet, don't make me hurt ya . . ." Beads of sweat shone on his forehead.

"Yeah, you're a tough guy with that gun," Berdin sneered. "I'm really tremblin' to think how you'd be if it was just you and me and no guns. You . . ."

"Don't be so quick to speak, Berdin," Ian interrupted. He turned to the Agent. "You are right to feel great fear, but your reasons are misguided. You need fear only one thing, and that is He who may pass judgment on you."

" . . . Pansy." Berdin muttered the end of his tirade, and the elevator buzzed to signal it had reached the top floor.

The three men stepped out, Berdin and Ian ahead of the Agent, who still flourished his gun. They stepped into a quiet reception hall, dimly lit, with simulated wood grain cabinets and artificial plants lining its walls. In the corner, in the gloom, sat a small metal desk guarding a small artificial man.

"Can-I-help-you?" the artificial man said, in a clacking, rhythmic cant. As he did so, he moved his head, owl-like, to look at his visitors.

"Yeah," the Agent stepped from behind his two prisoners, and spoke to the bald, riveted, metallic dummy while still staring at his charges. "Yeah, these two 'gentlemen' were creating a disturbance at Checkpoint EE7, flagrantly in violation of procedure and decorum. More details can be obtained through consultation with said Checkpoint's Morning Supervisor. That is all."

Immediately following Agent KB75's monologue, the elevator doors began to close, and the Agent quickly turned, dove between them, and disappeared.

"Please-approach-my-desk," clacked the artificial man. As they did so, Berdin realized why the agent had been so pointed in his efforts to avoid looking at the android: its two eyes closely resembled human eyeballs, staring unblinkingly from their metal casings. He felt vaguely sick.

Ian, too, was looking with disgust upon the receptionist. He frowned mightily as the android continued: "Welcome-citizens-I-am-an-AIA-Artificial-Intelligence-Android-built-with-some-hope-of-simulating-the-wonderful-capacities-of-our-most-important-advance-the-Evolutionary-Quantum-Leap-While-I-can-not-claim-the-power-or-brilliance-of-the-E-Q-L-I-can-claim-common-ancestry-and-as-such-am-of-the-same-species-It-is-my-somewhat-unenviable-task-to-restrict-you-from-exiting-until-you-have-been-reviewed-by-the-Jus-tice-Cabinet-Normally-they-would-not-serve-as-the-primary-review-board-for-citizen-misbehavior-but-your-infractions-are-of-a-most-unique-and-unquieting-nature-You-have-been-charged-with-"

"Silence, demon!" Ian struck his fist on the desk. The grisly android was quiet instantly, and neither moved its head nor clicked nor whirred again.

Berdin held his breath for a few seconds, anticipating a reprimand. When none was forthcoming, he allowed himself a nervous grin. "Phew! I'm glad you shut him up," he said, feeling generous enough to renew communication with Ian.

"He was a demon. You must understand that mere electricity and magnets cannot create genuine analytical thought and meaningful speech responses."

"Huh? Oh, yeah, I understand perfectly," Berdin said, as he moved toward the elevator. "Yeah, no speech repossession or nothing, I gotcha . . . Hey! Where's the button for this 'vator?"

Ian rolled his eyes. It was a startling expression; it made Berdin feel the same way a primitive tribesman must feel when the sun is covered in a partial eclipse. The robed, patient man answered: "Berdin, your Central Planning Agency is inept, but they're not so bungling as to leave a means for us to access the elevator and escape. The only way for us to exit this room is through the door next to that machine's desk, which of course leads to the Justice Cabinet's Conference Room. Now I know you'd rather not go through that door, but believe me, it's exactly where we should go. We haven't made it this far by chance or fate, but by design."

"Yeah, *your* design. That doesn't make us any less stupid for bein' where we are. Don't rock the boat, that's always been my motto—"

"And the motto of every citizen of this community."

"And I should have just stuck to it and kept my nose clean. But no, I go for the campfire in The Field and the next thing I know I'm an ACCESSORY to attempting to UNDERMINE SOCIETY! Of all the . . ."

A voice over a loudspeaker proclaimed, "The Justice Cabinet will review your case now."

Berdin paled. "No. Oh no. Do you think they heard me?"

"I think the people in Island Community Eight heard you. Now put on your brave face and let's go." Ian led the way through the far door. Despite himself, Berdin cast one last glance at the AIA receptionist. It winked.

The Justice Cabinet's quarters were enormous, and even more poorly lighted than the reception hall. At the far end of the room a giant picture window looked out on a concrete park, which lay in the center of the CPA building. This window provided the only light: the artificial light of the distant ceiling lamps high overhead "outside." Directly in front of the window sat twelve plush velvet chairs, facing Ian and Berdin, and a polished heavy table stretched endlessly in front of the chairs. Twelve figures showed dimly in the gloom, slumped in their richly-upholstered seats. A faint odor of cigar smoke hung in the air, as did the dry crackle of static electricity. An acrid taste settled on Berdin's tongue. He looked around for a place to sit, but no other furniture was in the room. The walls were dotted with CWO monitors and other communications screens.

"Approach the Bench," a steely female voice said.

"What's going—" Berdin started.

"Don't talk! Don't ask questions! You have severely eroded your usefulness to the community, and are facing the most grievous of correctional measures. It is quite possible that this Cabinet will recommend termination as the only means of reconciling yourselves to society. You have no say in the matter, and will speak only in accordance with our wishes. Is that clear?"

"Yes," Berdin bowed his head.

"Don't TALK!" the woman yelled hoarsely, jumping to her feet. "I will not tolerate imbeciles! You do not," she said, leaning over the table and lowering her voice, "know how much power I wield. But you will learn. And if you continue in spiting me, you will learn in ways more painful than you can imagine. Now . . ." she straightened up, looming tall in the gloom, "Approach the Bench!"

Ian strode forward, Berdin by his side. They stopped a few feet in front of the table and squinted at the members of the Justice Cabinet. The woman, apparently the Chief Justice, had seated herself in the right-hand middle chair. Berdin had already decided he didn't like her—or anything about her—but he supposed her features were of the kind that many men would call "striking." Her chin was a little too flat for his tastes, her nose a little too sharp—and her metallic blonde hair was cut like the male soldiers he had seen in history books. Still worse, her eyes gleamed with a kind of uncontained passion that made Berdin restless and even a little queasy. It was the kind of gleam that he had always imagined haunted the eyes of fanatics from the Close-Minded Age. The woman's garb was identical to the clothes worn by her companions—a black blouse with black pants—except her blouse had a large purple star in the center. Her hand gestures seemed contrived to bring attention to the star. She always seemed to be pointing toward her chest or making flapping motions that caused you to notice the odd emblem.

The other members of the Cabinet were, almost to the man, unworthy of notice. They slumped and fidgeted in their various seats with little change of expression—choosing almost always to appear stern yet somehow bored. Some were short, some thin, some tall—one was remarkably shaped like a toad—but none excited any real interest on Berdin's part, except for the man sitting on his extreme left. This man, whose features were all but lost in the twilight, seemed to be watching Berdin and Ian with an intent ferocity—not because his eyes followed them (one simply couldn't see to know), but because he sat ram-rod straight in his chair and gave a faint guttural growl whenever either man moved suddenly. This unnerved Berdin almost immediately, and kept him so shaken that it was many minutes before he noticed perhaps the single-most puzzling thing about the Justice Cabinet: eleven of its twelve members were male! Upon realizing this, Berdin became even more disturbed—clearly they were facing people above the law, people who could flaunt a government regulation as sacrosanct as the Absolute Equal Individual Opportunity Ultimatum (AEIOU) of Our Benevolent Liberator himself. How else could one explain such gender prejudice? It was at this point, confronted by the blatant injustice of the branch of the CPA that was supposed to defend justice, that Berdin began to feel something other than fear and outrage. Deep down, so deep he didn't really acknowledge it was there, a spark of the taste for absolutes began to kindle. Suddenly, truth was a little less something declared, a little more something discovered. He swallowed to force the feeling back down into his gut.

Even as he did so, he began to really hear what the Chief Justice was saying. He had paid attention long enough to hear her refer to herself as "Justice Brophy," but began tuning her out when she broke into a long monologue consisting almost entirely of state mottos. Apparently, such hearings began with a reprimand—Brophy had immediately begun explaining to them that "no one has the right to be their own boss" when some people "decide they are above society," and that, further, "Tolerance is a virtue which requires complete and unswerving devotion to the ideal of equal authority." Berdin began paying attention again as Brophy ran out of platitudes, closing with the old chestnut that "Fences and bars make men free to rebel."

"And," she added with a triumphant flourish that made Berdin start and the justice on his far left growl, "men like you severely threaten that freedom."

"You speak as if you have already found us guilty," Ian said. "Shouldn't you try us first?" Berdin stared openly at his companion, half expecting Justice Brophy to immediately terminate Ian for talking before he was granted permission.

"You don't understand, do you?" she said, ignoring Ian's breach of decorum. "What you did specifically is irrelevant. The fact that you behaved in a fashion deviant enough to merit the attention of Law Enforcement makes you guilty by default. Such actions lead men to believe you might be aware of an authority which supersedes their own personal authority, and that removes their freedom to serve only them selves. Such an effort to infringe on personal freedom is, in my opinion, the worst possible means one can choose to undermine society."

"But . . ." Berdin began.

"DON'T TALK!" Justice Brophy screamed. She stared violently at Berdin, who had jumped a little, and then she picked up her gavel and threw it at him, hitting him in the stomach. Berdin flinched but didn't make a noise.

"Pick that up!" she yelled in her scratchy, throaty voice. "Bring it here!"

Berdin reluctantly stepped forward and handed her the gavel. She snatched it with one hand and grabbed his wrist with the other. He felt her fingernails dig into his arm, and wondered at the frenzy of her grip. She leaned forward and hissed, "You'll not make that mistake again." As Berdin nodded, she released him—still staring with the odd gleam in her eyes.

Ian put his hand gently on Berdin's shoulder. "You're okay, right?" The smaller man nodded. Ian strode forward, resting his hands on the table. "Do not threaten him again. He is my friend."

The growling justice stood up with a rush, knocking over his chair. "Silence, dog!" he barked. "Chief Justice Brophy has spoken, and need not listen to your meaningless drivel! Speak again, and I'll strike you down myself!"

Ian drew himself to his full height, a pinnacle over the seated justices and the standing growler. An awful quiet hung in the room. The robed man opened his mouth to speak, but Brophy interrupted. "Thank you for your concern, Bila," she said icily. "Your attempts to entrench yourself in my good graces, however, annoy me. You intrigue me only as a lover, and even then only when I require you. Sit down." Bila turned his chair over and hastily sat down. Brophy, who had fixed her stare on Ian throughout this reprimand, lowered her voice and spoke to him: "Your point is well taken."

"No, I don't believe you sincerely understand," Ian said. Berdin felt his heart sink, awed at how shamelessly Ian pressed his luck. "Jane Brophy, you and your fellow cabinet members trust in just two tools: power and fear. It is your general belief that personal power is some kind of absolute good, and that the only means of maintaining that power is by constantly causing those below you to fear you."

"So? Why tell me what I believe—don't I already know?"

"You do—yes. Your mind is sharp, and your belief system is coherent. Further, even when I demonstrate that your beliefs are based on false precepts, you will ignore me, for your heart has been hardened since your personality was put together. But in your narcissism, you've forgotten your fellow Cabinet members. I tell you what you believe because, to one degree or another, each of your fellow justices believes the same thing—and not all of them are made in such a way that they cannot accept the truth. Never ask to whom I speak, only seek to understand the words I speak to you."

"I do understand. You are a throw-back, an antique— a fossil from the Close-Minded Age. You neither believe tolerance to be the ultimate good (as saps like he do)"—here Brophy gestured at Berdin, "nor power, as cynics like I do. You actually believe in—oh, I feel ridiculous saying it" (here she giggled in a high-pitched, joyless chirp) "in an authority higher than man. You may even believe in an after-life. Regardless, you are too full of pre-scientific hogwash to have anything of value to say to this Cabinet."

Ian lowered his chin and stared at her. "But I believe," he said, "that what I have to say is of immeasurable value. And since your community's only real standard is tolerance, who are you to censor my beliefs?"

The woman stared back, her upper lip twitching. The odd gleam in her eyes flamed higher. "Speak your piece," she murmured hoarsely.

"Thank you." Ian began to pace the length of the table. "Chief Justice Brophy speaks more truly than she knows when she calls me an 'antique.' I come from the International Wilderness, and I am from an Age even older than she can conceive. Tell me," he stopped pacing and peered at one of the nondescript justices, "are my ideas, my beliefs, inherently wrong because they are not modern? Does truth become outdated? Do you know? . . . No, you do not. You know nothing, nor does anyone in this society. You think you know—some have even guessed the truth—but it is not knowing. True knowledge requires a true foundation, not one built on Fashion or Progress or the Scientific Method. True knowledge requires a rock, not shifting winds. Listen to me now. These are the most important words you will ever hear: truth lies not in the Benevolent Liberator or the EQL, nor even in yourselves. These truths are relative; real truth is absolute. I am that truth."

The Justice Cabinet was less than pleased with that revelation. Fury swept the room in a dingy tumult. Angry words burst, justices turning this way or that, talking and shouting, pointing fingers, working loudly into chaos. Finding no one to listen, the black-garbed court talked louder and gestured more, boiling like the sea in a storm. Ian stood calmly in the eye of the swirling panic, flanked by Berdin, who had moved to his side when the confusion began. The wiry Field Engineer glared around the room, fists clenched at his side. He finally was beginning to understand.

With this understanding came a sudden, irrational burst of fear. Not the usual kind—that of imminent death—he'd been experiencing more or less since he met Ian, but rather a strange fear that Ian might also be about to die, leaving Coastal Community Twelve (and especially Berdin Dwate) very much the poorer. He intuited that separation from Ian was the very worst fate he could face. How crazy, he thought (at the same time making a mental note that he was crazy for reflecting so deeply in the midst of such a horrible tempest) that he would feel such an acute fear of being separated from a barefoot man he barely knew. And yet, he reflected, he did feel a powerful knowledge . . . a *quality* of knowledge. Unconsciously, he nodded his head. That was it.

His thoughts were drawn back into the mayhem slowly, as a man awakes in the early morning to the unsteady chirping of a cricket. Dimly, he became aware that Justice Brophy, who had leapt up at the inception of the commotion, was now literally howling with rage. It was a terrible, bestial sound and it tugged at him in a frightening way. As she howled, the Chief Justice gazed around the room, apparently unseeingly, blinded by the ferocious glow blazing in her eyes. Berdin quailed as her eyes turned on him. He resisted a temptation to cling to Ian like a scared child, and braced himself until she turned her gaze to another. But she didn't turn—she fixed him with that vacant, mad stare and continued her low howling. Unnerved, Berdin grabbed the sleeve of Ian's gown and closed his eyes.

He opened them to the sound of Brophy's gavel pounding the table and the subsiding wake of the storm. The justices were sitting down again, but many were still speaking hurriedly, attempting to finish their individual tirades. Brophy smashed the gavel down again, and screamed, "Quiet!" The room became still.

"I don't know what your whole name is," she said, looking at Ian, "and I don't particularly care. You could have come from the woods or you could have come from a can of tomato soup—either suits me fine. But what you've said today (incredibly, in the presence of the Justice Cabinet) is something this society has worked long and hard to avoid hearing. Some of these men are more idealistic than I, and therefore probably wouldn't resort to such primitive language—but I say to you: today you have blasphemed against our new world order. You have denied the only thing which our society unanimously believes in—relativity—and have claimed, in essence, to be the downfall of our way of life. Such authoritarian bigotry staggers the imagination. Indeed, I am more than a little surprised that your speech didn't incite these men to physically assault you. The bottom line is this: you are dangerous; perhaps—no, certainly—the most dangerous person to ever open his mouth in our community. Your 'friend,' the cowering former Field Engineer, would be insignificant beyond mentioning—easily cured by a few trips to Pharmaceutical Counselling—had he not been tainted by your influence. As it is, he is guilty by association. I see no need to list the charges that Coastal Community Twelve . . . assigns you. Your radical attempts to undermine society are so obvious even Justice Bila is capable of recognizing them . . ." (low growl from the corner). "Thus, I believe all that is necessary is to call for a verdict from my colleagues. Justice Cabinet of Coastal Community Twelve,"—here she raised her voice and folded her hands on her stomach with her thumbs pointing upward at the purple star—"what verdict do you assign the two men that stand before us today?"

Berdin knew what was coming, and searched himself for feelings of self-pity. The feelings were there, deep down—but they were not urgent. Mostly, he felt resignation mixed with the same odd melancholy over his imminent loss of Ian. He tried to stir himself, to form some plan of action, however desperate—but his normally headstrong nature resisted his prodding. He was conjuring mental pictures of horrible tortures and slow deaths in an effort to excite himself to action when Ian leaned over and whispered, "Don't worry. The time for action is not yet at hand. Just pray that you are ready when the day comes." The word "pray" cuffed Berdin's mind, like Latin words spoken in casual conversation.

Meanwhile, each member of the Justice Cabinet was, in turn, rising to his feet and solemnly stating, "Guilty to extremes." The man built like a toad attempted to add the reasons he chose to deliver such a verdict, but he was shouted down by the Chief Justice. When each of the eleven men had stood and intoned the same phrase, Brophy herself stood, looked at the men, and said: "I, too, find you guilty to extremes. And the punishment for such guilt is termination as directed by the Justice Cabinet."

Brophy spoke the words in her low, gruffled voice as ominously as she could, apparently taking delight in the fear she inflicted when assigning such penalties. This time, she was disappointed—Ian was as unmoved as the foundation of the CPA building, and Berdin, though dismayed, solemnly faced the Cabinet with the intuitive understanding that outward manifestations of fear would only reward Brophy.

Besides, a glimmer of hope was flickering dimly in his murky subconscious. Every termination the Justice Cabinet of Coastal Community Twelve ever carried out was done on the basis of a confession by the extremely guilty party. Indeed, in each case the terminated had literally pleaded with the Cabinet to end his societally-stunting life. Berdin knew this to be true because he witnessed such confessions on the CWO monitor. These scenes had always intrigued him, as he never understood the motives of the guilty. If they had acted in ways that drastically undermined society, why did they later repent and allow themselves to be terminated for the good of society? Why the sudden concern for a society they had previously flaunted? Guilt might explain such actions, but guilt was a concept from the Close-Minded Age. Individual guilt had been psycho-analyzed away years ago . . .

Out of his muddled reverie, Berdin wrested a reason for optimism. Termination required confession, even repentance! He and Ian could simply deny their extreme guilt and avoid the punishment. Forgetting the risk of incurring Brophy's wrath, Berdin exclaimed, "Hey! This can't apply—"

"SHUT UP!" Brophy was on her feet immediately. Ian raised his hand, as if to calm her. She sat down, still scowling. Only a low growl rumbled the tense silence.

"Have your say, then, farmer," Brophy sneered. "Grace us with the profound wisdom of the proletariat."

"I really must protest, Chief Justice," a voice said. Berdin looked around, surprised. The toad-shaped man was on his feet, and was speaking in a nervous, hurried tone. "Your attitude is coloring your language and causing you to breach decorum. I could tolerate your reference to blasphemy—in a curious way, it may have even been appropriate—but your use of the vulgar to describe a Field Engineer is really too much. Such outbursts betray the ideal of the community."

Upon finishing his discourse, the Justice flinched once, looked around, sat down, and tried to maintain his dignity while sweating. Berdin averted his eyes from Brophy, expecting her to fly into a rage. Instead, she laughed. The noise rang against the bare walls, echoing unkindly in Berdin's ears.

"You fool," she spoke calmly. "You haughty, ridiculous fool. You really do believe Our Benevolent Liberator's whole spiel, don't you? You probably think the EQL creates wisdom! Listen, Crashton: it doesn't matter a whit what the community does, and I don't care if anything I do 'contributes to the development of society' or makes the world a better place for the next generation. Know why? Because I'm all that matters. What's best for me"—she pointed at her purple star as her calm began to abandon her—"is my only concern. I'd be a hypocrite if I lived any other way. That's right, a hypocrite—like you, you old fool—because I'd be acting like I had some reason for caring about the community or the world. But I haven't got a reason! And neither have you. What would it be, Integrity? Conscience? Spiritual Obedience? No, those are all Close-Minded Age concepts, and you *earnestly*"—she sneered—"reject those. So what are you left with? I'll tell you! You! And I'm left with me. And I'm out to make sure that 'me' gets a better deal than 'you.' And if you were smart—which you most emphatically are not—you would act according to the same principles." Brophy paused for a breath, and regrouped her thoughts. "So why do I tolerate such an overbearing dinosaur as yourself? Simple: you're a useful figurehead for the Justice Cabinet. When the CWO Directors want someone from my Cabinet to spout Our Benevolent Liberator's tired rhetoric, I shove you in front of the cameras. But, believe me, should you ever outlive your usefulness I will revel in the opportunity to discredit, humiliate, and terminate you. Do not forget that!"

The toad-man's dignity had completely wilted before the tirade. He sat motionless in sweaty, gloomy silence. The quiet was broken by the timid scraping of a chair on the floor. Hesitantly, another justice stood. "But . . . I agree with Justice Crashton, and I b-believe in the ideals of our . . . Community."

The Chief Justice crossed her arms and glared. "Then that makes one of you expendable." The timid Justice fairly leapt back into his seat, trying to blend in with its upholstery.

"Now," the Chief Justice unfolded her arms, "I believe every dolt has had their say except for you, *farmer*." Her eyes flashed at Berdin.

The sunburned Field Engineer swallowed. "Uh, I, well, I, that is, I saw in CWO where nobody gets assigned termination unless they . . . uh . . . *wanted* it. You know, unless they believed they were extremely guilty. Well, I think I speak for both Ian and myself when I say we do *not*, uh, perceive ourselves as guilty and therefore do *not* grant you permission to terminate us."

Berdin noticed, out of the corner of his eye, that Ian was smiling. The barefoot man leaned over to Berdin and said, "You never will say die, will you? I bet you'd moo like a cow if you thought it would help in any way."

Chief Justice Brophy was also smiling, although only one corner of her mouth turned upwards, so that she appeared unbalanced. "Unbelievable," she said, shaking her head. "You are every bit as gullible—no, more gullible—than Crashton. You actually believe what you see on CWO monitors! Can the same be said for you, Mr. Back to Nature? Or have you, Ian of the International Wilderness, guessed the truth?!"

"I do not guess." Ian looked at her. "But I know the truth." He sighed. "You and your colleagues force those assigned extreme guilt to confess and plead for termination."

"Right, blasphemer." She stood, clenching the gavel in her left hand. "And we will employ any means to elicit such begging from you and your friend. We will tape take after take of your confession, and I will encourage you between takes to perform to my satisfaction. I will break your fingers, and stick thumbtacks in your eyes if I must, but the Justice Cabinet will hear your repentance. They deplore my means, but they are willing to look the other way for the good of society. Besides, they have little choice in the matter. Almost as little as you."

Ian surprised Berdin again at this point. He turned his back on Brophy and walked toward the door in a steady, measured pace. Berdin saw the Chief Justice's eyes gleam with rage. Three steps from the door, Ian turned around. He spoke in a loud, impassioned voice. "I have brought you the truth today. Most of you believe the ideals of your society closely mirror the truth. Justice Brophy has, ironically, made truth more accessible to you by demonstrating the folly of such ideals. She has revealed your precious community for what it is: a ship lost at sea, without an anchor or a port. Unfortunately, while she recognizes the inconsistency, she is blinded to the lie behind the inconsistency. She accepts the senseless world she finds herself in, and seeks to make sense of it by serving only herself. But I tell you, while she seeks power and you anesthetize yourselves with sex and drugs, you forget the One truly worthy to be served—"

"Stop it!" Bila was on his feet again. He was seething. "Have you no shame, no sense of decency?" Berdin stole a glance at Brophy, who (oddly) appeared slightly relieved. "Your babbling flaunts all that this court stands for, and will be tolerated no longer! We give you one pain-free chance to confess your extreme guilt to our satisfaction, and then we let Brophy have her way with you. And frankly, today I feel like helping her! Jermis," he turned to a fellow justice, "call down and have them prepare the studio!"

Jermis glanced at Brophy and then began to stand, but Ian held up his hand. "That won't be necessary, Jermis," he said. Berdin gaped at him, as did Bila and ten other justices. Brophy looked on with helpless fury, a hungry tigress in a cage. "Berdin and I will be leaving now. We have said all we wanted to say. All but this: you know, don't you, who the One worthy to be served is?" Incredibly, each justice dropped his or her eyes and gazed at the floor. "Yes, I thought you did. Well, the truth is yours, and now I charge you to loose it. Let's go, Berdin."

People talk about children's eyes being wide with delight at Christmastime, or cat's eyes widening with terror at the sight of a dog. But no man or animal, from the beginning of time to the end of the earth, has ever stared with wider eyes than Berdin Dwate as he walked away from the bench. Indeed, his mind was so staggered by the audacity of his friend and the apparent impotence of the Justice Cabinet he began to question reality. He looked around the dim room, suspiciously searching the back of his brain for memory of a recent journey to the Pharmaceutical Counseling Center; he knew the only possible explanation for this realistic delusion was the powerful hallucinatory effect of some TRRIP (Twisted Reality Resulting from Intravenous Pharmaceuticals).

To snap out of a TRRIP, Berdin knew, he had to use unpredictable behavior. Carefully, he put his hands palms down on the floor, and stood on his head. It didn't help. The illusory reality looked exactly the same except, of course, it was all upside down (and the Justice Cabinet now looked positively scandalized). Ian's voice sounded above him: "As you can see, Brophy, it would have been impossible to get a confession out of him anyway. He's crazy as a loon." Then Ian gripped one of Berdin's feet and gently pushed it forward till the small Field Engineer toppled. "Come on," he said.

Berdin never saw how Ian opened the door. When he scrambled to his feet, the barefoot man was already passing through the doorway. Berdin hesitated for a heartbeat, and then fled after him. He followed Ian closely, looking straight ahead so as to avoid the glare of the android. He tried to watch the way Ian opened the elevator door, but it seemed to require no more than a touch. Once inside the elevator, Ian pushed the button marked "ground floor," and smiled. His eyes sparkled as he looked at Berdin.

"You are not on a drug trip," he said. "Although for a moment there you certainly acted like you were." He smiled bigger. "Why didn't you just take my advice, and moo like a cow?"

"Because," Berdin said, staring dazedly at the elevator wall, "it was suggested to me by what I considered part of my hallucination, and therefore might not have been unpredictable enough." The elevator opened into the lobby on the ground floor.

The two men walked, unnoticed, through the lobby and emerged "outside" in the street. "Did that really happen?" Berdin asked.

"Yes. It really did."

"Then why aren't we having thumbtacks stuck in our eyes?"

"Because the time for me to be handed over has not yet come."

"This has got nothing to do with time. We just walked out on the highest judiciary branch of Coastal Community Twelve. That's not how it's supposed to go." Berdin had his hands on his hips.

"Well, if that's not how it's supposed to go, how come you're standing here arguing with me instead of running away so Justice Brophy doesn't run out here and nab you?"

Berdin dropped his hands to his sides and cocked his head. "Good point," he said. "Let's go." He started to move toward the gate, but Ian grabbed his arm.

"It's not a good point," Ian said. "They would have stopped us immediately if they had the power—but they don't. Not yet."

"So . . . you didn't just lead me into the jaws of death?"

Ian laughed. "No, I didn't. Besides, you must learn: there are some things worse than death."

"Yeah, like thumbtacks in the eyeballs. I get yer point. So now what? Can we just march in anywhere we want and give 'em a good talkin' to?"

"We can . . . yes. But *we* won't. I've got to do some things alone now, so you can head back to your unit. Rest up. You've had an eventful 24 hours."

Berdin looked a little hurt. "Yeah, but I can take more. Let me stay with you. I promise I won't gripe so much now."

"It's not a question of griping——although you are good at that—but of conforming to the plan. And right now the plan requires that I go it alone. Don't be upset, I'm not rejecting you. You'll see me again soon. Now go."

"I'm not upset," Berdin mumbled as he turned and began to shuffle away. "It's not like I've never been alone before . . . I can take care of myself . . ." Ian patiently watched him walk away. "It's just that—hey!" Berdin strode swiftly back to Ian. "How d'ya expect me to make it through the Zone all alone? Ya might as well tie a ham around my neck and throw me to the lions! . . . Guess that means I'll have to stay with you."

"No, it doesn't. No one in the Zone will hurt you, for the same reason no one hurt you on the way out here. It is not a part of the plan."

"Oh." Berdin looked at the ground. "So," he shuffled his feet, "so what's the plan for you? I mean, what are you gonna do right now without me?"

"I'm going to enter various doors in the CPA building, take the elevator to the top floor, and 'give 'em a good talking to.' Enough stalling. Get along, so I can get to work."

Berdin looked shocked. "Stalling? Oh no, I'm not stalling." Again he turned and began walking away. "Man, for someone who thinks he can read people's minds, you've got me figured all wrong," he muttered as he moved down the avenue. Ian watched him, smiling at the running commentary. When Berdin disappeared around the curve of the building, Ian turned and walked the other way.

Eventually, Berdin stopped talking to himself and began to ponder the road before him. The Zone was an ugly problem, despite Ian's reassurances. But an even uglier dilemma was rearing its meddlesome head—namely, how to get through the gate and out of the CPA complex? Berdin stopped to ponder this problem, but the appearance of an official-looking man from a nearby door reminded him of the Law Enforcement Agency and set him walking again. *Too many problems*, he thought. His mind was only capable of wrestling with one problem at a time; his stubborn nature was that of a bulldog: it could sink its teeth into a problem and shake it until it was dead—but each problem required his full, tenacious attention. When beset by a number of problems his inclination was to move forward at full speed, and hope to trample them underfoot.

He opted for this strategy now, hurrying toward the gate with his head hung low. If he kept moving, and maintained a low profile, he might make it through. Anyway, it was better than just standing around looking desperate, waiting for someone to get suspicious and call Justice Brophy and the thumbtack squad.

After a few moments of hurried walking, the nervous former Field Engineer (who had suddenly realized he was starving) reached his first obstacle: Checkpoint EE7. He looked around for an attendant's booth, but none was in sight. This puzzled him. No attendant, no one to tell to open the gate. What could this mean? He stepped forward to give the gate a nudge, and at that point noticed a sophisticated intercom housed in the wall on his right.

At least, it looked like an intercom—but there were no buttons to push. This froze Berdin for a moment. Logical progression was breaking down, and he was already feeling susceptible to panic. He opened his mouth, but doubted the value of speaking. He shut his mouth. He looked over his shoulders. (No one around.) He set his jaw, leaned in close, and opened his mouth.

"Hello," he said.

Long pause. "Yeah?" a familiar bored voice sighed.

"Open the gate." Berdin tried to sound commanding.

"Yeah, sure thing. Right after ya tell me your clearance code."

Berdin was in a gambling frame of mind. "XY6912-F."

Long pause. "What kind of a crazy code is that? You want me to go ahead and call the Law Enforcement?"

"Listen, you punk," Berdin growled, desperate and emboldened by his desperation. "This is Justice Bila of Coastal Community Twelve's Justice Cabinet. In case you haven't been informed, I'm dyslexic and therefore can't—can*not*—remember my code. Open this gate before I am forced to file a disciplinary report!"

"Citizen," the intercom squawked, "you're the worst liar I've ever heard. I'm gonna go ahead and open this gate just to have a look at you—and if ya give me any trouble I'll have Law Enforcers crawlin' all over you." With that, the gate began to move.

Naturally, Berdin's first inclination was to dart through the gate and make Law Enforcement chase him through the Zone. But a man running through the Zone was an instant victim—like a man hitting a wasp's nest with a stick. So Berdin opted instead to go on the offensive. He strode through the gate with his arms swinging brashly, his head up, and a leer (or a close approximation) on his lips. He fairly swaggered to the attendant's booth. The young attendant's mouth hung open.

"Y-you!"

"Yeah, it's me, you punk. What are ya gonna do about it? Call some more fancy men in uniforms? Why dontcha do that, kid—why not? and while we're waiting for 'em I'll show you what I showed the last set of Enforcement Pansies! How does that sound—Punk?!" As he snapped the last word, Berdin slammed his fist hard against the glass, rattling the booth and making the attendant jump from his chair.

The attendant was looking around wildly, backing away from Berdin, whining: "No-no problem, citizen. No sweat. I was just messin' with ya . . . I . . . "

"You're not worth it," Berdin growled, and he turned to stride away. As he swaggered down the avenue, he allowed himself a small smile.

CHAPTER SIX

"With them the Seed of Wisdom did I sow,
And with mine own hand wrought to make it grow;
And this was all the Harvest that I reap'd--
'I came like Water, and like Wind I go'."
—Edward Fitzgerald, *The Rubaiyat of Omar Khayyam*

Outside Coastal Community Twelve, raindrops spattered dustily on The Field and the SHELL. An early July windstorm swirled the big drops and moaned through the tree trunks. Pines creaked. Wheat stalks bent low, and slapped each other's backs in cadence with the wind. The air was profound with static electricity and the smell of the wrestle between bone-dry and wet. Gradually the wind grew purposeful, and drove the maturing angrier drops in a northeast slant. Field Engineers, scattering artificial curses, fled for the protection of the SHELL. No one stayed to see the lightning.

Inside, a sinewy redhead was talking to himself. Berdin

Dwate, painfully conscious of the stares he was eliciting, stood near the corner of a block on the edge of the Zone and convinced himself that Ian did not actually expect him to run the Zone alone. Once convinced, Berdin darted across an avenue into the monorail terminal, entered an elevator, and rode to the top. He stepped out of the elevator onto a small platform—surrounded by railings but still dizzyingly high—and awaited the arrival of the next train. No one else was on the platform, so Berdin closed his eyes and relaxed. It felt good to pause and contemplate his potential freedom.

He opened his eyes to the sound of an on-rushing train. Blinking rapidly—he was temporarily blinded by the intensity of the artificial ceiling lights, which were brighter at this altitude—he tried to pull himself together to face another challenge. The train pulled up quickly, effortlessly, and opened its door to allow two passengers to exit. Berdin dove in the open doorway, which closed behind him with a "whoosh."

Immediately he heard a bell ringing. An angry Transport Engineer had sounded the bell to delay the monorail's forward progress, and was now bearing down on Berdin.

"All right, citizen," he said in a nasal twang, "just who do you think you are and where're you going?"

"I'm Berdin Dwate, and I'm a former Field Engineer on my way to inform employers in the mercantile district of my recently imposed availability." Berdin spoke these words with little hope, wondering why he was such a lousy liar.

The Transport Engineer stared at him. He frowned. Then he reached above his head and pulled a cable which sounded the bell again. "That's good enough for me," he said, and the train began to move.

Berdin blinked. "Uh . . . thanks," he said, and sat

down. The Transport Engineer made a show of looking around the passenger car—which was empty except for the two men— and then sat down next to Berdin. He was exactly the kind of man who irritated Berdin the most—a gossipy, nosy type willing to cough up all his dignity for anyone who seemed vaguely predisposed to tolerate him. His eyes were in a permanent squint (as most all monorail employees' eyes were because of their prolonged exposure to the intense light), but his squint was different in that it made him look uncommonly like a mole. Berdin flinched and looked away, staring at the row of seats across from him.

"I've heard about you," the conductor said, tapping Berdin on the arm. "Oh, yes, I've heard it all. That's why, as soon as I recognized you I let you on without a fight. That's right. I was ready to give you what-for—who does this guy think he is, I said to myself when I saw you on the platform— but then I got a good look at you." The little man was leaning forward, imploring Berdin to condescend to look at him. "And when I saw who it was, I said to myself: look out, it's the very same man who was with the wild man from the International Wilderness. I know it is. Most people would hesitate, wouldn't believe their eyes or the stories they heard, but not me—I just saw you and I knew. I said, here he is, the man who people whisper actually spent a night in The Field, all alone with the stranger, being taught and seeing strange and wonderful things." Berdin was looking at him now, actually staring. "And I knew I *had* to let you on, just to get a chance to know: is it true? Is there such a stranger? What have you learned? What have you done and seen?"

Berdin was actually trembling a little. "How—how do you know all this?"

"Well," the conductor said, patting Berdin's arm again as if to see if he was real, "I don't of course *know* anything, I've only put together what I've heard, but as a Transit Authority I have access to all kinds of information and all I've heard this whole workday have been the wildest stories ever told in this Community. Some stories I had the good sense to ignore, of course, they were too crazy to be real. I mean, some people were saying nonsense like this stranger could fly like a bird or that you and he actually walked through the Zone unhurt, which I naturally dismissed as gossip. You *know* how easily unfounded rumors spread! But anyway after listening to these stories all day I'd heard enough to know that some things—probably those most often repeated—had to have some basis in the truth. Like, see, for example, the rumor that you spent the night in The Field—everyone was buzzing about that, claiming to have heard it from the lips of the very Arrival/Departure Monitor who saw you in the morning. Supposedly a wild, barefoot man with—dare I say it?—*soulful* eyes and a shining white robe and a Field Engineer with red hair, still dressed in his work clothes *entered* the Community instead of exiting it first thing in the morning. I can't tell you how many times I've heard that story today, often embellished of course, but based on the same central, eh, event . . ."

"So you recognized me because of my work clothes?"

The mole nodded eagerly. "Yes, yes, because as everyone knows . . ."

"Did anyone ever explain why the Arrival/Departure Monitor allowed us to enter the community?"

"Hmm. Hmm. Now that's a good question. Hmm . . . yes. Well, I suppose we all just assumed it had something to do with the wild man's power. I mean, anyone that could survive The Field at night must be quite, well, incredible . . . We heard he had fire! Is that true? Tell me, tell me about this man."

Berdin brushed aside the clutching hand and stood up. "This is my stop. Ring the bell, please."

The small conductor looked dismayed. "Oh, tell me," he muttered, even as he rose and shuffled toward the bellcord. "You've got to tell me, or how will I know what to believe?"

A bell rang; the train whooshed to a halt. Berdin looked at the pleading, squinted eyes and the eager mouth and turned away. He stepped out the door onto the platform and faced the elevator. With relief, he heard the whoosh of a door close behind him and then the rumble of the monorail leaving. Painfully, he imagined he could still hear the sniveling undercurrent of the conductor's pleas within the train.

"Those are the worst kinds of people," he muttered to himself. "I can stand anything except a grabby whiner. It's not my fault he's intolerable." Berdin was still muttering when the elevator opened and he stepped inside. The muttering, grumbling thoughts rumbled in his head long after he'd quit moving his mouth—in fact, the unsettled state of mind accompanied him all the way back to Unit A12G.

Once inside his unit, Berdin stripped off his Field Engineer uniform, an act that incited whistles from the Norvle sisters across the avenue. The absence of shades and modesty was supposed to demythologize sex, according to Our Benevolent Liberator, but all it seemed to accomplish practically was the heightening of societal interest in coupling. "The sex act is nothing special," was another slogan plastered all over the community; but really, if it wasn't special, would anyone have to tell people that? *Warts aren't special*, Berdin thought,

*and Our Benevolent Liberator isn't knocking himself out to
get that message across.*

He stepped into the hot shower, wishing fervently for
a shower curtain or at least a stall that didn't face the street.
Berdin let the water get so hot it hissed against his body. He
felt his blood duck and rush through his veins and flush his
skin. With his eyes closed, he hummed a small tune and imagined that a thin sheet of plastic hung between the Norvle sisters and him.

Outside the shower stall, Coastal Community Twelve
went about its business in much the same manner it always
did: monorails carried only those passengers in transit from
home to work or vice versa, Pharmaceutical Counselors doled
out a few more milligrams per patient than they had the day
before, CWO monitors preached tolerance and condemned
dogma (and mixed in some sex and violence), most Central
Planning Agency officials spent their days sending memos
explaining their absence from recent committee meetings, and
SLOTH marched almost three full blocks to protest intolerable workdays. Only two rumors distinguished this day from
any other in the community. The first rumor, of course, cen-
tered around Ian and even hinted at the events that took place
in the Justice Cabinet hearing. The second rumor asserted
that Our Benevolent Liberator was planning to visit (perhaps
even relocate his headquarters to) Coastal Community Twelve.
At present, Arthur Aphek resided in Mountain Community
One, but there had been suggestions and even a few veiled
threats which pointed toward a move. Citizens couldn't decide which was more exciting: the prospect of becoming the
world capitol, or the chance that an outlaw visionary walked
among them.

Berdin was at least temporarily unconcerned with such matters. After his shower he pulled on a pair of blue community pants and lay on the couch. For exactly thirty-five seconds he wondered what he should do next, and then he coasted easily into an open-mouthed, unmoving sleep.

Dreams prodded him; he saw a seed fall into a crack in the avenue right outside, and watched a stalk spring from the crack and grow higher than the blocks—higher even than the CPA building. The Avenue Maintenance Technicians tried to remove the massive plant, but it repelled both axe and shovel. Our Benevolent Liberator appeared, with fireballs in his hands, and set fire to the stalk—and Berdin ran. But it was too late. While citizens screamed, the vine-like plant ascended to the SHELL, coiled itself, and burst the dome. Berdin turned. He walked back to the plant—right through Our Benevolent Liberator—and climbed toward the light streaming through the SHELL . . .

His climb lasted well into the evening, when the ceiling lights were extinguished and the street lamps lit. Berdin awoke abruptly, with the sensation of a man on a roller coaster ride that has just ended, hitting awareness with the sudden speed that always marks the close of the most desperately-needed sleeps. He felt pleasantly foggy, and for a time he savored the muffled feeling in his mind. The realization that he was starving finally prodded him to action.

Scratching and yawning, Berdin moved toward the CWO monitor. He punched it on (he was forever losing the remote control), and turned it to the Dining Channel. He waited as it listed the menu for other blocks. Eventually his block appeared, followed by the words: "Options: Burger Factory, The Salad Works, Pizza Connection, or the Evolving

Palate." Berdin grimaced at the final option; the Evolving Palate constantly pushed new dishes recommended by the EQL—everything from broccoli juice to leather jam. He picked up the phone and pressed "O".

"Hello, this is Berdin Dwate in Unit A12G. I'd like to order from the Burger Factory's menu tonight."

The voice on the other end of the line—a voice that belonged to a silly girl with braces that worked in the Food Preparation Facility in Berdin's block—informed Berdin that all the Burger Factory's deliveries had long since been ordered by other block members.

"Oh. Well. In that case I'll have a pepperoni pizza."

The voice again informed Berdin, this time with a nervous giggle, that all Pizza Connection deliveries had been previously ordered.

Berdin's forehead wrinkled in irritation. "Don't TELL me all you've got left is Evolving Palate syntax!"

This time the food prep girl sounded a little offended, as she declared in an even tone that the Evolving Palate's selection of bacon pudding flambe was really *quite* satisfactory tonight, but that there was some leftover Chinese food from last night if Mr. Dwate insisted.

Mr. Dwate did insist. He requested two pounds of the Chinese stuff, whatever it was, and hung up. He wondered aloud why he even bothered to look at the stupid Dining Channel. Then he clicked the CWO monitor to the Informative Channel and flopped on the couch to wait.

The Informative Channel was even more annoying than he usually considered it to be. A woman with a moustache was ranting about gender prejudice, apparently offended by the fact that the best basketball players were men. Her contention was something to the effect that basketball must be abolished because its rules intrinsically favor athletes and therefore repress women. The usual bespectacled talk show host was interviewing her and periodically running around the studio to get the opinions from various men and women with nasal voices. Each person expressed his opinion excitedly, shifting his eyes around the room to make sure his comments met the audience's approval. Berdin's disgust was palpable; his mouth tasted acrid.

Unfortunately, his mouth tasted much the same after his dinner. No one in Coastal Community Twelve really knew how to make Chinese food, because no one had ever had the opportunity to compare it to what real Chinese food tasted like. Without such a standard, the hybrid restaurants constantly deteriorated. Without such a standard, Berdin had no way of knowing whether he was eating bad Chinese food or good Chinese food that he just happened to think was bad.

He had turned down the volume of the CWO monitor when his dinner had arrived via the Meal Shuttle, which was a tube that ran from the back of his unit to the Food Preparation Facility. Choosing to read a magazine instead of listen to the anti-basketball tripe, Berdin had thumbed through an older copy of *International Query*, a movie star tabloid. This, too, was suddenly offensive. Why, Berdin wondered, should Margo Lefluve's 18th divorce concern him at all? Who cares if Elvis's daughter is still alive?

He leafed through the rest of his coffee table library: *Sports Digest*, *Nudes Illustrated*, *Bloodsports Report*, *Big Muscles and Scantily-Clad Women*, and *From the Top* (a daily newsletter that contained the transcript of Our Benevolent Liberator's speech and the decrees of the EQL, delivered to each citizen free of charge). Berdin opened this last magazine to a random page and began reading. For the first time in about ten years, he tried to make sense of the words.

" . . . destined for greatness [the page began]. Citizens young and old can take pride in the fact that they are a part of the organism Mankind, an organism that has ascended to unparalleled heights in our universe, and gone on to hasten the evolution of an even more significant species. We have reached out and touched the stars! We have tamed this world and caused it to produce abundantly! We have humanized societal institutions in such a way that every man and woman is perfectly free to be fulfilled! And we have done all this in just a heartbeat, from the perspective of the evolutionary time scale. Mankind's appearance in the universe has been meteoric: we spun high and flamed bright, and now shall rapidly fall.

"We must not fear this fall. It is only those of the Close-Minded Age that would be concerned by an end. Modern man understands the indisputable facts of the life-cycle: organisms are born, they grow, they wither, and they die. The death is every bit as inescapable as the birth. And in our death, behold what we give birth to: an organism more advanced than any would dream! An Evolutionary Quantum Leap which will usher in a new Golden Age! Surely man, a being who has had his day in the sun, would not stand in the way of the next great leader of the world. Surely we will step aside. And I believe—because I believe in the character and nobility of man—that we will even step aside *graciously*, as stoically as the acorn abandons himself to the oak.

"But I shall not dwell on such matters. They are of interest only in passing, and have no bearing on our present situation. The time will come for standing aside, but only in the distant future. At present, we may busy ourselves with other . . . "

Berdin turned the page, and then another and another. Try as he might, the words had little meaning for him. That is, they meant something, in the same way that a grocery list or a cereal box means something, but the meaning was too small to be grasped, too irrelevant to his emotional and mental gymnastics to bother with. A whole stormy sea of thoughts sloshed in his stomach.

Out of habit, Berdin checked the LiST (Life Span Termination output) at the end of the magazine. Again, no names on the LiST were familiar—no friends, no acquaintances, not even a member of The Field Engineering Corps. For the first time, Berdin wondered at the odds of such a thing happening. And what of the odds of it happening week after week? One thousand names appeared on the LiST every day, and never— not once—had Berdin even recognized a name. Sure, there were 36 million people in the world, and Berdin probably knew only a thousand of them by name, but 365,000 names appeared on the LiST each year, and the LiST had been generated by the EQL since before Berdin was born. Suppose he had only paid close attention to the LiST for the last fifteen years; that would still mean he had seen over five million names LiSTed. Even by conservative estimate, that meant one out of every eight people had been designated for termination during that time frame. In other words, his inability to recognize one name on the LiST defied the odds exponentially.

Berdin put his chin in his hands and studied the math in his mind. No matter how he somersaulted the computations, he still finished with the same idea: he should know at least 100 people who had been terminated. He remembered Ian questioning the likelihood of such a scenario, and again wondered why it took someone from the International Wilderness to point out the inconsistencies of his society.

Berdin turned to the page that parroted the EQL's latest dictums. This page used to cause Berdin the greatest concern—in fact, he used to dread reading it. At length, however, he had realized that any of the dictums which were too outrageous or contradictory were always "re-interpreted" within the week by some branch of the CPA, and thus rendered unobtrusive. He had long since ceased to glance at the page. Now he found himself staring at a list of declarations and regulations which ranged from the bizarre to the logically impossible. Among a hodge-podge of other proclamations, the EQL stated that "frogs and men are baked species," that "nervous twitches light extra foxholes," and that "work is an absolute evil which must be abolished." It seemed to Berdin that the EQL was turning out much more brazen and befuddled "truths" than it had in the past. It seemed, indeed, that reality was becoming less and less recognizable, like a marble cracked and finally crushed by repeated blows from a hammer.

The newsletter slipped from Berdin's hands and splashed to the floor. He gazed distractedly at the wall opposite him, sorting various files in his brain. He cracked his knuckles, one by one. His big, calloused hands fidgeted— uncertain of their place in this type of work. Dimly, he recognized the fact that the answering machine across from him was blinking. He gradually closed the drawer on his pondering process, and pressed the "play" button on the machine.

"BEEP! Hello, Berdin Dwate, this is your *good friend* Willis. Rumor has it that you welshed on our deal. I hope that's not the case. [Pause] Call me and we'll arrange a re-negotiation. 854778335 . . . BEEP!"

The words slapped Berdin. He switched the machine off, walked toward the bathroom, turned abruptly, walked to the phone, and dialed. Practicing his straight-ahead approach to unpredictable situations, he chose to call his fellow Field Engineer before he had time to think of explanations, ramifications, or the like. Better to face it quickly than to fuss.

He winced at the sound of Willis answering. "Citizen of the Globe, Willis speaking."

"Hello, fellow citizen," Berdin responded mechanically. "This is B—"

"Berdin! My *good friend*! I'm very anxious to meet with you this evening! Can we, uh, can I expect you on the balcony at 9:00?" Willis spoke his words pointedly, as if he were speaking in code.

Absently, Berdin glanced at the clock. "Well, sure, Willis. If that's all right—convenient—with you . . ."

"It is! See you then." He hung up with a clang.

Berdin hung up more slowly, wondering at his apparent good fortune. Willis was excited to see him, and in fact was willing to meet with him in fifteen minutes. What could that mean? Willis was rarely positive about anything other than quitting time. And he certainly should not be happy with Berdin's irresponsibility. *If this were a spy movie*, Berdin thought, *this would be a trap*. Indeed, it was possible that Willis was anxious to meet with him solely for the opportunity to pummel him. But it was unlikely. Willis was too disinterested in anything resembling work to fight, and he had to know that Berdin was capable of holding his own.

Berdin toyed with the idea that Willis might just kill

him, but he decided it was too easy. He was beginning to believe that the road Berdin Dwate had to walk was a more difficult route—for him, oblivion was too convenient; it tied up too many loose ends. The answer, if there was one that he could grasp, would be more complex (and more intriguing) than he could have guessed.

So instead of guessing, Berdin concentrated his energy for the next fifteen minutes on "straightening up." All this really meant for Berdin—as it does for most every male— was that he arranged the furniture at right angles, dusted his coffee table with his sweatshirt, and threw stuff away. This last operation included the remnants of the Chinese dinner and, after some thought, all his magazines. He watched, a little in awe of his decision, as the various tabloids and glossies slid down the garbage chute, to be transported on conveyor belts to an underground incinerator. He wondered whether or not he should have saved *From the Top*. Cawly Jons, in Unit A12B down the way, saved every issue—had a whole closet full of chronologically filed community newsletters. Berdin shrugged, and let the lid to the garbage chute swing shut.

A whistle from Jan, the huskier of the two Norvle sisters, reminded Berdin he was not fully clothed. He shook his fist vaguely and yelled through the bars, "What about my right to privacy?"

"What about our right to choose?" The sisters called back, almost in unison.

Berdin clenched his teeth. He wanted to respond, but he already despised the attention he had called upon himself. In a haze, he rummaged through his chest of drawers, found a semi-clean red polyester community shirt, and put it on. He checked the clock, hastily slipped on his white vinyl shoes (shoes with a shine no amount of scuffing could erase), and summoned his courage. Time to face Willis.

Willis was willing to meet Berdin on the balcony at such an unsafe hour for the simple reason that he lived in the same block, and therefore shared access with Berdin to the same rooftop balcony. The proximity of their living quarters was not as coincidental as it might seem: Our Benevolent Liberator had seen fit long ago to group men and women with similar jobs in "neighborhoods" within the community. It was his belief that such an arrangement promoted comradery and would eventually strengthen the "organism that we call Humanity". Thus, all Field Engineers lived in an area within a four-block radius. Thanks to such precautions by Our Benevolent Liberator, Berdin found an unscathed Willis leaning against the railing on the deserted balcony.

Willis smiled and walked toward him. He extended his hand, and Berdin shook it. "Hello, Berdin," the smiling blond said, "You've made quite a stir in the last 24 hours."

"You mean my not gettin' our work done in The Field? I—I know, and I . . ."

"No, that's not what I mean at all. Bytes! Don't play me for a fool. I fell for it yesterday morning, but I won't fall for it now. See, I thought you were just another citizen—a little slow, not much fun. The work scheme surprised me—it didn't seem like something you'd come up with. But then when I heard what you've been up to since quitting time yesterday—then I understood . . . You're a wild man! You're the original—"

"What have you heard?" Berdin spoke sharply, surprising himself.

"I've heard it all, Berdin. I've heard stuff that no one will ever believe! I heard," he lowered his voice, "that you spent the *night* in The Field. I heard," (his voice gradually rising), "you walked the Zone! I heard you appeared before the Justice Cabinet and thumbed your NOSE AT THEM!"

"Quiet!"

"Right, right. See, when I called I was fried about The Field thing. I figured you were yanking me around, planning only to punch my clock for me half the time. I didn't see how you thought you'd get away with it, but it seemed obvious you were trying. Then I started hearing things. First I didn't pay much attention, then it dawned on me a lot of the stories were describing you. Then I started listening. And hearing the *craziest* stuff." He laughed his pleasant laugh. "You wouldn't believe the rumors going around. You—say, was the other guy for real? The big barefoot boy in a white dress?"

"Yeah." Berdin said. Then, "Yeah" again. He paused. He opened his mouth. He closed it. He looked closely at Willis. He moved to one of the rickety cast-iron lawn chairs beside a table and sat down, passing his hand over his face.

"He's real." Berdin drew a deep breath. When he spoke again, he spoke quickly, his words tumbling and frothing in their haste to capture a slippery perspective: "Most of this is going to sound even more crazy than the stuff you've already heard today. You can believe what you want, but you have my word that what I say is true. This man—he called himself 'Ian'—just appeared when I was working in your section of The Field late yesterday. He was—he is—not at all like you or me, except that he's a man. See, he said he came from the International Wilderness, and really—yeah, I know it sounds nuts—it really seems possible once you've spent time with him. Like, for example, his eyes—Willis, they're . . . unyielding . . . formless, and depth-less. They're the most *real* eyes I've ever seen, and everything he says and does—its authenticity shows in his eyes and gives him . . . an aura of reality. I'm . . . I'm saying this badly and won't ever be able to say it well, but I'm certain that he actually knows, no, *is* truth. He's the most important part of our world to get to know, because he's the only one who can really tell you somethin' worth hearing. And it's worth hearing, it's *valuable*, because he backs it up. If he says it, he doesn't just mean it, he lives by it. He doesn't just sell truth and buy truth, he employs truth—*real* truth, something that doesn't change. If you get my meaning, his truth gets more *true* all the time because its applications are explored by him daily." Finally, Berdin stopped for air. "Does any of this make sense?"

"No," Willis said, and the word hit Berdin like a sledge and numbed him.

"Wh-what . . ." he started.

"No," Willis said again. "None of it makes sense. Mainly 'cause you haven't told me a thing the guy did when he was with you."

Berdin tried to gather his emotions and tie them down so they'd lie still long enough for him to explain. "Well, well, it doesn't much matter what he did, except he did what was true and tried to teach others the same, and was a . . . friend to me. I mean, he did things that were amazing—"

"Like what?"

"That's not why you need to hear about him. You need to hear about Ian because he's true, because he can lead us all—the whole world—back to the truth and the foundation for all reality. And because he . . . he *cares* enough about us to want to lead us back."

"He's certainly sold you," Willis sneered. But he became suddenly serious, and leaned forward with his eyes fixed on Berdin. "However, you *still* haven't told me one concrete thing he did."

Berdin's eyes flared. "I thought you wanted to hear my story! To hear the truth!"

"You're right about the story part. But so far I've heard lots of words and very little action."

"All right. Here's action! How do you think we made it through the Zone? How do you think we escaped the Justice Cabinet? Ian did it!"

"How?"

This question set Berdin back a bit. "How? Well, with words . . . that is, he talked to this big guy in the Zone and,"

"Forget it, Berdin. You're being too bitmapped cagey. If you want to be dull, fine, but I'm not buying it. If you don't want to talk about it, fine. Just shut up."

Berdin leapt to his feet. "Why don't you start listening? You just hear what ya want, and what you don't want ya yawn at! Why dontcha get yer thumbs out of yer ears and start thinkin' instead of reacting?"

Willis took two steps closer to Berdin and pointed his finger at him. "Because I prefer to be my own boss, if you don't mind. I don't listen to . . . throwbacks, I listen to my own voice. And you might want to listen to it, too, when it tells you this: nobody likes a new king when he's the old one—nobody likes to hear about it. So keep quiet, get back to The Field, and hope that the CPA forgets your involvement in this whole mess. Hope like a fiend. Because they like new kings even less than I do!" With this, Willis turned on his heels and started down the stairs.

"I WON'T be back in The Field!" Berdin shouted after him. "So don't expect me to do any work for you!" ("Shut up!" someone yelled from the street). "And another thing," Berdin barked, incensed by the yell, "I certainly don't need advice fr'm you! It would be like talkin' to a parrot that had lived in the same room with the EQL!"

Berdin heard a pause on the stairs, then footsteps, and saw Willis reappear at the top of them. "I wouldn't say that so loud, if I were you," he said. He started back down, stopped again, and added in a sarcastic tone, "And really, I'd think that a man who knew 'truth' so well would be a little more gracious than you." He turned and clanked down the stairs.

With the end of the footsteps, the air was completely still. No breeze moved. The rooftop balcony, where Berdin stood fuming, was not at all an appropriate setting for his funk. He looked neither noble nor tragic, standing on a bare tile floor surrounded by cluttered herds of iron chairs and drooping artificial plants. No moon shone; the only light came from dingy street lamps glowing at eye level. In the bleak, unnatural setting, Berdin appeared to be merely another artifact, as gross and common as a plastic statue of a pagan god.

Such things weigh upon a man. It is tolerable, even strangely pleasurable, for a man to reflect on his alienation and the choices before him when he stands in a place touched by nature with pathos and mystery. A wind, moonlight, shooting stars, fierce rains, delicate sunsets, swaying tree shadows, or the chill of morning touch man with the wonder of his predicament and make him feel justified. But Berdin, in a climate-controlled dome, stood alone with his sense of dread, effectively separated from any consolation—even the odd, awful consolation of nature's indifference.

The dread wore on him quickly, and he returned to his unit. It, too, was little comfort. Nothing distinguished it from any unit in his block, for there were no books (most books were relics of the Close-Minded Age; the only new ones were intolerable romances and psychotic thrillers), no pictures, and no family. Berdin wanted to turn on the CWO and fall asleep listening to Our Benevolent Liberator's latest plea for tolerance, but too much was moving in his mind. Something important was happening, and he had to figure it out.

The resolution didn't come to him immediately. First, he had to ponder why he was gloomy, why Willis had angered him so much, where his restless energy should be directed, and what it meant to quit The Field. The answers, when formulated, drove him to the conclusion in a rush: something important had happened in his life, and it was the first time anything important had happened to him. Most of the other inhabitants of Coastal Community Twelve had never had such an experience; this was obvious from the way they led their lives. Berdin owed it to the community, then, to tell them about his important experience—an experience which lived in the form of a man.

It was an easy conclusion, but it had hard implications. Justice Brophy and her purple star still lurked in the back of his mind, and even if Brophy couldn't get him, there were plenty of global-minded citizens who could. Once they figured he'd quit The Field, his superiors would take pains to track him down. And how hard would it be? His address was in every CPA database, and the dome over the community sealed off his escape routes as effectively as a prison. Ian might be able to protect him, but that was assuming he'd see Ian again. His friend was trustworthy, he knew, but clearly willing to spread himself too thin. Ian may just never find the time to think of him again.

And even assuming all these problems corrected themselves, there were more mundane considerations. How to pay the bills? What will his acquaintances think? Wouldn't it be less strenuous to make a gradual, less radical change in lifestyle? Doubts like these assaulted Berdin, but the trick in his personality that caused him to plunge ahead asserted itself, and he put the questions aside. The course of action he'd chosen made sense, and there was no use trying to get around it. Better to bull straight along the path and hope no cliffs were ahead.

Of course, it was hard to feel that way in the morning. When he awoke on the couch to the "whoosh" of a monorail, his mind was tired and in favor of the status quo. He lay still, staving off thoughts of living comfortably in his unit until Ian returned for him. But lying still wasn't the answer. The easy thoughts were beginning to arouse his lust for the easy path. Berdin glanced at his clock—9:30. He'd overslept breakfast, and now would suffer the consequences.

Yawning and scratching, he stood and walked to the phone.

"Hello, this is Berdin Dwate down in A12G. What've you got left for breakfast this morning?"

"Well," a sleepy voice answered, "not much of anything. Some pickle omelettes—"

"The Evolving Palate, I know. Forget it." Berdin hung up the receiver and groaned. Bad start.

Things, unfortunately, did not get better. In the back of his mind, Berdin had clung to the thought—as most people do—that since he was doing the right thing he would be instantly rewarded. He was not. If anything, it seemed that he was punished. He had decided to begin telling his remarkable story of Ian to close acquaintances—people he was reasonably certain would listen and at the very least refrain from reporting him to the CPA. As he had expected, he did a poor job of articulating his story. Still worse, people were not even sympathetic toward his halting, sincere narrative. Everyone had been happy enough to welcome him into their unit, but once they heard his fervent description of a man bent on unsettling Coastal Community Twelve, they seemed even more happy to usher Berdin out. A few went so far as to recommend trips to Pharmaceutical Counseling or to the Gaming Commission Resort.

Berdin's pleas became more and more impassioned with each successive rejection. Working under the assumption that he hadn't tried hard enough, he redoubled his efforts after each failure, only to find himself failing again. Soon he came to blame his listeners, believing they were too stubborn to tolerate truth. He felt enraged after every encounter, like a teacher faced with an apathetic, illiterate class. His mood became darker as the day wore on—though, to his credit, he swallowed his anger when approaching each new person.

He stopped his efforts early, around 5 o'clock, not because he was tired but because he was tired of failing. Also, he wanted to get back to his unit in time for dinner—something real, rather than highly advanced. For the first time that day, things went right: the Meal Prep Facility sent down a steak sandwich and french fries and a strong cup of coffee.

They even sent down seconds when he called. An odd thought presented itself as he leisurely sipped his second coffee: it seemed that he was being rewarded for quitting, rather than for trying. The horror he felt at this thought shook his hands. He had always lived with an unspoken belief that effort, when directed properly, was right, and quitting short of the proper goal was wrong. He had never before asked himself whether or not he had grounds to believe this, so now it shook him to think that his assumptions might be unfounded. Perhaps quitting was sometimes good; perhaps it was right to be apathetic about one's fellow man upon occasion. These thoughts were hideous to Berdin. But he couldn't turn from them; he had come to the point where he might have to consider them as true. And the truth, wicked or glorious, was what he wanted.

It frustrated him that so few others were interested in truth. Most everyone Berdin had spoken with today knew him to be truthful, yet they either brushed aside his honest testimony about Ian as though it hadn't happened, or ignored his honest conclusion, as if Ian's statements and actions didn't pertain to their little world. But if Ian was real, and Berdin's account of him was true, it affected everyone's world—powerfully and unapologetically. It grabbed reality and shook it hard, until life revealed the sense it guarded so dearly. You couldn't turn away from that. At least, Berdin hadn't believed man could turn from that until today.

Now he believed. Fourteen people had opened their doors to him; and then fourteen people had turned their backs. After each rejection, Berdin found himself looking up at the ceiling lights as he walked away. It was almost (he realized now) as if he had been looking up to implore some distant watcher to help him.

CHAPTER SEVEN

"I thought I could not breathe in that fine air
That pure severity of perfect light—"
—Alfred, Lord Tennyson, "Guinevere"

In the morning, Coastal Community Twelve was humming with excitement. Berdin had fallen asleep before the announcement made during Our Benevolent Liberator's nightly address, but one of his closer acquaintances phoned to make sure he'd heard the news. While Berdin had slept, Our Benevolent Liberator had declared his intention to travel to Coastal Community Twelve.

The acquaintance, Deborah Aksen, was a pushy low-level CPA official who had gone to school with Berdin. She had heard Berdin's version of the truth yesterday with some degree of patience, but when it became obvious that she wasn't listening so much as hearing what interested her, Berdin had left, gazing skyward. Today she called Berdin to tell him about Our Benevolent Liberator's decision because she was the type that has to be the first to tell someone something they hadn't heard, and because (as she said), "With the bigwig of all bigwigs on his way to the community, citizen, you know the CPA's going to demand the pinnacle of actualization from each and every one of us, and it just won't *do* for you to run around insinuating that the central planners at any level haven't got things figured out. You know? I mean, of course, we're tolerant of all views in our community and all, but still you've got to maintain a sense of . . . *decorum* when Our Benevolent Liberator's around."

"Why?" Berdin had asked. Deborah had sputtered so he spelled it out: "Why do I have to maintain a sense of decorum around the—I mean—'Our' Benevolent Liberator? Why is he such hot stuff?"

This hadn't gone over well with his informant. She hissed something about "talking nonsense to a CPA official" and hung up. Berdin chuckled a little at her panic, but he also felt slightly uneasy—he hoped he hadn't offended Deborah. He enjoyed her flighty, serious company.

He had just started to dial for breakfast when a familiar voice spoke outside his unit door.

"No time for that now, my friend. We've got work."

Berdin turned to look through the bars at a figure that made his heart leap: Ian! Still barefoot, still in his outlandish white robe, Ian stood looking in with laughing eyes.

"W-work?" was all Berdin could manage to say.

"Yes, work. Or have you forgotten what that is, after a couple of days away from your crops?" Ian swung open the heavy door easily, and strode inside.

Berdin laughed. "No, I've been learnin' what real work is. I've been tryin' to come ta grips with who you are, and then tell other people."

Ian became suddenly serious, which further unnerved Berdin. "And who do you say I am?" He sat down next to his friend and looked straight at him.

His eyes were clear—not just in the sense that they were undimmed, but in some positive sense, like the blue winter sky above a hilly horizon of snow-covered spruce. The clarity was terrifying and exhilarating at the same time. *Oh, to see with those eyes* flashed through Berdin's mind and stung him. With a sense of abandonment, Berdin shoved his selfish nature aside and said firmly, "You are the central Truth that has come to save men from the lies." This single statement exhausted him, and he wept.

Ian comforted him, with his arm around his shoulders. "It was to hear those words freely spoken that I have borne, and will bear, so much. You are right to cry. But know this: you are forgiven. All will be well." A cloud passed over Ian's eyes when he spoke the final sentence, but it went unnoticed. Berdin was busy pulling himself together, hardening his facial expression with clenched teeth, while the silent tears ran down his cheeks.

"Haven't—sniff!—haven't cried like this since I was a baby. N-not since I was born." He managed a weak smile.

"Birth will do that to you," Ian said. He helped Berdin to his feet and told him to change clothes. "It's time we get to work. There's much to be done."

"Like what?" Berdin asked, still wiping tears from his eyes and trying to unbutton his shirt.

"Like what you did yesterday, only with more convincing evidence," Ian said grimly.

"How—" Berdin started, and then said, "Did I do

somethin' wrong yesterday? I thought I was doin' the right thing."

"Of course you did something wrong—you always do. But that's beside the point. The point is, why weren't your efforts rewarded yesterday? And the answer is one I should think would be obvious to a 'Field Engineer': people do not plant and harvest on the same day. You see—yes, this is going to be another one of my stories which you never seem to grasp—a seed must be nurtured and also buffeted before it gives forth life and matures. The sun must warm it and strong rains must drench it as part of its growth process. The farmer does the right thing by planting the seed, but he is a fool if he thinks that guarantees wheat. Many things must happen before the harvest, not the least of which is the protection of the tender plant from her enemies, locust and rodents. A farmer does well to plant; he is wise to leave the seed to processes outside his control (that is, he must not dig up the seed each day to see if it indeed has taken root, but instead must trust the sun and rain and soil) and he must give protection from destroyers. No farmer does his job perfectly, but the attentive, caring farmer usually does enough. Often, he is *eventually* blessed by processes beyond his control with a crop ripe for harvest. Sometimes he still faces drought. But overall, in a lifetime, his efforts bear fruit. You can know a farmer by his harvest. But be not quick to judge with each new season."

"I may've gotten part of that," Berdin said.

"Yes, miraculously, you may have."

"That word's from the Close-Minded Age. You're not supposed to say it, you know."

Ian winked. "Why? Aren't I my own boss?" Then he took the newly-dressed Berdin by the arm and guided him outside. The ceiling lights were shining abrasively, and the blocks were remarkably quiet.

Ian said, "So, you had some trouble yesterday?"

"Yeah, I couldn't get anybody ta listen to me. It finally hit me that the most important thing I could do while you were gone was tell people about you, but everyone acted like I was talkin' in a foreign language. So then I kind of figured I wasn't doin' the right thing. And then I didn't know what to do."

"I am sorry, Berdin. It's never easy for someone who cares about truth to realize that others may not value it at all. It's simply something you must experience. But, as you say, the experience is not enjoyable." Ian paused and looked thoughtful. "Then again, some things in life supersede the primacy of your personal enjoyment."

"What?"

"Again, it's something only experience, and not words, can teach. Do not think you're done growing just because you shave. The truth is, you're never done. Not even after you grow old and die."

Berdin stopped. "Wait a minute. You aren't sayin' that . . ."

"And why not? Surely there is more to a man, and his world, than just the material. Are we all just atoms crashing around? Oh, I know, I know. What I am saying is from the Close-Minded Age and so it is hateful to such a 'modern' man as you. But do you know why your people call it the Close-Minded Age? Do you? Because people at that time actually believed there was such a thing as truth—real truth you could base your life on—and consequently, falsehood. Now your truth evolves every day, and so of course you must remain open-minded—open-minded toward everything except the outdated ideas of the Close-Minded Age. Can't you see the hypocrisy? Can't you feel it bearing down all around you, like a massive sponge saturated with chloroform crushing and dulling you? The truth is, you are more than just an animal hanging clothes on itself. There's something about you that worries, and laughs, and cries, and revels in honest labor. Coastal Community Twelve and the Benevolent Liberator don't want you to remember that. I do."

Ian stopped his far-ranging hand gestures with the end of his lecture, and encouraged Berdin to start walking again, guiding him toward the outer limits of the community. They walked in silence for a few blocks, and then Ian spoke again. "I know this is a lot for you to digest. But there's something else you must think about as well. Ask yourself this question: why all the excitement about your so-called Benevolent Liberator visiting the community?"

"Oh, that's an easy one," Berdin looked slightly relieved. "He hasn't visited our community in twenty years, not since right after his inauguration."

"Yes, but why not? He has a private helicopter, and there are only twelve communities now in your entire world. Surely, as the world leader, Arthur Aphek could find the time to visit each one at least yearly. It's not as though he doesn't have enough Cabinets to share his duties—and anyway, how hard can it be to write the same speech over and over? So why has it taken your leader so long to come calling?"

"Oh, I see what you mean . . . well, I guess it's because he feels like he has to stick close to the EQL, in case it comes up with any really important mandates or whatever."

"Yes, but the EQL is solar and fully portable. Why

can't it also travel with Arthur Aphek?"

"Hmm." Berdin looked a little distracted, typically uninterested in a discussion which seemed irrelevant to him. "Oh, I don't know—maybe he's concerned about the envir'nment and doesn't want to pollute by flyin' anymore than he has to. I don't know. What differ'nce does it make?"

Berdin's barefoot friend was grim. "A great deal, as you and I shall see. But not before we finish our work." With this, Ian made a sharp turn, walked to the nearest unit, and rattled the bars.

"Hey!" Berdin hissed. "Whadda you think you're doing? It's barely ten in the morning!" He glanced around quickly, like a squirrel looking for a tree he might climb to safety.

A quiet female voice spoke from within the unit. "Y-yes?"

"Come here," Ian spoke firmly.

The girl—and it was clear she was a girl no more than eighteen years of age—came slowly forward out of the gloom, wrapped in her blanket. Her eyes were wide and her hair was tousled. She looked, Berdin thought, oddly like a dandelion. She even swayed slightly, moved by the incredible awakening she faced this morning.

"Follow me," Ian said, and Berdin felt a stirring in his breast.

The dandelion-girl turned and walked toward the back of her unit, disappearing in the darkness. *Calling the Law Enforcement agents*, Berdin thought. But he couldn't speak.

Neither did Ian speak. He stood in front of the unit patiently, and when the girl reappeared fully dressed in her red and blue community clothes, he opened the door for her. She passed through quickly, looking awe-struck. In that sense, Berdin's face mirrored hers.

"I am Ian," the barefoot man introduced himself. "And this is Berdin. Berdin, meet Nila."

Berdin smiled and nodded hello to the girl, but she didn't notice. It was all she could do to spare him one quick, unseeing glance before she riveted her gaze again on Ian's face. She kept searching his eyes for their secret.

Ian returned her gaze and then began climbing the stairs to the second floor, with the girl a step behind him. Reluctantly, Berdin followed. He had a bad feeling he knew what would happen next, and his hunch was all too quickly confirmed. His friend was rattling the door to another unit.

Before Berdin had even formulated the hope that this was the home of another timid teenage girl, the hope was dispelled. "Who the byte is it?" a gruff voice, made still deeper with the heaviness of sleep, demanded.

"A friend who comes and calls you to follow." Ian's voice boomed into the dark recesses of the unit. Berdin, quite afraid, shouldered Nila behind him and stood at Ian's side, ready for a scuffle.

He needn't have worried. After much snorting and scratching, a heavyset man lumbered to the front of the unit and said simply, "Well, let's go then." He frowned at Berdin and Nila, and stepped in line behind Ian, who was on his way to yet another unit. Introductions were again hastily passed out, and then another barred door was rattled.

Most of the morning was spent this way. Not everyone chose to follow Ian—some wouldn't miss work, or risk derision from their friends, or cancel their scheduled visit to the Gaming Commission Resort. One man even excused himself because he said he had to oversee his deceased father's consciousness-programming session. But for the most part, people followed, usually with a submissiveness that was eerie in its sincerity.

As the crowd following Ian grew, people began to join the ranks unbidden. Berdin found himself more and more distanced from his friend. At first, Berdin tried a number of ploys to distinguish himself as Ian's right-hand man—even going so far as to rattle one unit's door himself. But when the unit's occupant proved to be an angry sixteen year-old boy with a bat, Berdin retreated to the edge of the throng and abandoned his efforts to assert himself.

Had Our Benevolent Liberator chosen to enter Coastal Community Twelve through Gate M74 around noon that day, he would have been greeted with a remarkable (and for him, highly distasteful) sight. He would have found a throng of almost 13,000 people humming with questions marching behind one tall man in a blazing white robe. Still more remarkable, the throng would not have been impressed by Our Benevolent Liberator's arrival—indeed, they would not have acknowledged him. They were too enchanted by the one man who had shaken them from their scheduled, protected lethargy and trumpeted life.

That one man walked now as an armed cowboy walks the main street at high noon. He strode purposively, somehow larger than the dingy reality around him, and his eyes were so clear and so focused he could have detected the movement of a starfish in the bottom of the sea.

When Ian reached the gate, it slid open. Berdin, some distance behind Ian, was treated to a rare sight: the Arrival/ Departure Monitor, in his haste to join Ian and his followers, broke the glass out of the window in his booth and leapt outside, rather than passing through the various checkpoints between his post and the door. Sirens sounded immediately, frightening some of the crowd enough to send them back to their units inside the community. Most, however, ignored the sirens. Berdin was likewise unconcerned, believing he was finally outside the jurisdiction of the Law Enforcement Agency. He was certain that Ian was leading his followers through The Field into their new home, the International Wilderness.

But Ian had other plans. He led the crowd of men and women along a side road and asked them to stop. He then doubled back, walking along the east flank of the throng, until he reached a toolshed, the toolshed of plot R3. With one deft move, he hoisted himself to the roof of the shed and stood up. Then he addressed the crowd that stretched along the road to his left and right.

"I am Ian," he said, his voice thundering over the heads of the people. "You have acted wisely in following me. And yet you know not what you do. It is time you learned."

Each man and woman stood quietly staring up at Ian, rooted to the spot where he had asked them to stop. Each person, that is, except for Berdin. He had been watching the way nearby Field Engineers reacted, and when he saw plot R3's Engineer pick up his hoe and walk toward his toolshed, he moved to intercept him.

Thus, while Ian continued teaching, Berdin met an irate Field Engineer in a row of corn twenty feet from the toolshed. R3's Engineer was tall and angular, and wore a worn and worried straw hat. Up close, he seemed more unnerved than angry.

"Just what in the binomial is going on here, citizen?"

the Engineer said softly. "You've got some boy in serious need of re-educating hanging off my roof and I don't like it one byte! I'm going to . . .".

"You're not gonna do anything," Berdin said, clenching his fists and grasping at the one innocuous explanation for Ian's deviant behavior. "Apparently you haven't paid attention to the EQL's latest dictums, have you? *Have* you?"

Caught, the Engineer blinked and backpedaled. "Well . . ."

"Well, what? And you call yerself a citizen! I can't tell you what I'd call you! But I *will* tell you—because I'm concerned for the people of our community—what the latest dictum entails. The EQL has provided us with a new stress-management technique. It's premise is simple: every person in a company meets together and is lectured by one member of that company for as long as that member desires. One lecture is heard per day, for as many days as is required. According to the EQL, this affords employees the opportunity to . . . express their individuality and appease their ego. We— that is, my company, Edison Solar Power—have been selected to be the first to employ this technique."

R3's Engineer scratched his head. "But . . . that still doesn't mean old bright boy there can just go ahead and stand on my shed," he said hesitantly.

"OH YES IT DOES!" Berdin boomed indignantly, causing the field worker to take a step back. "I don't know who you think you are," Berdin continued forcefully, "to be questioning the wisdom of the highest life-form on our planet. But I *do* know that the EQL *specifically* designated the toolshed of plot R3 as the official base for this technique, so that it is every person in the community's DUTY to stand on your toolshed!"

"Y-you don't mean I'll be listening to every speech that . . ."

"THAT'S PRECISELY WHAT I MEAN! And I should think . . ."

"Enough." Ian slung his command at Berdin, and it produced the desired result immediately. Berdin shut his mouth and looked up at Ian, who was glaring at him. "It is wrong for you to lie to this man, and you know it," Ian said.

"Is this guy your boss?" the field worker whispered.

"Yes," Ian said, turning his gaze to the other man, whose eyes had grown very wide. "And I am his friend as well. I now offer you the truth: I would call you my friend, too, if you join these people in following me."

The dazed field worker looked at Berdin. "The EQL?" he asked.

"That was all a lie," Berdin said hastily. "This man is truth. Come on." He took the man by the arm and led him around the toolshed into the throng of people. The poor puzzled worker clutched his hoe close to him, but he did not flee. Berdin, too, was a little concerned—he was ashamed to face the people who had seen him evoke Ian's wrath—but he tried to appear undaunted as he and his charge walked to the front of the crowd.

Ian resumed his lesson immediately. Apparently he had been discussing the way people ought to act, because he began with, "And so you can see that there are blessings and punishments according to a person's choices. There are laws which govern your universe, and not only with respect to the physical. The law of gravity dictates a certain effect upon a stone when it is dropped, and the second law of thermodynamics describes the manner in which molecules in a gaseous state may diffuse within a container. Likewise, there are moral laws which describe what will happen to a person or a . . . community when it chooses a specific course of action." He paused, surveyed the crowd, and continued: "Now, you may not like to hear me say this. You have heard, for too long, that you are your own boss and may therefore act any way you please—but I tell you that this conclusion is based on lies. Were you your own creator, you might argue for your right to be ruled by your own whims. But you are not. Indeed, you were shaped in the womb by an artist far more intrepid than your finest sculptor and your wisest author. He gave you life and laughter and the ability to interact with and even power-fully impact the world around you from a vantage point in-side—not just inside your body or inside your brain but *deep* within you, from the core of your being, from a point too deep inside to be described as a temporal/spatial designation. Can't you feel it? Haven't you always known it? When you consciously assessed your thought process, did you ever pin-point the spot in your head where thinking originates? Of course not. The thoughts don't come from your head or your heart. They come from a place inside you that is deeper than the deepest well—too far away to be contained in any physi-cal body, and yet incredibly, so close that thoughts bubble up like a spring always at your lips. Why? Because man is more than flesh and bone and hair and water. Man is a poor frail animal with a heart of fire that makes him love and hate and strive and fail and strive and *strive*. It is this which renders each person more lovely or pitiful than any other creation stand-ing. It is this which makes *living* infinitely more significant than *being*."

Again Ian paused, his eyes flashing to underline his next words: "And so I say to you: I come bearing good news—strange good news. It will sound hard against your ears, like the thud of a body falling from a throne of great height; but the more you reflect on this strange good news, the more it will comfort you, until you realize it is the only news which could truly render you sane. The news—the hard, poignant, welcome and terrifying news is this: your anguish is real. Do you hear? Your anguish is real. The morning you awake and wonder if you can bear another day; the sudden swelling, choking fear; the sharpest caustic stab of careless words—is *real*. You've always suspected this, of course, but you never knew. Why? Because everyone hides the anguish. They hide it because it is difficult to express the boundless, engulfing flood of emotion—but more importantly because each individual sees himself in isolation. No one else, you think, could possibly feel the same, because they function steadily every day and almost never question the parameters of our little society. It is only you, Berdin Dwate, or you, Nila Kerry, that experiences an anguish based on the conviction that life—not just your life, but all life—could be fantastically better. The very weight of history calls your anguish into question, proclaiming that men throughout time have simply accepted circumstances and gone about their business gingerly to avoid making waves. If those dark, potent moments of anguish were real, wouldn't mankind have dedicated itself to earnestly seeking out truth years ago? Wouldn't fewer have anesthetized themselves with liquor or work or routine if they, too, experienced a real pain and despair when faced with what you perceive as man's grasping at nobility? Unfortunately, the answer is no—they wouldn't. Because they, too, choked back the anguish and despaired in their isolation, unwilling to believe in the standard they saw themselves and the rest of mankind fail to achieve. They didn't trust the law written on their hearts, just as you fail to trust it now. But the time for distrust is passed. Today I say unto you: the law written on your hearts by He who made you is True. Therefore, your anguish is well-founded; man has much cause to despair. He has chosen a crooked, downhill path that leads him away from that for which he was intended. When you lie in bed disgusted with the prospect of another day, you are realizing a basic truth: man apart from meaning can only make things worse."

Berdin glanced at the people around him. They stood in awe. He understood their emotions: he felt like a man struggling the last few yards to the top of a ridge, his view still obscured by the rounding of the hill, his mind anxiously anticipating the panoramic enlightenment.

Ian continued: "So in one sense, at least, my news is good. Your faculties have not betrayed you. Each man or woman standing here today has felt the despair, and it is a signal which is reliable. But my news is far, far better than this simple assurance. Once you understand that your anguish is logical—that mankind is really failing to realize its potential for nobility—then you must soon conclude that one real path exists which will lead mankind in the proper direction; indeed, that if you could only arrive at Truth—tangible, concrete truth which speaks to both theoretical problems and the real dilemmas of daily existence—mankind could achieve the triumphant level you are haunted by in your desperate moments. Simply discover the lamp which will guide you to that promised land, and your anguish will be replaced with eternal joy. Today,"

Ian said—and his eyes grew so bright the sky seemed dim—
"I tell you that I am that lamp, I am that path, I am Truth.
Only I can heal your anguish."

As if on cue, the mob of people began muttering among
themselves, buzzing and humming like a giant cloud of lo-
custs. Berdin heard a tall man on his right say, "He sounds
like a refugee from the Close-Minded Age," and a shorter,
pleasant-faced man respond, "Yes, it seems a little too primitive and a little too dramatic. I think a lot of people lead
triumphant lives." Berdin was turning to answer them when
Ian spoke again.

"I warned you my words would not be easy. The
path—the real road that a man seeking to follow me must
walk—is difficult. It leads ever upward over uneven terrain,
like a mountain trail. When you think you have achieved the
highest peak, a higher peak will rear its head. The air will
grow thinner and colder, and your only reward will be its purity and that of the people you meet along the path. Someday,
however, you will achieve the true peak—not because you
earned it, but because my Father sees fit to allow me to carry
you. When you achieve that peak, the rigors of your travel
and the work of my hands will render you truly noble, the
being you were created to be. You will stand on top of the
world and your anguish will fall from you like a needless co-
coon. Remember this day. It will be the day all your strife
began to bear fruit. Until then, do not fear the anguish, but
rather treat it as a spur encouraging you ever closer to your
goal."

People began to drift away from the crowd—half a
dozen here, a solitary man or woman there. Many of the remaining people shifted their feet nervously. Berdin saw the

pleasant-faced man walk away. He wished desperately that he could bring the man back—but he understood the absurdity of his hope. A man who can turn his back on such unpolluted honesty was beyond Berdin's grasp—perhaps even beyond Ian's. He wondered fleetingly whether Ian should have spoken so forthrightly so quickly. Yet even the thought of watering down truth tasted faintly of betrayal. The thought burst away.

"People leave," Ian said. "And you, too, may choose to leave. Do not concern yourselves with decorum, fear, or misplaced loyalty. The issue at hand is truth. Either I speak the truth or I deceive you—you know the answer. Seek it earnestly." He paused and scanned the crowd, now and again locking eyes with various people. More men and women slunk away. The silence grew tangible in its endurance. Everyone moved nervously, like children near the edge of a cliff.

Finally, Ian spoke again. "There are two things, and two things only, I require of you. Your willingness to obey these requirements needs manifest itself in countless ways, but the requirements themselves are basic: love each other and my Father as yourself. *Love* them. Do not simply engage in niceties; do not tolerate lies in the name of kindness. Instead, serve everyone with generous portions of truth. Forget yourself in your desire to be used by your Creator to be beacons. These are the hardest words I will ever speak to you, but they are hard and pure as diamonds, and every bit as precious. Follow my commands and your rewards will be bountiful—but first you must endure many trials. Your rewards will store themselves to be showered upon you in an Age that knows no time. Until then you, the prisoners of time, can only serve and be assured. It is a high calling. But it is true.

Better you should choose once always for the truth than run forever after lies. Better to mount once the wings of eagles and taste the dizzying fear of heights than to taste nothing but the bitter seeds of groundless life."

Berdin felt his shoulder blades tense, tightening his throat. This man had called him friend! This man—if man he was—held all the magic and beauty Berdin had sensed was somewhere just beyond his grasp in an open hand, and extended them to a stumbling, stubborn Field Engineer with wounded dreams! A stabbing pain rended his heart, and he yearned to cry out. The Field Engineer next to him actually sank to his knees, tears on his cheeks and passion on his face.

Ian looked directly at the two men. "Now you have heard enough for one day. It is time we ate. Mr. Patchett, will you allow these people to enjoy the harvest from your plot of land?"

The Engineer kneeling beside Berdin looked stunned. He fumbled and fumbled for words and finally managed: "I don't . . . that is, the harvest—my plot has only young corn. It, it isn't ready for harvest . . . it . . ."

"It is ready, Mr. Patchett," Ian thundered. "Berdin, go and inspect the harvest."

With a sense of wonder, Berdin walked heavily past the toolshed and into the vegetation behind it. He gasped.

"Show us," Ian said.

Berdin bent down, and then arose with an enormous watermelon held over his head. Patchett stuttered and gaped. "I—i—t can't . . ."

"It can." Ian lifted his eyes and addressed the crowd. "Go and enjoy," he said.

The people nearest R3 walked gingerly, almost shyly,

into the vegetation. Gradually, those behind followed, talking earnestly and quietly among themselves. As soon as every man and woman had made their way into the rows of plants, a profound silence ensued. Berdin, still holding the melon, watched curiously as those around him sat on the rich, earthy ground and ate their watermelons with raptured expressions. He looked curiously at his own melon. Suddenly, Ian spoke from directly beside him.

"Taste," he said. "And know that it is good." Berdin stared for a moment at his friend, and then obediently sat down and broke open the melon. He smelled the sweet, clean scent and then bit into the meat of the fruit. His mind swam. The melon tasted golden—like a cloudy sunset after a long, gentle rain. Nothing, nothing Berdin had ever known, could match the purity of that melon. He chewed slowly, almost reverently, and marvelled at the world.

An unbroken quiet engulfed The Field. No bird chirped, no worker whistled—and no one in plot R3 even seemed to breathe. When Berdin again thought to look at Ian, the white-robed man was gone.

No one counted the minutes that the silence prevailed. Berdin was finally jarred from his meditation by the faint rustling of various members of the crowd slowly rising and moving toward the community. They moved like sleepwalkers, the way Rip Van Winkle must have moved after awaking from his twenty years' sleep. Berdin watched in a daze as Patchett gently arose from where he had been contemplating his own melon and approached. When he reached Berdin he sat down beside him and stared at the sky.

"Never," Patchett said, "*never* has so much as the seed from a melon fallen on this plot. And then . . . today . . . the

finest watermelons I've ever tasted grew up among my corn."
Berdin began to speak, but the other Engineer stopped him.
"Look around," he said. "We just ate watermelon, didn't we?
Why, the sweetest sticky taste is on your fingertips—and yet,
do you see even one vine among the stalks? Do you? Look
around, citizen. The vines are already gone."

Berdin was looking around, open-mouthed. He could
not find words to answer the other Field Engineer. Both men
had been too close to the land, had wrestled too hard with it,
to underestimate the power they had just seen and tasted.
Berdin could only shake his head.

The other man sighed. "Well, at least you went through
it too. I know then it wasn't a dream." With these words he
stood up, moved to his toolshed, put his hoe away, and locked
the door. He waved uncertainly at Berdin and then turned
south toward the domed city.

For his part, Berdin sat among the rows of corn and
scattered rinds until every other person had left and the sun
just showed above the tree-tops. Now and again, he licked
his fingers to remind himself. Finally, he hoisted himself to his
feet, and glanced self-consciously around The Field. He started
at the sight of Ian, not fifteen feet away.

"Well, my friend, did you learn anything today?" Ian
was smiling faintly.

"Yes." Berdin confined his response to one word with
an effort. He knew he must, because a more detailed answer
would take months—years—to articulate.

Ian stared at him. "Yes," he said, "you did. And somehow you always manage to get yourself in situations which
require more learning than anyone else needs." He smiled
broadly.

Berdin smiled too. "I will follow you wherever you go," he said before he thought.

Ian laughed a halting, melancholy laugh. "Ah, yes, the lion's heart. You are brave, my friend." He paused. "Well, following me tonight will be a pleasant task. For tonight I must stay in The Field."

Berdin's heart leapt at the announcement. To see another star—to again smell the woodsmoke of the fire!

"Yes, it will be pleasant," Ian said. "But it must also be serious. I must prepare myself tonight, for tomorrow I confront the Benevolent Liberator and his demon machine."

"He's coming tomorrow? I didn't hear that."

"He's coming." Ian looked grim. "And that's not good news for you or anyone in your community."

"Why not? It probably means a holiday and . . . sure, his speeches are boring, but—"

"I'll tell you. But first, let's enjoy dinner and a fire."

This time, Ian produced eggs, a loaf of wheat bread, and cheese. Berdin watched closely to see how his friend lit the fire, but he only saw Ian's hand pass over the wood and flames leap up. A strange idea bounded through Berdin's mind: miracles were all around him. Our Benevolent Liberator and every Growth and Development Supervisor he'd ever known had promised that miracles were, by definition, impossible— even in the face of the miraculous tint of the natural world. Was Ian's creation of this particular campfire any more miraculous than the qualities of fire itself? Could any man clench his fist and see the tendons and veins in his forearm bulge and sway, and never confront awe? Why did it take Ian's strange conjurer's hands to make misdirection direction?

The two men ate in silence, enjoying the sunset's fade

into twilight and a thousand shining stars. Berdin rested with his back against the toolshed, struggling to frame his emotions in a way that he could always duplicate. He loved the crickets and the breeze and the smell and the stars, and he loved Ian deeply for showing him life and the proper way to live it.

Finally, Ian spoke. "You think, I know, that my trepidation is misguided. You are puzzled by my antagonism toward your so-called 'Liberator.' But am I not the Truth? Could I find the way to speak a lie? Listen, what I say is real and tragically true: that man and the 'EQL' bring death. Do you know why they have abandoned their previous community?"

Berdin shook his head.

"Because there was no community left. Oh, your innocence—if only you were truly innocent! You have never recognized a name on the EQL's LiST, because it only contains the names of men and women in the community in which it is located. Don't you see? You believe there are 36 million people in your small world—in truth, there are little more than 3 million." Berdin gaped. "That's right—three. Your community is all that's left. Slowly, inexorably, like snow melting before flames, the people of your planet have been systematically terminated. Some—painfully few—have climbed the mountain to the International Wilderness. Most have simply turned their back on truth and submitted to death. And it will happen again here. In four days, the EQL will generate its next LiST, and this time it will concern you—for this time, it will claim the lives of men and women all around you. Perhaps it will even beckon . . . Berdin Dwate."

"I . . . it . . . it can't be!" Berdin was sitting chairback-straight, his eyes wide. "It's not right. The EQL . . . *needs* us."

"Oh, it needs you. It needs to absorb your consciousness—to, in a sense, win your soul. But it is quite content to kill you in the process. Do not fool yourself. Heed my words. A battle is about to rage, and there will be winners and losers. People must choose life or death. Many will choose death."

"Then we've gotta save them!"

"No." Ian looked away, and his eyes were strangely lit. "I must save them. Your job is to follow me."

CHAPTER EIGHT

"Though our smoke may hide the Heavens from
your eyes,
It will vanish and the stars will shine again,
Because, for all our power and weight and size,
We are nothing more than children of your brain!"
—Rudyard Kipling, "The Secret of the Machines"

Berdin's shivering awakened him. His body ached from
a cold, hard night on the ground. His spirit ached, too—he
felt an anguish that deadened his desire to move. Only the
cold forced him to stand and stamp his feet, cursing the dew
and the yellowing sky.

He looked at Ian. His friend sat cross-legged, staring
straight ahead, apparently unmoved from the position he had
adopted eight hours ago. "Don't blame you for not bothering
with sleep," Berdin said huskily. "It wasn't worth anything
anyway."

"Quit grumbling," Ian said. He breathed the fire to

life, and handed Berdin a loaf of bread and a flask of spring water. The Field Engineer ate, grudgingly at first, but with increasing intensity.

"You sure do bake good bread in that robe of yours," he said. "Aren't you gonna eat?"

"No, I choose to fast." Ian watched Berdin. "Are you done? Good. Warm yourself by the fire and then we must go."

Jackrabbits with absurdly long ears wrangled through the crops as the two men walked the choppy road back to the SHELL. Ian paced, while Berdin shuffled and kicked at loose pieces of asphalt. They didn't speak.

The two men trudged past Checkpoint M74, where workers were busy replacing the pane of glass in the checkpoint booth. As they walked through the community, men and women peeped through their bars and whispered among themselves. Occasionally, one or two persons sheepishly scurried after Ian and Berdin, until a crowd of nearly 200 traipsed at their heels. No one spoke above a whisper, so that the procession seemed eerily like a funeral from days long ago.

When the informal procession turned on to avenue 772 East, they were greeted—much to Berdin's surprise—by another throng, much larger, lining either side of the cement street. Ian led his followers between the on-lookers, till they reached Checkpoint P36. There they stopped.

"Are you sure we should just be standin' in the middle of the road like this?" Berdin whispered out of the corner of his mouth.

"I am sure." Ian's voice boomed in the morning quiet.

"Are all these people waitin' on Our ... the Benevolent Liberator, too?"

"They are. The news broke on your CWO late last night."

"Do you . . ."

"Quiet. The time for fretting has passed. Fear only Him who made you."

Berdin shifted uneasily. He shouldn't be afraid, he knew—in fact, he hated the feeling—but still . . . Maybe the Benevolent Liberator would choose another entrance. Sure, the heliport was closest to P36, but maybe he knew he'd be mobbed and would therefore choose a quieter way. Maybe . . . Berdin caught his breath. Maybe not. He had just noticed a small circle of people standing apart from the rest of the onlookers. Immediately, he recognized the Lieutenant Liberator and his Secretary of Cabinets, Lucias Bakke. These were men who would not be stood up. The circle obviously consisted of local dignitaries waiting to welcome their leader, and they wouldn't brave an early morning on the streets unless they had some guarantee.

Well, what of it? Berdin felt himself clenching his fists, accepting his fate with the stubborn bravado that was so much a part of him. He felt himself relaxing and yet somehow becoming more intense, as a man readies himself for an unavoidable fight.

But his calm resolve was short-lived, crumbling before it solidified. For the second time in as many minutes, his heart leapt and his breath caught in his throat. Bakke had stepped aside, revealing behind him a statuesque woman dressed all in black—all except for the purple star on her chest. Justice Brophy stood with fierce pride, her eyes made more fierce by her recognition of Ian and Berdin. Her stare fixed on the Field Engineer and wrapped ice around his heart. He felt his knees unlock and flutter.

"Do you . . . do you see what I see?"

"I don't have to see her," Ian replied. "I can feel her hatred raging."

"But . . ."

"Fear not." Ian's voice boomed, echoing in the concrete canyon. Berdin swallowed his words with an effort, wishing he could tell Ian that Brophy was marching their way.

His wish, however, was unnecessary. As the Chief Justice drew closer, Ian turned to look at her. She gave a visible start when faced again with the clarity of Ian's terrible eyes, but she continued her advance toward the men. Berdin found himself sidling closer to Ian, his adrenaline pulsing. When Brophy drew within speaking distance, she loudly proclaimed that "Loitering at this time threatens the security. Please do not continue such socially irresponsible behavior patterns." As she said this, her flashing eyes swept the crowd of followers behind Ian. Sixteen of them slunk quietly away.

Then, in a whisper, Brophy hissed at Ian, "You've crossed the line this time, blasphemer. Our Benevolent Liberator won't stand any of your reactionary propaganda—not for a minute. And your simple-minded followers—including this corn farmer—" she waved a deprecating hand toward Berdin "will probably fall down on their faces and worship the Evolutionary Quantum Leap, assuming it really exists. You think you're some kind of hero, don't you? Well, this is your high noon, citizen, and you're about to be gunned down." Her words trailed off into a frantic sneer.

"What do you mean 'if' the EQL exists?" Berdin said before thinking. He regretted the words as soon as they escaped—and he regretted them still more when Brophy turned on him.

"That DOES it!" She half-whispered, half-shrieked. For a moment Berdin expected her to strike him, but instead she composed herself quickly and hissed, "I'm on my best behavior now, of course, but don't think I'll forget this or anything about you, Dwate. Yes—Dwate! I remember your name—and I remember your crimes. And now you've sealed it; you can know that sometime, somewhere . . . soon . . . I'll get you. And I'll preside over your confession myself, and I'll make sure it's a slow, agonizing one. And . . ."

"He makes a good point though," Ian interrupted. "Why are you suspicious about the EQL's actual existence?"

Brophy turned to look at Ian and immediately straightened up, looking for all the world like a guilty bully caught by a teacher. She blinked, collected her thoughts, and said softly, "You know the answer. Must I explain myself to some farmer?"

"Yes. I want you to say it. To hear the hopelessness put into words."

"Well." She looked smug. "I think I'm capable of facing that." She turned toward Berdin. "I think the EQL may not exist because I, like you, do not believe in the system. You, however, are a groveling failure, and so choose to believe in a lot of reactionary fantasies; whereas I, understanding the purposelessness of this world, live only for myself— seeking pleasure, fame, and riches and serving one wise master: Jane Brophy. Perhaps if I were a toad like you, I would believe the same things you do; as it is, I am free to follow my every whim."

Ian looked grim. "That certainly conveys the hopelessness," he said. "But it doesn't directly answer my friend's question. Why might the EQL not actually exist?"

A prickly smile showed on Brophy's lips. "You know the answer better than anyone," she purred. "Men lie." Her twisted smile grew broader.

"Isn't it true that you've met one man that doesn't lie?" Ian looked hard into her eyes. Her smile took on a permanence which mocked it.

"BROPHY!" The moment flickered out quickly, doused by the yell. "Brophy, my dear!" George Beaker, the Lieutenant Liberator, was calling her. "The gatekeeper's preparing to open the gate! Come here!"

Brophy's cunning eyes stayed fixed on Ian. "He's a buffoon, I know, but he *was* useful. Not as useful as Our Benevolent Liberator will prove to be, of course, but he had his moments." She hesitated. "I won't see you again. Strong as I am, I wouldn't have the courage to oversee your termination." She looked at Berdin. "Yours, however, I wouldn't miss for the world. In fact, I think I'll just seal your fate now." She reached across to Berdin, grabbed both sides of his face, and kissed him. Her cold lips completely engulfed his mouth and pressed it violently. Berdin's esophagus convulsed.

With a contrived sorrowful look, Brophy gazed one last time at Berdin and Ian, and then turned back to join the circle of dignitaries. Berdin wiped his lips with the back of his hand and shuddered. "Even her lips are cold," he said to Ian.

Ian looked at his pale friend. "I'm sorry you had to go through that. But now you have plumbed the depths of your fear and survived. There is something to be said for that."

Even as Ian spoke this last sentence, the gate was sliding and the dignitaries were advancing eagerly toward the opening. A squadron of Law Enforcement agents, armed with stunguns and wearing plexiglass face shields, were the first to pass through the gateway. They scowled at the sight of Ian and his followers, who were blocking their path one hundred feet away, and marched forward to control Ian's group. Our Benevolent Liberator followed, surrounded by a ring of twelve men and women—his Governing, Allocating, and Bowdlerization Cabinet.

Arthur Aphek, Our Benevolent Liberator, did not appear as a knight on a gleaming white stallion. He looked more like an absent-minded college professor. His expression was placid, though somewhat dazed, and his grey-white thick hair stuck up wildly. He didn't stride; he shuffled—and every once in awhile he would stop and put his hands on his hips, as if he needed to regroup his thoughts. His dark brown eyes were set deep in his head, guarded by bushy eyebrows. Very few wrinkles showed on his face—only his brow was deeply grooved with marks of concentration.

The Lieutenant Liberator, Brophy, and two other men stepped briskly forward to welcome their highest government officials. Berdin was too far away to hear what they said (and besides, he was a little distracted by the unflinching advance of the agents), but he did notice that the Lieutenant handed his superior a book, and that Brophy had already managed to get hold of Our Benevolent Liberator's arm. Berdin shivered a little at the thought of her touch, but quickly forgot his discomfort when he noticed the next link in the procession.

Behind the official welcoming and kissing up that was taking place around Our Benevolent Liberator, thirty men carried a large wooden platform (similar to a litter from the days of Egyptian pharaohs) over their heads. On the platform rested an enormous gleaming block of steel and glass with raised letters on three sides proclaiming "Evolutionary Quantum

Leap." The computer was six feet high and almost ten feet in length and width. Its edges were sharp, and no seams were visible. The keyboard system and printer were nowhere to be seen—apparently they were remotes, carried separately in the interest of international security. Curiously, the monitor was built into the box, so that the system looked like an enormous aquarium. Even from his vantage point, Berdin could see that the EQL was secured to its platform with huge titanium bolts.

The sight of the machine which had dictated so much of his life, and its uncanny resemblance to a fishtank, had a profound effect on Berdin—but not in the way that Brophy predicted. He felt a wave of nausea engulf him, and through the dimness a pounding in his head.

"At last you understand the sin of Idolatry." Ian's words floated through the nausea to register in Berdin's mind. Berdin summoned his courage and again looked at the EQL. Aside from its size and lustre, it was hardly remarkable. What most impressed him—and, in truth, stabbed Ian through to his heart—was the obvious pride of the EQL's entourage, the men and women carrying the litter. Each one stood erect, chest out, their faces belying their awareness that they were a part of the center of attention. Whereas slaves were forced to carry royalty in the ancient days, these men and women had battled for the honor, and were esteemed throughout society. Each one chaired a CPA Cabinet, and each reveled in the opportunity to serve their evolutionary superior.

Berdin was so preoccupied with the EQL and its entourage and his own queasy state, he forgot about the agents until they were almost on top of him. In a haze, he watched Ian step forward to meet them.

"We'll have to ask you to step aside, citizen," the captain of the squad said impatiently.

"My followers will step aside. We don't mean to make your job hard. But my friend and I must be allowed to pass." The captain stared at Ian for a moment, blinked, and then signaled his squad to step aside. Ian thanked him and moved forward, followed by a dimly awed Field Engineer. Had Berdin thought to look back, he would have seen a still more incredible sight: the captain removed his star-studded helmet, handed it to his second in command, and joined the throng of people behind them.

As it was, Berdin was busy watching the shock register upon the faces of the men and women in front of him. The Lieutenant Liberator looked outraged, Our Benevolent Liberator looked puzzled—only Brophy appeared calm, even smug.

Ian raised his hand in greeting and began: "Some of you already have heard or seen me, some have not. I am Ian. I've come to tell you your world is founded on lies, and to call you to repentance. I . . ."

"Who is this Nazi?" Our Benevolent Liberator turned to the Lieutenant, who was staring wide-eyed and shaking his head. Brophy opened her mouth, thought again, and closed it. Some of the men from the Governing, Allocating, and Bowdlerization Cabinet stepped forward saying things like "We'll handle this," but retreated quickly when Ian looked at them and said, "No you won't." Unable to get a response from the various dignitaries, Our Benevolent Liberator turned to Ian and demanded, "Who are you?"

"I have already told you," Ian said. "But I must also tell you this: you and your machine bring only death to this community. I offer you life."

Our Benevolent Liberator furrowed his brow and pushed his hands through his hair. "Do you mean to tell me," he said, "that you come to hinder man's evolution—to save him from himself? You believe yourself to be . . . in authority over every man, to be my boss?"

"It is as you say."

"You would have men listen to *you* rather than the Evolutionary Quantum Leap?"

"I would."

The group of dignitaries—except for Brophy of course—gasped at Ian's words. Our Benevolent Liberator simply frowned. "Then I have heard enough. Your own Justice Cabinet will deal with you."

"They already have," Ian said mildly. "Isn't that true, Justice Brophy?" He turned toward her quickly, shaking her smug expression from her face.

"Well . . ." she began.

"The truth!" Ian snapped.

"Yes," she said, looking a little puzzled.

Berdin felt his queasiness gradually slipping away, as he marveled at the new mess in which Ian had placed them. It wasn't so much that Berdin feared Our Benevolent Liberator himself—he looked small compared to Ian, and much less intimidating than on the CWO. His nose was flat and his eyes were small, and his forehead was much too high. His gestures suggested his authority, but he had a habit of shuffling his feet that made him seem boyish. No, it wasn't Our Benevolent Liberator's presence which made the situation threatening— it was just the overwhelming odds—the sense of being trapped in a box canyon by countless armed deputies and too many people brandishing ropes. *Let's see Ian get us out of this one,*

Berdin found himself thinking.

Meanwhile, Ian seemed only interested in digging a deeper hole. He was saying, "So you see Arthur, my time has not yet come. When it does, you will be the first to know. For now, I must proclaim the truth—to you and to those you rule through the curious delusion that they rule themselves." He turned to face the mob of loyal citizens swarming behind the Law Enforcement agents. "Hear me!" he said, and the throng pressed closer to the harried LEA squad, followers of Ian mixing with the citizens who had come to welcome their leader and the EQL. "Hear me!" Ian again said, his voice echoing off the nearby unit blocks. "There are those among you still concerned with truth—those who know the universe is more than an empty void that greedily inhales your dreams. To you I say: take heart! The troubles of this world are real, and I shall overcome them for you. You who are tired of being ruled by yourselves—by your every whim and appetite—hear me when I say that your true ruler has arrived!"

"Yes, he has arrived!" Our Benevolent Liberator stepped forward, next to Ian, and yelled as loud as he could, in a flat tone that almost equaled Ian's spoken oratory. "He has arrived, the EQL is here!" He began clapping feverishly, and his applause was taken up by the dignitaries and some scattered men and women in the audience pressing up against the slowly retreating line of Law Enforcement agents. The clapping sounded ominously hollow, like the first big raindrops before a harsh afternoon hailstorm.

Ian stared Our Benevolent Liberator and the crowd into silence. Then he addressed the throng again, his voice like thunderclaps punctuating the raindrops: "That is the lie you have heard for too long. I tell you now the truth: you mock yourselves when you fall prostrate before a box of circuits and microchips. Man has a soul! Each of you knows this as surely as you know you have imprisoned the soul in the flesh. Repent! Free your soul! Turn from the machine which has no soul and drink from the spring of everlasting life! Turn from a life of lies and embrace the truth! Today I set before you life and death; choose once and always for life."

Our Benevolent Liberator was shuffling his feet in earnest now, and the crowd was swarming and boiling with questions. The Law Enforcement squad was being overrun by the mob, like sandbags before a swollen, seething flood.

Ian's eyes glowed with the sense that he was orchestrating the storm. He continued, stirring the sea of people with expansive gestures and strong words: "I tell you there are two kinds of sheep. There are those that huddle together soft and satiated on the valley floor, never lifting their heads from the patch of ground they graze. They are herded in any direction, and they do not question because their stomachs are full. But another kind of sheep lives above them—the mountain sheep, who tread delicately on cliffs over precipices, seeking the tough wind-driven tundra that hides in dangerous places. These sheep grow strong, hardened by living in a way the domestic sheep will never know. The mountain sheep need only one shepherd—the true shepherd that guides their feet and watches over their path. Today I tell you: I am that Shepherd . . . and you, you are my sheep!"

The crowd boiled louder with weeping and cursing. Our Benevolent Liberator yelled, "Enough! We've heard enough!" But his words were drowned out by the raging storm. Berdin sidled closer to Ian.

"You may never hear the truth again," Ian said, his

spoken word sounding with the power of sonic booms, "but today this truth will suffice for all time. I offer you freedom from your prison; I offer the key to your chains. Do not turn away from me, or I will turn from you. Choose living, my friends! Choose Life!"

Berdin moved still closer to Ian, until he was actually touching his friend's robe. They stood together, an island in a storm of shouting and jostling. The Lieutenant Liberator was screaming, "Arrest him! Arrest this fascist!" at the circle of dignitaries, who were busily shouting orders at each other. The sea behind the Enforcement squad swelled and crested, poised to break. In a frenzy, George Beaker burst toward the squad, grabbed the newly-appointed captain and howled for Ian's arrest. His move startled the squad enough to allow the wave behind them to break. The mob poured over and though the agents, engulfing the Lieutenant Liberator and streaming toward Ian.

The fury of the storm stunned Berdin and froze him. As the wave crashed around him, clutching and pulling him down, he saw Ian begin to wade through the throng. The robed man walked coolly, his head held high—clearly untouched by the seething flood of people. Men and women grabbed at him, swung their fists at him, and fell at his feet. Yet no one touched him. While the storm raged around him, he moved as if alone on the avenue.

Berdin felt himself being swamped by people demanding information about his friend. He was pulled down, desperately close to the suffocation of being sucked under. In a panic, with what felt like his last breath, he cried out to Ian.

Instantly, Ian's voice rang in his ears. "Have faith," it said. "Walk, and trust in me, and you shall not falter."

Berdin obeyed—he couldn't help but obey. He stood up and took a step. And another, and another. While the howling mob raged, he found himself walking untouched down the avenue. The hand of stillness rested on his soul, and his strides became assured, determined. He could not see Ian, but he fixed his thought on him and strode forward as one certain of his goal.

The moment lasted forever in Berdin's mind. How long he walked against the tide he didn't know; it felt like a time outside of time. When he finally realized where he was, he was walking through a knot of people pleading with him to stop. A man grabbed at his arm and seemed to touch it. As Berdin marveled at that, he felt the certain grip of another hand on his shoulder. A blitz of panic slashed through him. The hand squeezed his shoulder tightly; another pulled his hair. Again he cried out—and as he fell, he felt Ian's strong hand close around his own, and the other hands slip away.

Ian pulled him through the throng to a nearby block, where they splashed through the last of the crowd and climbed the outer stairs to the wrought-iron catwalk on the second floor. When they reached their perch, Ian released Berdin's hand and the Field Engineer leaned over the railing, gulping in air in short pants.

Ian allowed Berdin to clutch his breath and then said, "You took your eyes off me."

"What?" Berdin's voice was incredulous; he was a little angered by his friend's calm.

"You took your eyes off me. Faith requires a fixed point in a shifting world. You lost your point of reference."

"My point of reference keeps getting me in LOTS OF TROUBLE!"

"And out of it. Weren't you listening to my parable of the mountain sheep?"

Berdin looked uncertain. "Yeah . . ."

"Then hear this as well: I must leave you again. This time you are better prepared for my departure, and have something of an understanding of the love that will bring me back." Ian paused and surveyed the scene below them. The storm was beginning to subside; Our Benevolent Liberator's voice could be heard plainly, demanding Ian's arrest. The throng became quieter as their bewilderment over Ian's disappearance grew. Men climbed on each other's shoulders and talked earnestly about where they had last seen the barefoot man.

"Why can't they see us?" Berdin whispered.

"A few can, but they hold their tongues. Here is one that I have allowed to approach," Ian said, gesturing expansively toward a solitary woman climbing the stairs that led to their perch.

Berdin opened his mouth to express his concern, but he closed it when he saw that the crowd was oblivious to the woman's movement. The woman walked to them and threw herself at Ian's feet. Kneeling and weeping, she said, "My son is sick and losing blood. Please heal him."

"Hey, lady . . ." Berdin began.

But Ian's voice drowned him out. "Go home. Your faith will heal him."

"What?" Berdin said. The woman was on her feet, thanking Ian and bowing slightly. She turned and scampered down the stairs.

"Since when did you become the Physician?" Berdin grumbled as he watched the woman leave. When he turned to face Ian the answer was burning in the big man's eyes.

"Since the beginning of time," he said. He looked stern. "Berdin Dwate, you should know this by now. Why must you be so brash?"

Berdin felt bad and shy immediately. "I'm sorry," he looked down and timidly stamped his feet on the metal catwalk.

"In the future, try to do things you won't have to apologize for. Now to the point: during the time we are separated you will face great trials (as will I). Justice Brophy was not making idle threats when she vowed to catch you. And once she realizes I am not with you, she will do everything within her power to avenge herself."

Automatically, Berdin turned his gaze toward the circle of dignitaries. Most were milling around, but the woman with the star on her chest stood still. She seemed to be staring back at Berdin. "She—she can't see us, can she?" Berdin asked, fearing the answer.

"She can. But she also must hold her tongue. Be assured, though, that she is seething with rage." Ian clenched his long, sturdy hands to accentuate the point.

"Great. Really reassuring. So how long will it take her to realize we're apart? And how long till we're together again?"

"I should think it won't take her long to notice we're apart—I must leave you as soon as the procession resumes. As for how long we'll be separated, I cannot say."

"You can't *say* or you don't know?" Berdin asked, and was again met with a stern gaze. He began to mumble and stamp, but Ian interrupted.

"As soon as Aphek finishes his address"—even now Our Benevolent Liberator was speaking to the crowd—"I must follow the procession. You would be wise to climb higher up and hide on the balcony. From there, you must fix your thoughts on my goals and stay away from the authorities. Do you understand?"

"Oh, I understand all right. I just . . . don't . . . feel like I'm up to it. I—"

"You are 'up to it.' And besides, I have too much planned for you to see you fail. Summon that courage that was built into your very core, and don't turn your eyes from me. Be brave, my friend. I will see you presently." With these words, Ian turned toward the stairs and began to descend to the avenue.

"Wait!" Berdin said, but Ian ignored him. The barefoot man walked to the bottom of the stairs and melted into the oblivious crowd.

Berdin took a step toward him, checked himself, looked around quickly, and then lunged up the second and third flights of stairs to the balcony. He ducked behind a large-leafed artificial palm near the railing, and peeked at the scene below him.

" . . . touched by this show of support," Our Benevolent Liberator was saying in his loud hollow voice. "And I vow to you now that the presence of a few cranks in our society will in no way influence me to inhibit your freedom. You are free, my friends! Free to fulfill your every desire! As the Evolutionary Quantum Leap so aptly put it: 'Serve yourself, or forever be another's servant!' Today, I promise you: our arrival in your community guarantees your right to serve yourself. Revel in it!"

The crowd, or most of the crowd, roared its approval. Berdin noticed that a scattered few were not applauding, but instead were slowly retreating. They moved nonchalantly, like criminals leaving the scene of the crime. In a wave of self-pity, Berdin realized that he, too, was condemned to such shadowy movements. He mourned his horrible deserted position.

Far below, the CWO camera-crews squeezed closer, and Arthur Aphek shook hands awkwardly for a second time with most of Coastal Community Twelve's high-profile public servants. Much of the footage of these formalities, however, was left on the floor of the news stations' editing rooms; the 11:00 news teams preferred shots of the EQL and its entourage. The camera angles were necessarily dramatic, framing humanity's evolutionary superior against cityscapes from a worm's-eye view. News anchors poignantly described their first glimpse of the EQL. The viewing public saw only a triumphant entry.

Berdin, meanwhile, saw things from above. He watched the crowd move toward the sides of the avenue. He saw the Law Enforcement Squad resume their authoritative march westward into the community, parting the crowd as they went. Our Benevolent Liberator and his cabinet followed, with the local dignitaries a short distance behind them. Justice Brophy moved distractedly, her eyes fixed on Berdin's balcony perch. Her fury was so intense she completely ignored the Lieutenant Liberator, who was striding beside her and talking harshly. At last, as the procession unfolded, the EQL and its attendants fell into line. The throng swelled behind it, crowding after their honored guest. Berdin had the sensation of watching a snake uncoil and gradually slither away, leaving only emptiness in its wake.

But a final figure strode on the scene and shattered the illusion of desertion. Barefoot, tall in his glistening white robe, Ian appeared at the middle of the avenue and washed away

Berdin's self-pity. As Berdin's heart thrilled, Ian paused in a way that framed itself in his friend's mind, and then moved decisively after the procession. He knifed through the crowd, reached the EQL, and lightly hoisted himself onto the platform. Ian stood tall and shone bright next to the EQL, but no one in the procession even acknowledged his existence.

Awed (and a little pleased) at Ian's audacity, Berdin hid on the balcony and watched the procession till it disappeared around a corner. Then he stood up from his hunched position and smiled a swashbuckling smile. He might get caught—in fact, he probably would get caught—but he wouldn't go down without giving 'em a run for it. If Justice Brophy was going to catch him, he was going to make her work for it, and he was going to go down with at least a shadow of the bravado his friend showed. Most importantly, he was going to be true to Ian. He owed him that much.

The first step was easy. Berdin understood instinctively that his unit was no longer safe, and that anything he needed from it he would have to get now, before Brophy could deploy a squad to intercept him. He moved quickly down the stairs to the avenue, and then hustled along its north side, close to the buildings. His heart beat fast, filled with adrenaline at this latest, most brash, defiance of society. He moved fast enough to keep from imagining how things would end.

Anyone glancing through the bars of their unit at the sound of Berdin's footsteps was treated to a rare sight: a thin and muscular redhead in rumpled overalls half-walking, half-running, with an oddly triumphant smile on his face. Now and again he would laugh one sharp, sarcastic bark, seize a "Fences and bars make men free to rebel" flyer from the wall, crumple it, and hurl it to the ground. Occasionally he would start at the sound of someone yelling after him, and redouble his pace. He repeatedly looked over his shoulder to see if anyone yelling was also pursuing, but no one bothered. It took more courage to chase the wide-eyed unbalanced friend of Ian than anyone cared to muster.

While Berdin's feet carried him on this merry dance toward his unit, his mind raced through a maze of contingencies, assumptions, scenarios, and practicalities. What did he need? Where would he go? If he went there, what if? Could Willis be trusted? Could he survive in The Field? Dare he? The International Wilderness? The Zone? Pharmaceutical Counseling? Act? Run and hide? Trust? His mind whirred as his feet danced.

He reached his block quickly, but moved cautiously as he approached his unit. His eyes scanned nearby balcony rooftops, and he listened attentively. When he finally reached the barred door of his own unit, he unlocked it quickly and ducked inside.

The front room was a mess—just the way he had left it. Somehow incited by the disarray, Berdin began moving frantically, grabbing clothes, blankets, a kitchen knife, matches. When his arms were full he ran back into his bedroom, dumped the pile of supplies on his bed, and then rushed back to the front room for more gear: more clothes, a radio, a hammer, the remote control . . . he stopped, and stared at the remote in his hand. What was he doing? Where was he going? He threw the odd collection on the floor and dashed to the bedroom. His habit of always pressing ahead in clutch situations was finally betraying him. Pressing onward without a goal just meant running in circles. He had to stop, to collect his thoughts. He sat down on the bed and put his head in his hands.

And thought about nothing. The pressure was blocking his mental processes—he felt a sickening emptiness in his stomach that mirrored the state of his brain. He sweat nervously, and thought about his sweating instead of the problem at hand. Then he thought how desperately he needed to think. He thought of Ian and how he wished the barefoot man was with him. The thought of Ian steadied him for a moment, and he found himself focusing on his friend. His heartbeat didn't slow down, he still fidgeted nervously, but somehow he felt better. His feet were touching solid ground.

A sound at his door rocked him bolt upright. Someone was clanging at the bars, and calling his name. It took him a moment to focus on the words—words he had been praying not to hear: "Berdin Dwate, this is Captain Marshall of the Law Enforcement Special Forces! Citizens have already informed us of your presence in this unit. It is our duty to bring you to justice for your socially reckless behavioral tendencies. Surrender yourself! You have no choice."

If I don't have a choice, Berdin thought, *why don't you come get me?* He peeked around the doorjamb to see what he didn't want to see. It was worse than he had imagined: six armored agents, complete with helmets, stood outside his unit door. One was lighting a blowtorch in preparation to disable the lock on his door.

The Captain saw him and said sternly, "You can't hide, citizen. It's time to pay the price."

"I don't want to!" Berdin hollered, still peeking around the door. He looked around nervously, his mind racing. "I thought I was supposed to be my own boss!"

"You forfeited the right to be your own boss when you acted in ways detrimental to societal progress. And besides," he said, lowering his voice, "you crossed Jane Brophy."

The agent with the torch began melting the point where the bar of the lock secured the door. Near panic, Berdin ran back to his bed, shoved the matches in his pocket and grabbed the knife. He ran into the front flourishing the blade. "Whoever comes in first will get cut!" he said, trying to look fierce. "I'm going to take some of you with me!"

The Captain actually laughed. "We may not be allowed to carry pistols, but we've still got stunguns. You . . . won't . . . touch . . . us." He bared his teeth.

Defeated, Berdin collapsed on the couch. He resigned himself to watching the inexorable path of the flame through the lock. His mind still raced, but his body was numb. No action seemed appropriate to him. Again, he thought of Ian. The rebel from the International Wilderness was responsible for all this—had in a sense, condemned him to torture—and yet he felt no rage. Strangely, he even felt a little peace.

At the same time, he sensed a thought stirring around in the back of his mind. It was a young, ill-formed thought, and it fumbled around instead of getting to the point. Berdin knew it as his last ray of hope, and grabbed it tightly—but that only made it stutter and shy away. As he watched the last shred of metal melt before the flame, Berdin clung to the prenatal idea even as it drug him deeper subconsciously. The agent turned off her torch and set her shoulder to the door. Berdin wrestled with his last hope. The door heaved open with a bang, and with the same bang the thought breathed an impulse.

Berdin acted on the impulse with all the conviction of a rash man finally called to action. As the agents poured through the door, he darted to the food service portal and dove inside. It was a tight fit, even for his small frame, but he didn't much care about that. He was too busy pounding elbows, shoulders, and knees against the sheet-metal tube in a frantic effort to get out of reach. He heard his panicked breathing rattle loud in the small space, and the noise of someone forcing their way behind them. The sound of pursuit meant it would be best to keep moving—which in a way relieved him, since it stripped him of a decision and forced him to rely on what he did best: pressing onward.

I thought fugitives were supposed to be quiet and avoid drawing attention to themselves, flashed through Berdin's mind as he clambered and wedged his noisy way in the dark, moving steadily upward. He found himself grading the quality of the darkness, yearning for the hint of grey which would signal his approach to the food preparation room. He also wished vaguely that he could plan his next step, but his mind was given over to reacting—urging each movement to maximum efficiency.

Things didn't happen like he imagined. In a second, a grey twilight was around him, and in that same second he was tumbling through a plastic hinged door and into the food prep room. Without thinking, he was up and running past a startled Food Preparation Engineer toward the exit.

A sudden instinctual flash of self-preservation overrode his unthinking scramble and jerked him through another plastic hinged door. Mercifully, this chute aimed down to the first floor, so that he was able to make good progress just by stretching his arms ahead of him and kicking his legs frantically. He slid quickly down the conveyor belt, muscled a little straightaway, and emerged into a unit very similar to his own. He blinked, stared at a man staring wide-eyed back at him, and then ran to the front door. His new-found luck held true, the door opened, and Berdin dashed into the street.

The Law Enforcement squad was, of course, well-trained; an agent was posted near the side of the block from which Berdin emerged. At the sight of the wiry, frantic red-head the agent began shouting directions into the wireless communication system in his helmet, and moved carefully toward the fugitive. Berdin didn't hesitate; he turned and sprinted north along the avenue.

A shout to his left warned him that another agent saw him and had begun pursuit. Berdin was already breathing hard—both because of anxiety and his hurried thrashing in the food chutes—but he wouldn't acknowledge the signs of impending fatigue. He would run till he dropped, he knew, because this last defiant freedom—no matter how painful—was infinitely better than confinement and torture. This knowledge made him dart and dash like a frightened, awkward colt, and gradually distance himself from his pursuers. He ran haphazardly, often on the same avenue for blocks at a time, turning occasionally either north or west but never in a direction that would cause him to lose ground to an agent trailing him.

Berdin recognized, however, that such a guileless route would eventually ruin him. Even now the agents were summoning back-ups on their helmet radios. It would be an easy matter for agents stationed elsewhere in the community to extrapolate his progress and lay in ambush. The choice Berdin must make, then, was obvious: eventually he had to double back either south or east around a block and effectively disappear. Where? There was only one hiding place he could imagine. And he would have to get there quickly and quietly.

The nearest pursuing agent was now almost a block and a half behind Berdin. Despite the LEA's training and the athleticism of the squad members, they could not gain on a scared man with few options and a body conditioned by years of physical labor in The Field. The agents trained with weights and an obstacle course; Berdin had the less-contrived stamina of a man who worked with his hands and loved his work. Slowly, inexorably, his panic, conditioning, and determination prevailed. A quick glance over his shoulder showed the only pursuant in sight to be about two blocks away. Berdin gasped a huge breath, dodged right to the north, sprinted one block, and then ducked right again to the east. In a heartbeat he was mounting the stairs two at a time, moving as silently as his breathing and footsteps allowed. He arrived at the rooftop balcony just 35 seconds later, and dove behind an artificial plant in the corner. There he trembled and panted, praying that his ploy had worked.

At the same time he realized he couldn't relax for long. As soon as the agent behind him acknowledged Berdin's disappearance, the squad would be able to narrow down the possible hiding places to an area of perhaps six blocks. Even assuming the squad chose to search the units in the blocks before the balconies, the web would have closed too tightly around Berdin to allow his escape. He had to abandon his perch quickly, before an ordered search could begin.

Realistically, there was only one place to go: the rooftop balcony on the block due east from his hiding place. Even that move would be risky, but it increased his chances of avoiding detection drastically. If the agents chose to search each block that Berdin could possibly have disappeared into after his initial disappearance, they would be forced to cover an area containing at least 14 blocks. Berdin would have to gamble that they didn't have the manpower or the desire for such an extensive manhunt.

And he would have to gamble quickly. Despite the pleading of his heart and lungs, Berdin forced himself to crawl away from his hiding place to the south side of the balcony. He carefully rose to a squatting position and peered over the railing at the avenue below. He watched as two of the slower agents jogged past and turned right on the street beyond his block. Then he counted ten, took a deep breath, and moved quickly to the east stairs and down them in a rush. He flashed across the avenue, up the stairs, and onto the other balcony. The whole move took perhaps a minute and a half—but Berdin felt the sensation of years of anguish.

Again he dove behind an artificial plant, and again he prayed. Before him stretched the most difficult task of all: waiting. In an odd, disjointed way he had felt equal to the challenge of outrunning the agents, but nowhere in his heart could he find the same confidence in his ability to exercise the patience now demanded of him. The time for action was over; the time for faith had begun. Berdin dreaded the hours till dawn.

He began his forced immobility by collecting himself physically. He concentrated on his breathing and his pulse, trying to slow them with a controlled pattern of inhaling and exhaling. Gradually, his body trembled less and his heart thudded quietly.

This relaxation was dulled by fatigue. Every muscle felt heavy; a weight pressed down on him. He found himself worrying he might fall asleep. In an effort to allay that fear, he tried to discern what was happening on the streets below. Berdin strained his ears—acutely aware of distance and his inability to see—and found that his hearing could pick up sounds but not distinguish words. Occasional shouts, the sounds of distant footsteps, could mean anything: weary citizens returning to their units from work, or a crack Special Force squadron zeroing in on Berdin. He decided not to endure the uneasiness of guessing games played at a distance; he turned his thoughts inward in an effort to devise a long-range plan.

The ceiling lights dimmed to simulate twilight and the streetlights below flickered on. Berdin shifted his position behind the plant quite often, both because his body was weary and because he was nervous. He ran his fingers through his hair, he sighed, he rubbed his eyes, he stretched his legs, he murmured his bad luck, he rolled his shoulders, he cracked his knuckles. He fidgeted like a third-grader in math class. He thought about Ian and wondered whether or not he could regain the mental state that allowed him to move through a stormy mob untouched. He wished fervently he had grabbed a sandwich or something on his way through the food prep room. He began to remember stories he had heard in school about men who had died of thirst and how their tongues had swollen and their lips had turned black. He asked himself why he remembered such stories and yet couldn't remember half of what Ian had taught him. He worried again and again that the footsteps he was trying so hard to ignore were on their way to the balcony.

He maintained a constant flurry of mental activity and fidgeting for more than four hours, and then finally his voluminous capacity for such impatient practices wore out. He found himself succumbing to an exhaustion which numbed him. Berdin didn't sleep—his iron will power could still control that—but the pressure and the fatigue left him in a state approaching suspended animation. Aches and ideas hovered just outside his consciousness, but he no longer had the capacity to catalog them. In the dark before dawn, Berdin Dwate experienced the strange sensations of a cornered animal—feeling, and yet somehow only responding in a vacuous state.

He was still in this odd twilight fog when the ceiling lights began to hum. He vaguely remembered that the lights were warming up to begin casting their artificial sunrise. Like a man starting from a nightmare, he sat bolt upright and set his mind racing. Wherever his thoughts had been, they returned post-haste—prodding and urging him to action. He had survived the wait. Time again to be brash.

Berdin's next destination called him with an assurance he could not resist. He hadn't formally evaluated his next move; in a sense, he was only reacting. But the reaction felt right, like the first instinctive step of a basketball player driving the lane. With that step, the player knows the joy of knifing through defenders for an uncontested lay-up, and he never looks back at the thought process that suggested the initial move—he only accepts and keeps running. Berdin knew this emotion—not intimately, but he had tasted it—and he knew it to be, in an immediate sense, the highest gift. For a moment, the wisdom in his soul was made known to him without first being tarnished and manhandled by tedious synapse firings and other physical middlemen. For a moment, his judgment was not weighed down by his fumbling humanness.

Even as Berdin worried this emotion in his heart—unable to express it, but moved deeply by it—it occurred to him that part of Ian's mystique was a result of this very emotion. Ian never appeared to suffer the lapses of wisdom that seemed to define the human condition; indeed, he possessed the grandeur of a being always in touch with a soul unhampered by imperfect physical means of communication. His impulses were always right. And yet, it was inaccurate even to call them impulses; they were thoughts in the highest sense of the word—what thought was intended to be. Not only did Ian possess the intimate knowledge of his own soul—he possessed a soul omniscient and faithfully good.

These concepts flashed (not in so many words) through Berdin's conscious in a matter of moments. They were punctuated by the final, tangible thought: *Well, what did you expect?* This thought rang through Berdin's head and caused him to smile. Well, what did he expect? He was still smiling when he emerged from his hiding place and began his journey-based-on-impulse.

He slipped down the stairs quickly, and then moved along the avenue self-consciously close to the blocks, losing himself in the artificial shadows. His steps guided him to the north in general, but he dodged a block east or west occasionally to avoid prolonged exposure to any curious tenant's line of sight. Eventually he stopped ducking and dodging and began sauntering in an effort to appear to be an average commuter on his way to the nearest monorail. The sauntering took its toll on him: it was an act he knew he performed poorly, and it made his neck-hairs bristle. But he had little choice.

He was comforted by the knowledge that virtually every citizen was asleep. Late-night CWO gossip shows, the Home Liquor Network, the Gaming Commission, and the conscientious lobbying of SLOTH combined to form a powerful inducement for citizens to play late and sleep late. Only those workers with early shifts in The Field need be awake, and even they had over an hour before it was necessary to report. Still, Law Enforcement agents might be anywhere; Brophy's hatred of Berdin seemed to be without bounds, and she clearly had agents who respected her wishes.

Berdin pushed this last thought from his mind, and tried to focus on his next obstacle. With a little luck, this would be the final hurdle he must clear; if he made it, he could wait safely for Ian in his new haven. All he had to do was convince the Arrival/Departure Monitor to let him reach The Field.

Two things, he knew, would work in his favor. First, the A/D Monitor was new to the job; the old morning monitor had abandoned his post to follow Ian on the day of the Incredible Watermelon Harvest. Secondly, Berdin was familiar with standard Coastal Arrival/Departure procedure. He was a lousy actor, it was true—but it should require very little skill for him to act like a Field Engineer on his way to work. The catch, of course, was that he didn't have a passport, but . . .

But he did have a passport! It wasn't valid because he had quit, and he couldn't risk letting the gatekeeper see his name—but a quick flash of the document and the right words might still do the trick. Berdin walked taller with the realization that his chances of success had increased.

He consciously changed his walk as he approached the gate. Once in sight of the mammoth sliding door and the bulging bubble-window of the gatekeeper's booth, he tried to walk even slower, as a sleepy man with a hard day's work ahead of him would walk. His heart raced faster, and he struggled to channel the burst of energy into his trudging performance. He yawned and he blinked; he looked for all the world like a hyperactive sleepwalker. He approached the window fearing his habit of truthfulness would betray him.

"Mornin'," he said to the slot in the window, his eyes downcast. "Headin' out to work old R3."

"You're a little early, aren't you?" asked the peevish middle-aged woman behind the plexiglass.

"What if I am? I thought I was my own boss." Berdin looked sullen and yawned.

"And who are you?" the woman asked in her coldest, most unconcerned voice.

"Patchett." He flipped open his wallet to show his passport and quickly flipped it shut. A painful silence followed. Berdin didn't dare look up.

"First name?" Was there a note of suspicion in her voice? He couldn't tell. His fists clenched and unclenched.

"Martha. What do you think? Good Megabyte, lady, you see me every day, you ought to know me by now." He shoved his hands in his pockets.

"Ye-es," she said pointedly. "And you look different today."

Berdin finally raised his clear grey eyes in a desperate, defiant stare. "Well so do you, and I ain't sayin' it's for the better. Now OPEN UP!" He roared his last words, hoping they were in keeping with his sullen character, and then marched over to the gate and stood with his hands on his hips, glaring at the crack which he hoped desperately would grow wide and set him free.

He waited fifteen rapid heartbeats as his nerve faltered and began to plummet. Then the door groaned open and the sweet, sweet smell of The Field filled his senses. He let the door creak completely open, threw one last glare at the A/D Monitor, and sauntered into freedom. He wanted to run and shout and laugh at the earnest singing birds, but with a supreme effort he stayed in character. He trudged down the cracked asphalt road with his head down and his feet shuffling. But his heart danced. Brophy couldn't touch him now.

CHAPTER NINE

"If one falls down, his friend can help him up.
But pity the man who falls and has no one to
help him up!"
—Ecclesiastes 4:10

Berdin would have felt less secure if he could have witnessed the scene that occurred at the gate fifteen minutes after he had blustered his way into The Field. Poor Mr. Patchett, sleepy and quiet, found himself, his character, and even his citizenship challenged by an A/D Monitor bordering on hysteria. Only after he produced three different forms of I.D. *and* his passport was he acknowledged as "the real Patchett," and then only grudgingly. Through it all, he maintained an air of patient humility—an attitude he had assumed ever since the "magnificent day of words and watermelons," as he called it. The Monitor, though, was frantic. Even now, with the real Patchett in front of her, she hesitated to open the gate. She nurtured vague fears of evil identical twins or a cunning plot by CPA officials to trap her in mistakes, and her fears were paralyzing her. While Patchett stood facing the gate, the older woman struggled with who to tell and how much to incriminate herself. She finally allowed Patchett into The Field, and then kicked herself for delaying him. Would he now suspect her error? Indecisive and distracted, she tapped her fingers near the red "indescribable tragedy" button . . .

Patchett, of course, did not suspect her (of anything other than neurosis). He walked quickly down the red asphalt lane, shaking his head slightly. He subconsciously catalogued the birds chirping and the wind in the distant pine tops, but his central thought processes were focused on the impropriety of everything. Lately he found himself constantly befuddled by fellow citizens and their goals. He was disgusted with CWO programming, Pharmaceutical Counselling, tolerance, slogans, bars, Violence Cinema, and the fear he saw writ deep in people's eyes. These feelings of disgust produced a strange uneasiness in Patchett, because he saw them as his judgment of others, and felt he did not have the right to set himself over others to judge. He found himself thinking that he thought too much (something he'd never had to worry about before). He wondered why life had become more complex rather than easier. In the old days, he coasted—now he swam upstream. How long before he was sucked under?

These strange thoughts accompanied Patchett as he logged in at BAE building #4, changed clothes, and walked to his section of The Field. Distracted, he began walking the furrows between his rows of corn, a routine he followed each work day. Now and again he stooped to pull a weed or absently caressed a young ear of corn. Then a voice froze him.

"Sure wish you'd grow watermelon instead of corn."

A frightened Patchett stepped through two rows of corn and found a dishevelled Berdin. The redhead laughed at Patchett's surprise and said, "Who were you expectin', the EQL?" Berdin shook the other's hand happily, not bothering to stand up.

"Wh-why are you sitting in my corn field?" Patchett looked glad and scared and absent-minded, all at the same time.

"Oh, so it's *your* corn field," Berdin teased. "That's funny—all these other sections b'long to the citizenry of the Globe. You must really be something."

"You know what I mean." Fear suddenly overwhelmed Patchett's other emotions, so that he was terse.

Berdin recognized his consternation and answered more seriously, "I'm on the run. Ian . . . well, you know how the EQL and the . . . Benevolent Liberator arrived yesterday?"

Patchett interrupted him. "I know all about that. You mean Ian's public defiance of our governing officials? Yes, the whole community knows of that by now. At . . . at first I was shocked, I couldn't believe. And then it hit me: what did I expect? Of course Ian must defy the unjust, of course he must make a public stand. It's so . . . *appropriate*. It made me learn more about, um, about, well, the world, the universe. I . . . oh, never mind."

"I think I know what you mean. Once you *see*, some things are just appropriate—the way they should be—I know. Anyway . . . wait. What have you heard? Tell me exactly."

"Well, the parade for Our Benevolent Liberator was just beginning inside Checkpoint P36, and apparently he was making some kind of opening statement when Ian interrupted him and began lecturing the masses. I don't . . . well, from what I've heard, it was less complex than what he said out here . . ."

"Yes, that's right. I know all that. But what have you heard about when he finished, and the crowd began to riot? What happened after that?"

"Well—this is all second-hand you realize—" Patchett cocked his ears and looked away. "What's that?" he yelled in the direction of the main avenue. "Oh, I'm just out here . . . talking to the corn! Seems it grows sweeter that way! Oh. Thank you!"

"What's going on?" Berdin hissed from a new hiding place two rows over. "What just happened?"

Patchett lowered his voice. "Just one of the inspectors. Saw me standing here talking and thought I was acting crazy. I basically told him he was right."

Now it was Berdin's turn to be scared. "Well would your please get over here and hunker down so you won't attract any more attention? Thank you."

"You're welcome." Patchett sat down next to him. Berdin's fear rekindled the older man's fear. Patchett looked puzzled, but slowly remembered he had been interrupted: "Anyway, like I was saying, nobody really knows what happened after that."

"What do you mean?" Berdin's mind was spinning— it seemed he had time to think about fourteen other things while listening to one of Patchett's drawn-out sentences.

"I mean just that. Ian stirred the crowd up, the crowd swamped him and his 'lackey'—I guessed that was you—and they just disappeared. No one's seen either Ian or you since. I mean, I've seen you, but just now."

"How is the population reacting? What do people think?" Berdin's eyes were wide and his tongue nervously licked his teeth.

"Oh, some this and some . . . Well, you remember how people acted after he gave his talk on my toolshed? How some got mad, some just left, and some of us caught fire? It went kind of like that. When the crowd rioted, I guess some were trying to kill him and some just wanted to be near him, to follow him. But, um, they couldn't touch him and then they couldn't see him. He disappeared."

"And where do you think he is?" Berdin didn't know why he asked that question. He knew the answer himself. He wondered if he was testing this simple man.

"I figured, that is, I thought you'd know."

"I . . . I do. I just, I don't know, wondered what you thought. Do you have a guess?"

"I'd guess he's with the EQL."

Berdin gaped. "W-What made you say that? I mean, that's right but how . . ."

Patchett scratched behind his ear. "I kind of looked at it this way: The EQL is our—our society's—uh, um, *idol*. The thing we worship that we shouldn't. So he's gone to destroy what we worship so we can worship what is right."

"That makes sense." Berdin was distracted for a moment by the Field Engineer's simple logic, and forgot the gist of the conversation. He wondered why he hadn't guessed Ian's plan for the EQL, and then realized that he hadn't guessed it because he hadn't even thought about his friend's plans. *All I think about is me*, Berdin thought with a wince. But then he formulated an excuse: *Well, after all, I've been running for my life. This time I had to focus on myself.*

A sweet breeze moved the corn stalks around Berdin and drew his mind back to the reality of chalky dirt furrows, blue sky and hunkering. He sat down and stretched his legs straight in front of him. The action relieved his mind as well as his joints. He still felt vaguely uneasy about his selfish mindset, but the guilt submerged itself under his renewed focus on practical communication.

"Yeah, that makes sense. I hadn't thought about it 'cause I was too busy running. You're right, Ian is with the EQL, and he left me to fend for myself for awhile. He promised, *promised*, though, that he'd be back with me again and, uh, everyone else who trusts him. So I'm sure we'll be seeing him shortly."

Berdin stopped. "So—" Patchett prompted him.

"So, oh—so I'm here in your corn field because Brophy's out ta get me. I mean, all the higher-ups are after me because I quit workin' and've been with Ian when he stirred up trouble, but Brophy's *really* out to get me. And—"

"Who's Brophy?"

"Brophy?" Berdin was indignant. "Don't you know the members of your own community's Justice Cabinet?"

Patchett thought. "No, I'm sorry, I don't. So Brophy's on the Justice Cabinet. Who else is there?"

"Well, she's the Chief Justice. And then there's some guy named Bila and a guy that looks like a toad and some other guys. But they're not important. The important one's Brophy, because she's got some kinda personal thing against me. And because she's powerful, and she's mobilized the whole LEA. They came after me yesterday with a blowtorch and stunguns and I just barely out—ah—witted them. So . . . I decided the only place I might be safe is in The Field, and I, I knew I could count on you to help me." Here Berdin became particularly inarticulate, as he was whenever he showed he was vulnerable to caring about someone. "See, uh, I knew I could come here because we—you and I—um, think alike. You know? We don't *think* alike, but we feel, no, believe alike. Does that make sense?"

Patchett blinked.

"Well, anyway, I'm desperate and I need yer help. What do you say? As one Field Engineer to another?"

As always, Patchett was slow to answer. "I won't help you because you . . . were once a Field Engineer, but I will help you because you're a friend of Ian's. No, that's not right. I should say, I'll help you because I'm a friend of Ian's."

Berdin was losing patience. "What are you sayin'?"

Patchett smiled. "What can I do for you?"

Berdin wasn't sure. He had made it to The Field—he had focused on his goal and attained it. Now what? He didn't know, so he told Patchett the truth: he didn't know. Patchett, like anyone, was refreshed by the truth, and earnestly set out to help Berdin formulate his plan.

The plan, of course, wasn't difficult to discern, nor was it complex: Berdin must wait in The Field until Ian returned. Berdin had trouble digesting this plan, as he had trouble accepting any advice which required patience. He suggested a number of alternative plans, including everything from disguising himself as an EQL repairman to storming the CPA building single-handedly. But he finally was forced to concede the wisdom of staying put. The knowledge that he would sleep again under a star-swept quilt made it easier for him, but only a little. He did not like to be without direction.

In the course of this planning meeting, Patchett remembered his morning problems at the Checkpoint. He waited until Berdin had sold himself on staying in The Field and then gently chastised his new friend: "You used my name to get past the Arrival/Departure Monitor this morning, didn't you?"

Berdin tried to look guilty, although he felt rather pleased with himself for having been so resourceful. "Yeah," he said, looking more smug than ashamed.

"Well, that could cause a bit of a problem," Patchett said slowly.

"What . . . oh my MEGABYTE!" Berdin hissed, "Bytes! You're right, you're right . . . I'm done for! . . . Oh, what was I thinking?"

"Don't panic," Patchett said, feeling a little frightened himself by Berdin's over-reaction. "The gatekeeper let me in, remember? She, she couldn't be too suspicious. But—" he paused.

"But what?" Berdin was looking fierce.

"But just to be on the safe side . . . let's hide you in the toolshed today."

Berdin balked. "The toolshed?"

"Yes. No one will ever check my toolshed. Because I'll lock it and tell anybody who asks that it's been locked all day. And then if they're pushy, I'll raise a ruckus and give you time to . . . to tunnel out or something."

Berdin eyed the toolshed. It was a modest four foot by six foot structure, made completely of corrugated tin. The door fit poorly, and the whole building seemed to be settling into the ground. Berdin felt claustrophobic inside the SHELL; he knew he would not like being locked in a toolshed.

Patchett was enthusiastic about the idea, however. "You won't have to hunker, you won't have to crawl. Heck, it's roomy. All I got in there is a rototiller, a 'barrow and some odds and ends. I'll show you."

After more discussion, and Berdin's reluctant acknowledgment that Patchett's toolshed was very tidy and even cobweb-free, the fugitive resigned himself to his fate. Berdin stepped in the toolshed, sat on the wheelbarrow, and watched daylight swing shut behind the door. He listened longingly as Patchett whistled his way back to work, the sound growing fainter as he lost himself in his plot of land. Berdin's ears focused intently on the whistling, his soul savoring it the way a man savors his last bite of food. He wished the last hollow note would not end, that it would hum in his mind forever.

But the note ended, and loneliness closed on him. Berdin responded by concentrating his big confined thoughts on a minor task: rearranging tools so he could stretch out. In the dusk of the shed (it was lighted by the crack at the bottom of the door), he set the wheelbarrow on end against a wall and moved the rototiller to a corner. Then he took off his sweatshirt, bunched it into a pillow, and stretched out on the soft, musty ground. His thoughts swelled. He stared at the ceiling.

I did the right thing, he decided. He had known that Patchett was frightened, and probably a little confused, by his sudden appearance. Berdin's move to the toolshed put Patchett's mind at ease, which allowed him to return to work. Further, it put Patchett in his debt (according to Berdin's way of thinking), because Berdin had acceded to his wishes. *Now the old guy owes me one*, Berdin thought. *But I won't take advantage of him. He's a good guy and he'll come through for me.* Berdin closed his eyes.

When Berdin opened his eyes, he was no longer convinced that Patchett was such a good fellow. The light under the door was gone, replaced by a cool breeze and darkness. Birds no longer chirped, having long ago retired to their nests and perches. Berdin wondered why he had never heard Patchett put his tools away. Sleepily, Berdin kicked at the door. It rattled, but stayed closed. That made him stand up fast.

He pushed at the door with both hands, and felt immediately what he had feared: the door flexed but was held fast by the lock. Berdin shoved the door again just to vent his rage, but quickly backed up when he heard how loud it sounded in the otherwise still night. He looked uncomprehendingly around the shed.

So Patchett had betrayed him. How badly? He considered the worst: Patchett had willfully left him locked in after finishing work, and had gone straight to the authorities. Clearly, this was not the case. Patchett could have notified the authorities as late as 6 p.m., and they would have already come for Berdin. So what was the best-case scenario? Patchett had simply forgotten?

Berdin winced and again scanned the dark walls of the shed. In the gloom, he could make out two-dimensional shapes and nothing more. The shovel was gone—at least as far as he could see—and so was the hoe. Feeling a weight in his stomach, Berdin grabbed a pitchfork. It would have to do. He moved the rototiller away from the corner of the shed and sifted the soil in the corner through his fingers. Quite soft. He raised the pitchfork and stabbed at the ground ten, fifteen, twenty times, sinking the tines over a foot deep with each thrust. Then he cast the pitchfork aside, knelt, and scooped the loose dirt away from the corner with his hands. He repeated the entire process again and again.

In one sense, the process was rewarding for him. Berdin had not worked in The Field for days, and his heart rejoiced at the smooth weight of the pitchfork and the crumbly rich soil. But a deeper part of him suffered. What had Patchett done? What would Brophy do? He tried to keep his mind clear of such thoughts, but he found himself dwelling on the last question when he stopped digging. Oddly, it didn't scare him like the first one did. Brophy scared him, but he was beginning to doubt she had power over him. Ian always seemed to bail him out when there was trouble, so maybe he ought not to worry when trouble arose. It seemed reasonable. Ian was his friend, and as such, would protect him. Not from getting into trouble—just from the dire consequences the trouble seemed to bear.

As his thoughts dwelt on Ian, Berdin grew more calm. Somewhere, Ian was out there. And he had promised. This realization brought Berdin down from irrational panic to rational uneasiness. The uneasiness still caused him to dig, but it allowed him to think clearly, focusing on Ian, as he tunnelled. *Why couldn't Patchett be trusted like Ian? Why couldn't anyone?* He knew the answer, and it empowered him. *That such a man would call him friend!*

There are two ways to be hungry and thirsty. The first, and most human, is to concentrate on the absence of relief for your pangs, thus becoming more and more discouraged. The second way, the path Berdin chose now in spite of his natural urges, is to welcome the pangs as reminders that you are deprived for a cause. Ian was indirectly responsible for Berdin's suffering. But instead of allowing the pangs to beat against him like the senseless tide, Berdin allowed them to caress him like a gentle breeze carrying a welcome scent. The scent was Ian's smile. Berdin understood that by bearing his suffering graciously he would be pleasing Ian. And so, not in spite of but in cooperation with his hunger and thirst, Berdin dug, and dug faithfully.

His efforts were rewarded sooner than he expected. He had just expanded his tunnel to the point directly beneath the wall when starlight illuminated the little shed. But the light didn't shine through his hole—it came through the suddenly-open doorway. On his feet in an instant, Berdin stared at his new opportunity for freedom and muttered a hasty "Thank you, Ian." But before he could move through the doorway, it was blocked by a man's figure. Patchett! Berdin looked around for a shovel.

"Hold, hold, hold, citizen!" Patchett whispered as hastily as his slow-moving mouth allowed. "Sorry I startled you, but I'm trying to be quiet out here because . . . well—now hold on!" (This last piece Patchett really did say quickly, because Berdin had grabbed him and dragged him in the shed.)

Berdin closed the shed door quickly and said in a loud voice (but not a yell), "All right, whoever's out there and I'm sure there's a lot of you listen up! Listen! I've got the dupe and I'm not lettin' go till yer gone! Understand? I'd sooner kill him than look at him you know! You know! You—I'll kill him I mean it!"

Patchett, however, was not taking things lying down. He struggled in Berdin's grip while the young man babbled and then stuck a well-aimed elbow in Berdin's breadbasket. This not only caused Berdin to lose his grip, but also left him lying on the ground, gasping for air.

"Now, listen to me," Patchett drawled. "You listen. I

didn't—well, I did mean to lock you up. In fact, as soon as I locked the shed I had decided you were staying there till the authorities hauled you away. I—I mean, it was nothing personal. You just were too dangerous to me to be hiding in my field. So I made up my mind . . ."

"Too dangerous to you!" Berdin gabbled. "Too —"

"Hush. I know, I was wrong. I was being a coward. More afraid for me than willing to help someone else. And someone so important to Ian! That was what really got me. Ian protected you and so it, I, it seemed like betraying Ian to betray you. Fact, it seems like betraying Ian not to help you or anybody. But that, that takes courage. And even though I always thought—well, I need courage. So this is my first step." He helped Berdin up. "Sorry," he said.

Berdin was feeling put out. "Oh, you're sorry! Oh, fine, fine, let's shake and forget it happened. How do I know you're not going to slap handcuffs on me while I'm shaking your hand? How do I know? Why should I trust you?"

Berdin stared angrily at Patchett. The blow to his stomach had hurt—had made him feel vulnerable—but now he was revving himself up to act the rash hero again. Patchett looked quite scared as he reflected on Berdin's words, but his response smothered the impatient man's bravado: "I finally know that some things are more important than life working out smoothly. If the hard road follows Ian, then I'm ready to walk it. And to, to get hurt if necessary. So what I'm saying is, you can trust me because now I trust Ian."

"And that's it?" Berdin said softly.

"It's all I've got." Patchett spread his bony hands.

"Well, then it'll have to do," Berdin said with the last of his bravado. But he felt bad about it, so he added, "Thanks for coming back."

"Well, now I've got to go. But I've brought you some food—some hot coffee and rolls and water and this weird Yahtzee Surprise from the Evolving Pallet—it was all they had left . . ."

"Fine, fine," Berdin said. "But wasn't the A/D Monitor suspicious when you came back into The Field at night?"

"No. At least, I don't think so. I can't be certain, of course." Patchett was growing still more scared. "I gotta go. I'll bring more in the morning." And then he was gone, leaving Berdin in an open toolshed, shaking his head at the Yahtzee Surprise.

Things weren't going like they were supposed to. Sure, Ian had disappeared before and things had been okay, but this time nothing happened according to script. Patchett should be trustworthy—and now it seemed he was trustworthy—but not like Ian. And certainly no one else was going to help Berdin. He had to keep moving, to trust himself and his impulses.

He began by moving out of the shed. That helped his uneasiness, and brought with it a rush of exultation. Freedom! Berdin wasn't free of meddling CPA officials and Law Enforcement agents and loyal citizens, but at least he was free of that hulking dome in the distance, with its artificial lights and grey streets. The faint starlight cast dim shadows in The Field and made the night seem enormous, and almost eternal. Rustlings in the corn made Berdin feel less alone. Freedom! His soul expanded, growing large to accommodate the swirl of beauty and the starkness of the night.

The only thing that bound him now was The Fence around The Field. In the International Wilderness—oh! A man could go anywhere, do anything. He could walk with Ian beside cool streams—catching trout! Scaring deer just to see them leap and zig and zag through a maze of trunks and wind-fall! Berdin contemplatively munched on a roll, turning the possibilities over and over in his mind.

The roll distracted him. He had forgotten his hunger. He ate another and another, and then gulped down water in deep swallows. He ate all six of the rolls, finished the water, and poured a cup of coffee from the thermos. He even poked at the Yahtzee Surprise.

He decided he wasn't *that* hungry. But he finished his coffee and poured another cup. The sounds of the night be-gan to entrance him again, and he stared at a horizon full of treetops and stars. The furthest, dimmest stars enchanted him; they jumped from invisible to visible with irresponsible whims. He stared a long time before replacing the lid on his thermos and walking north along the asphalt road. He tried to whistle a song he remembered from grade school.

The Fence, strung fifteen feet high, stopped him. Just beyond sprawled a quiet, sparse forest of lodgepole pines and spruce and scattered scrub oak. He imagined standing in the pines, on the other side, and felt a longing that many have called homesickness. He inspected the strands of barbed wire, strung impossibly close, on The Fence. He took the knife from his pocket and dropped it against the strands. A light flashed—as he had been told, an electrical current ran through each wire on The Fence. Exit from the community was im-possible. Our Benevolent Liberator had seen to that.

Berdin retrieved his knife, slowly, and put it back in his pocket. He stared a moment longer at the wilderness, and then turned east, walking through a section of The Field that bordered The Fence. He walked until he reached his own section of The Field.

He wandered to his toolshed, which stood forlorn in the starlight, tools scattered around it. He picked up a hoe and tested its weight in his hand. He dug a small hole with the hoe, and then widened it. Again he looked at the hoe.

He snapped it over his knee. He grabbed a rake and did the same. Then he gathered the pieces and threw them in the hole. He fished in his pocket for his matches. Then he arranged the pieces of wood in a pile and tried to light them. And tried again. And again.

He used thirteen matches before he understood that only the splinters would burn and rearranged his pile so that he could actually build a fire. He huddled nervously over his new blaze, like a mother over her sick child, as it sputtered, caught flame, sputtered again, and finally seemed to catch. Only when he noticed that a bigger piece of the hoe handle was burning did he rock backwards and sit calmly watching his fire. He inhaled deeply so that he could taste the woodsmoke. He watched a single spark drift upward. He thought absently of Ian, wishing his friend could be a part of that beautiful night.

When the fire had burned to embers, and Berdin's mind came swimming back from that glorious blank abyss that opens when staring into a campfire, he thought again of Patchett. He was uncertain of Patchett. His friend seemed to follow Ian, but he did it poorly. Why be afraid, when you're doing what Ian requires of you? Why hesitate? Couldn't Patchett just take Ian at his word, as Berdin always . . . Berdin stopped, feeling guilty. He reassessed his judgment of Patchett. Maybe he was being too harsh. Maybe a little uncertainty was to be expected. As he kicked dirt over the ashes and embers, he tried to forgive Patchett. He couldn't tell whether he had succeeded.

Berdin decided to sleep in his old section of The Field that night. He picked up the head of the rake and threw it far back into the corn, and then did the same with the hoe. He picked up the Yahtzee Surprise, thought better of it, and slid the whole dish under the door of the toolshed. Then he wandered sleepily into the corn, relieved himself, and walked to the corner on the brink of the International Wilderness. He yawned happily at the trees, lay down, and drifted silently to sleep.

The night passed, as all nights passed. Inside the dome, the artificial lights hummed dimly to simulate starlight, and some of the population slept. Others, on the night shift, sleepily rode monorails, clocked in at work, yawned their way through their six-hour "day," and clocked out. Still others—unable or unwilling to sleep—entertained themselves or "took care of business." In Block 768, a disheveled man with a hairy chest and balding head passed the night feverishly scratching losing lottery tickets. He fell into a hopeless sleep, in a sea of stubs, at dawn. Two women—lovers—spent the night at the Recreational Hallucinogenics Center, tasting various drugs and holding each other through hideous and angelic visions. The Gaming Resort collected over seven million lottery tickets—better than the usual night's take—with a few tired men and women retiring to their rented suites having beat the system. In Block 443, a grim sixteen year-old girl took a deep breath, swallowed two tablets of Lilopristone, and waited quietly for the abortion pills to erase the life in her womb. Another sixteen year-old girl climbed a ladder and put her head in a noose.

27,000 people attended the Community Gladiator game, in which teams of athletic men and women fought for the right to survive a lethal obstacle-course playing field. Countless CWO monitors screeched "Cannibal Run," "Loving Daddy," and "Late Night With the Serial Killer." In a sumptuous five bedroom suite at the top of the CPA building, a smiling woman slipped out of a black robe marked with a purple star and touched Our Benevolent Liberator . . .

And in a corner of The Field, stars wheeled overhead and a breeze caressed a tired fugitive.

The cold woke Berdin. The night was still dark, but seemed less dark at the horizon in the east. Berdin curled up to warm himself, but was unable to break the chill in his bones. With a grunt, he sat up, found his thermos, and poured a cup of coffee. He warmed his hands and face with the steam from the mug, and drank deeply. A sparrow in a tree near him chirped tentatively. With a few nervous flits of its wings, it flew to the top of the fence, perched, and then fell to the ground electrocuted. Berdin grimaced.

But he had little time for reflection. More birds had taken up the song, and it was evident that dawn was breaking. In an hour, punctual Field Engineers would be passing through the final checkpoint and into The Field. Most likely a new Engineer had been assigned to Berdin's old section, which would create major problems for a loitering rebel. Berdin realized he would have to pass the day in Patchett's section again, and so he gathered his few possessions and quickly moved to his position of "safety." And he waited.

Patchett arrived at his section early. He still felt ashamed of his actions the day before, and had made a conscious effort to make further amends by bringing Berdin a sumptuous breakfast. He stumbled through his corn self-consciously until he found Berdin.

"Mornin'," Berdin said, seeing Patchett first.

"Morning." Patchett hurried to him and knelt down in the soft dirt beside him. They glanced at each other and looked away, studying the cornstalks.

"I had a fire last night." He didn't know why he said that.

"Really?" Patchett looked startled. "Don't, don't you think that might attract attention?"

"Yeah, probably. I just had to have one. They're so . . . I won't do it again."

"Oh, oh no, it's, it's up to you," Patchett said quickly. "I was just making an observation."

Berdin looked at Patchett. The older man's face was long and tan, made longer and darker by the old straw hat perched on his head. His brown eyes were set close together; thin and sturdy wrinkles made the unremarkable eyes expressive. Uneven teeth showed distractedly through taut, brown lips. Patchett's body was also long. He seemed to have especially pointy elbows and knees; when he squatted by Berdin he looked like a partially-assembled folding cot. He was developing the habit of chewing the fingernails on his left hand.

Still staring, Berdin asked, "What'd you bring me?"

Patchett reached into his bulging lunch bag. "An orange, some milk, some bread, a peanut butter sandwich, two sausage patties—they're still almost warm, a beer, some doughnuts, and a drumstick. Is that enough?"

Berdin laughed. "At least for this week. Thanks."

"Sure," Patchett said, feeling good. He glanced at Berdin with approval as the latter munched a sausage.

"What—what's it like in The Field at night?"

"Terrific." Berdin kept chewing. "The stars are out—real stars, not those hacking fake lights—and there are a million of 'em. Nothin's more beautiful than all those points stretchin' from corner to corner in the sky. And the air! And the crickets! The birds! Nothin' else—nothing's like it. Patchett, it makes you feel so close to the International Wilderness you just want to jump The Fence. Do you know what's out there? Neither do I, but just thinking about it makes me crazy. That's reality. Everybody," (here he waved his hand directly at the dome), "everybody in there thinks they're livin' reality when they fight with all their insignificant little problems and live their insignificant, hemmed-in lives. But that's only the tip of the iceberg! It's only a secluded, dull piece of what's real! What's *really* real—what's real and exciting—is out here, and especially out there!" He moved his hand in a sweeping gesture.

"But all the people are in there." Patchett pointed to the dome.

"I know, but—don't you get it? It's like Ian was sayin' when we were out here listening to 'm—what's real in there is mostly lousy (your loneliness and alienation and belief that people could be so much better friends), but, but what's real out here—in the International Wilderness I mean—is good. You know? The good part of reality we've always felt is somewhere and only get glimpses of is, uh, beyond."

The two men fell silent. Patchett nodded his head thoughtfully. Then he summoned his courage again. "Why did you quit The Field?"

Berdin shrugged his shoulders. "Ian told me to." He shifted nervously.

"Why didn't Ian tell me to?"

"I knew that was coming," Berdin said. "And I don't know the answer. I guess if everyone stopped working The Field no one would eat. But . . . well, I envy you in a way. I sure miss—"

"You envy me?" Patchett drawled. "You get to spend so much time with the teacher, and you envy me?"

"But The Field . . ."

"Ah, so what? The Field only borders the International Wilderness. You walk with the man who owns it."

They were silent again, each deep in his own thoughts. After a while, they remembered their manners.

"So, you need anything else?" Patchett said.

"Oh, thanks, no. You've done more 'n enough—I mean it's terrific of you to bring me food and all. Here's your thermos back."

"I'll buy another, so I can alternate them each day."

"You don't have to do that. But—it is getting colder. Could you bring me another old sweatshirt or somethin'?"

"Here." Patchett peeled off his sweatshirt, ignoring Berdin's protests. "It's big so it'll fit over yours, and I'll just tell the higher-ups it wore out. They'll get me a new one."

"Thanks."

More silence. Berdin remembered his other sausage.

"Well, off to work," Patchett said, straightening up.

"Tell me if you need me to move."

"I will. You'll be fine there." Patchett moved off toward the toolshed.

Berdin finished his sausage and the orange (carefully burying the orange peels), and drank the milk. He lay back with his hands behind his head, letting the sun warm him. He wondered how Ian was destroying the EQL, and what Brophy and Arthur Aphek would think. Eventually he dozed.

He awoke refreshed and instantly bored. It would be a long day. He watched Patchett work as best he could, and was surprised by the man's methodical dedication. Patchett didn't always do things the way Berdin would have—he snapped weeds off at the base, for one thing—but he tried hard. It was much more than most Field Engineers managed.

Eventually Patchett finished his work, stowed his tools, and turned to go. "Goodbye Section R3," he said softly in the direction of Berdin.

Berdin understood. "Goodbye," he answered. And then Patchett was gone.

Berdin spent the better part of the rest of the day crawling around R3, digging out weed roots with his hands. He gathered them in a pile and then carried them across an open space to a neighboring section, where he buried them. He was quite glad to see the sun disappear behind the treetops, and to hear the birds welcoming the evening.

When it was dark, Berdin stretched himself and then walked back to his old section. "Might as well get something done," he muttered. He tested the door of the toolshed. Locked. He looked under the door. The Yahtzee Surprise sat undisturbed. "Fine day's work this guy put in," he grumbled.

He set himself to the back-breaking task of weeding his old section by hand. The work warmed him, both body and soul. He became so engrossed he forgot the wheeling of the stars overhead. He didn't stop till dawn threatened on the horizon. Then he simply threw the weeds over The Fence and walked back to section R3 to await Patchett's arrival.

"Over here," he whispered when he saw Patchett blundering through the corn. "Mornin'."

He knew something was wrong when Patchett didn't return his greeting. The older man just paced quickly toward him and knelt down beside him.

"What'd you bring me?" Berdin asked, feeling sour in his stomach.

"Uh—this." Patchett handed him a bag stuffed with food. "And—this." He thrust a copy of *From the Top* into Berdin's hands. The newsletter was folded to the page that contained the EQL-generated life-span termination list. Berdin stared at Patchett.

"You're kidding. I made the LiST?"

"You didn't just make it. Look at it."

Berdin looked down, seeing first his white knuckles on the borders of the printed page, and then the page itself. Beneath the heading "Life-Span Termination" sprawled columns and columns of a thousand names. Except this time, each name was the same. Printed one thousand times in bold letters was one name: Berdin Dwate.

CHAPTER TEN

"I hear my own soul tremble and heave.
Nothing else?
I hear, I hear
The silent night thoughts
Of my fellow sufferers asleep or awake,
As if voices, cries,
As if shouts for planks to save them.
I hear the uneasy creak of the beds,
I hear chains."
—Dietrich Bonhoeffer, *Letters and Papers
from Prison*

"Well," Berdin said, trying to sound philosophical, "you had to figure I'd make the LiST." His head was swimming.

Patchett was animated. "Bytes, Berdin. You *are* the LiST! The EQL is fixated on you! And no, I didn't have to figure you'd make the LiST—it's supposed to be randomly generated. This sure is planned. It's almost like, like the EQL hates you. Like you threaten it, and so it's got to kill you."

"Yeah, but maybe—" here a comforting idea flashed in Berdin's mind and warmed him—"maybe . . . this is all part of Ian trashing the EQL! I mean, maybe he's thrown a monkey wrench in the whole thing and this is the . . . *symptom* of the EQL's imminent destruction—it could be! It could be that Ian's giving us a good sign!"

Patchett looked doubtful. "Drawing up your death warrant a thousand times over isn't exactly a good sign."

"But that's just Ian's sense of humor! I mean, you haven't heard anything of Ian, have you? He hasn't been caught, right?"

"No . . ." Patchett's long face was further extended by a frown.

"So what's he doing? Destroying the EQL, you said it yourself! And what better way than to kill it slowly, so people think it just malfunctioned? You know?"

Patchett still looked unconvinced, but Berdin had sold himself on the idea. He made one last effort to cheer his friend: "Hey, look at it this way, Patchett. Even if they do kill me, they can't kill me a thousand times. We saved 999 people from life-span termination today. And who knows? If I live to see tomorrow, maybe it'll save a thousand more. *That's* good news anyway."

Patchett had to admit that was good news. "It's good, but not necessarily for you."

Berdin became impatient. "Look, Ian said I'd see him again. He sure ain't lyin'. So I'll see him again."

"How do you know it will be on this side of the grave?"

Exasperated, Berdin threw aside the newsletter and began rummaging through the sack of food. "You're the gloomiest guy this side of the Zone, Patchett. Think what you want." He found an apple and crunched it loudly, to show his impatience.

Patchett gathered himself and headed for the toolshed. In truth, he was feeling more stubborn than gloomy. He was one of those odd kinds of people who like to cause a fuss and are disappointed when no one else wants to panic. It wasn't spiteful—he was genuinely concerned for Berdin—but he thought it a mean trick that Berdin didn't share his concern.

Berdin, on the other hand, was a straightforward brave man who liked to convince himself there's no cause to worry. He'd face fear when he had to, but he'd just as soon make it disappear. Now that he felt he'd dispelled cause to fear, Berdin's spirit was as placid as a glassy meadow lake. He hadn't deceived himself, he thought, just rearranged his perspective to properly understand the situation. Many people panicked, he knew, when there was no need to fear—therefore the truthful perspective must rarely admit reason to worry. To some, this sounds as foreign as a dance on the stars. To others it's self-evident. This second class of people make much better companions on adventures.

Berdin finished his breakfast, buried the apple core, and began reading the newsletter. He was bored, he knew. He was so bored, in fact, he read the entire transcript of Arthur Aphek's latest speech. It contained no mention of Ian or Berdin, but was full of allusions to the misfits in society who forgot who was their boss. Berdin understood almost nothing of it.

He read the latest dictums from the EQL next, weighing in his mind whether they sounded more haywire than in the past. He couldn't tell. One declaration that "Toxic waste generates herds of sheep" seemed stranger than any he could remember, but it was hard to say. When you want to believe something, you can believe it almost instantly without any cause, but you will also question the quality of your belief no matter how convincing the cause.

Eventually Berdin stretched out to sleep. The anxiety of the morning had passed from his mind, and he slept soundly until a hand gently shook his shoulder.

"Sorry to wake you," Patchett said. "Just wanted to apologize for being worried. It's my nature. But I'm working on it."

"That's okay." Berdin felt awkward, largely because he didn't think Patchett had anything to be sorry for. "I'm, uh, sorry I lost my temper." He felt a pang of guilt for lying— he didn't believe he owed Patchett an apology either.

"See you tomorrow, Berdin."

"Yeah, we'll see you Patchett. Uh—Patchett? What's your first name? I mean, I feel dumb always callin' you Patchett."

The older man smiled. "Greg." He turned and left.

Berdin felt vaguely happy he had asked that question, though he didn't know why. In this disjointed frame of mind, he rolled over and drifted absently back to sleep.

That night, Berdin awoke and went back to work in his old section of The Field. At the first hint of dawn, he returned to section R3, visited with Patchett over breakfast, and then slept for most of the day.

He repeated this pattern many days following, with little variation. What could vary? Berdin knew he'd seen the last of the inside of the dome—at least until Ian returned— and there were only so many ways to pass time in The Field. He wanted to build a campfire each night, but he wasn't willing to take the chance. He grew to enjoy Greg Patchett's company, and wished for more time to visit with him, but couldn't justify the danger. Pulling Patchett away from his work was irresponsible, and spending time with Patchett afterward risked making the Arrival/Departure Monitor suspicious.

So Berdin worked and ate and slept, and relished his time with Patchett. The older man's methodical manner—the very thing that irritated Berdin originally—endeared him to Berdin over time. Patchett carefully out-did himself with each successive lunch sack, and gently laughed when Berdin laughed at his extravagance. They came to know each other's idiosyncracies, and to succeed in expressing them in ways that made the men smile at their understanding. The tense moments caused by the locked toolshed appeared to be forgotten.

Occasionally, Patchett brought news of events in the community. Followers of Ian had begun meeting together in small groups to discuss his words and try to discern a course of action, and one such group met in Patchett's unit each Wednesday. Consequently, Thursday became Berdin's favorite day of the week. Each Thursday Patchett would recount the key discussions from the night before, and he and Berdin would wrangle until they reached a satisfactory conclusion. These morning brainstorms covered a wide range of topics, from "How vocal should a follower be?" to "What did Ian's parable of the farmer mean?" Patchett, always respectful, was willing to accept Berdin's conclusions as absolute truth, but Berdin wouldn't tolerate such a deferential attitude. He insisted, until Patchett promised, that Patchett present his conclusions to the group and ask their response. It was these responses Berdin enjoyed most of all.

The very existence of the group reflected the maturation of Greg Patchett. His responsible nature rebelled at the thought of the trouble a meeting of followers would create, but his new resolve mastered that fear. Now each week he bravely opened his door to nine people with just one thing in common, and weathered the suspicion of his neighbors. When the couple next door demanded an explanation, he told them the truth, tersely describing the integrity and majesty of Ian. The potential consequences of his honesty caused him to shudder, but he pressed onward with unexpected determination. He had one hope, and he held fast to it: Ian had promised that those who did not abandon him would neither find themselves abandoned. It was enough.

Patchett also brought Berdin news of the rest of the community, which seemed to have forgotten Ian. Patchett recounted the "news stories" presented by the CWO, and any changes in CPA policy. He found himself paying much more attention to the EQL and Our Benevolent Liberator. Even lesser public figures, like Jane Brophy and the Director of the LEA, commanded his attention. In turn, Patchett would faithfully relay significant events to Berdin.

Most of the news was bad. The EQL seemed to have regained a modicum of sanity after creating one deviant LiST, and had resumed generating 1,000 different names each day. Two things about these new LiSTs distinguished them: names familiar to Berdin now regularly appeared on the LiST, and Berdin's own name occupied its place (in alphabetical order) on each one. Ian seemed to be faltering in his efforts to destroy the machine.

Further, no one had heard a word of Ian's whereabouts.

He had disappeared. A tight network of his followers regularly communicated with each other, and yet none of them could so much as claim to have seen a white robe. Rumors that Ian had been rehabilitated by Our Benevolent Liberator, or had returned to the International Wilderness, grew popular. Some men and women lost hope and returned to lives cluttered with lottery tickets, rhetoric, and pharmaceuticals.

Berdin wavered but would not drown. He had been so certain of the EQL's imminent malfunction that its unceasing dictums and LiSTs unnerved him for more than a week, but he found he could reassure himself with reminders of the inscrutability of Ian. Nothing ever seemed to go as Berdin expected, so he tried to ignore his expectations. Still, the disappearance of Ian scared him, much the same way a child separated from his parents is scared in a crowd. For days he would refuse to face the logical conclusions, and then a dark hour would overwhelm him. The depression brought on by these hours was compounded for Berdin by his own anger at his unfaithfulness. His doubt fueled his fury and his fury fueled his doubt in a cycle that was difficult to break. During these times he most needed Patchett, though he couldn't say why. The two men added their doubts together in a way that somehow equalled assurance, and then would bravely face another day (or night) alone.

Apparently as a result of Berdin's loneliness, he began "talking" to Ian when he worked in The Field at night. Not that Ian ever answered—Berdin didn't expect that—but it reassured him to think that Ian somehow heard his complaints, petitions, failings, and successes. He knew he was behaving deviantly, according to society, to mumble aloud as he went about his tasks, but he was beyond caring about social mores.

His interest was focused on retaining the hope within him. He was trying to be brave.

After a week's work, Berdin had restored his old section to its proper condition, and began rehabilitating Willis's plot. That job took longer—Willis had always hated manual labor—but in two weeks' time Berdin had done everything that could be done for his friend's bean crop. For a week, Willis didn't even notice the improvement, but by the time Berdin had finished, he couldn't help but see the change. He had no idea how it had occurred, and (fortunately for Berdin) he wasn't curious. Willis simply figured "his luck had turned," and concentrated his energy on finding more excuses to miss work. Come harvest time, Willis thought, he would work harder. But in the back of his mind he knew he couldn't stay away from The Free Love Society Banquets that long.

From Willis's section, Berdin moved to Sherryl Lento's plot. Patchett had discovered that Sherryl was a member of another group that claimed to follow Ian, and had shared this information with Berdin. It seemed logical to Berdin that she should be the next to benefit from his night labor, and it was clear her section needed help. Sherryl was a talented teacher, but the bureaucracy of Coastal Community Twelve was uninterested in talents. So she struggled at a vocation for which she was ill-suited. Her plot reflected her ineptitude.

Berdin was glad to find her section in disarray. Hard work helped chase his doubt from his soul, and lately the doubts were growing at a rate that frightened him. He had been in The Field for thirty days, and still had not seen or heard from Ian. Patchett seemed more terse of late, and Brophy appeared to be zeroing in on Berdin. Even before he had moved to Sherryl's section, Berdin had become the subject of wanted posters scattered intermittently in the community's sea of fly-ers. Now the slow-moving machinery of the LEA had reached an important conclusion: Berdin was hiding in The Field. This conclusion, of course, should have been reached weeks ago—a fugitive inside the dome would be quickly reported by bored and nervous block monitors—but for some time the Director of the LEA subscribed to a theory that Berdin was hiding in the food service chutes of various blocks.

Now, faced with the inevitable, the Director escalated his efforts to locate Berdin by posting warnings at each gate to The Field. The warnings declared that Berdin was violent and "socially deranged," and that anyone found giving sanc-tuary or other forms of aid to him would also be deemed de-ranged and worthy of termination. The warnings were amended each day so that they became increasingly stern—so much so that even apathetic Field Engineers could no longer ignore them. The decrees unsettled them because they were worded in a way that "forgot who was boss" with regard to this situation. Field Engineers read them, shook their heads, and muttered "Don't tell me what to do" or "You be your boss and I'll be mine." But they began to keep an eye out for Berdin all the same. The presumptuousness of the warning was troublesome, but the severity of the punishment more so. Better to live and suffer a minor infringement on your rights than to die preserving the ideal.

Naturally, Brophy was the mastermind behind the manhunt. She muscled the LEA into action and then settled back to watch events take their course, but when she heard the Director's food service chute theory she realized she would have to assume an active role in the execution of the details of the search. Brophy was wise enough not to become so ob-

sessed with finding Berdin that she lost her influence over
Our Benevolent Liberator, but the former Field Engineer's
disappearance did distract her. Her temper grew even more
unruly, and she treated everyone except Arthur Aphek poorly.

Berdin knew it was just a matter of time until The
Field was searched. He and Patchett talked about possible
hiding places, but couldn't agree on a feasible one (without
mentioning the toolshed, which neither wanted to consider).
Sunlight touching the tree tops just before dawn became a
hateful sight for Berdin, because it heralded the tense moments he spent hiding in Patchett's plot, hoping his friend would
arrive unaccompanied by Law Enforcement agents. Each
morning he held his breath at the sound of footsteps in the
corn, and each morning he breathed easier when Patchett knelt
down beside him and said, "Morning."

But on the 38th day, Patchett did not say good morn-
ing. He was far too excited—more excited than the day
Berdin's name had appeared on the LiST a thousand times.
He knelt beside Berdin and said simply, "This is it."

"What?" Berdin felt adrenaline surge in his chest, kick-
starting his heart. "What?"

"There were agents milling around the gate this morning. They're organizing to search The Field. What are we
going to do?"

Berdin stared at Patchett, expecting more. Patchett
stared back, too startled to expound. "How—" Berdin began. He stopped. He stood up and peeked over the corn,
unable to see anyone. He considered a desperate assault on
The Fence. The pain from barbs and electric shock did not
deter him—Brophy was sure to do worse if she caught him
alive—but the land mines on the other side were daunting.

Not so much because they could kill, but because they could kill him before he saw Ian. He knew he was supposed to see Ian on this side of death, although he couldn't explain *how* he knew it. Perhaps he felt that way because suicide seemed too much like quitting.

His mind whirled in a frantic search for a solution. To his dismay, Berdin soon noticed that his thoughts spun around a central course of action that served as a locus for his search. With a feeling of dread, he surfaced from his mental maelstrom and acknowledged the fixed conclusion.

"Lock me in the toolshed," he said.

"What?!"

"Will you?" Berdin asked, remembering it meant Patchett would assume a great risk if he were to protect him. "I mean, it would . . . it *is* a huge favor and I know I don't have the right to ask it of you but would you please lock me in your toolshed and then make up some kind of lie, *story* to tell the agents when they come to search your section which they will any minute. Will you? Please? For my sake?"

"I—" Patchett had been nearly speechless when he first approached Berdin this morning, and now he was as stunned as a staggering boxer one punch away from being knocked down. He tried again to voice the emotions and rationale clattering in his brain: "I—yes." He clamped his mouth shut.

Berdin crouched down, grabbed his lunch sack from Patchett's fist, and ran toward the toolshed with a stooping, shuffling gait. Patchett followed in a similar posture. But before he could ask Berdin what to tell the agents, or provide the reassurance he knew his friend needed to hear, the wiry redhead had darted in the shed and closed the door.

Patchett straightened up. He glanced down the asphalt road: no one, not even a Field Engineer. He walked slowly, in measured steps, to the toolshed door and locked it. He whispered hoarsely, "What should I say?"

"What?" Berdin strained his ears in the twilit room.

"What—what do I tell them to keep them out of my shed?"

"I don't know. Tell them—oh, I don't know." Berdin was nervous, and he hated himself for it. "Just think of something, Greg. Go away and think of something and stop drawing attention to the shed."

Patchett lingered for a moment by the door, hoping Berdin might change his mind and volunteer an idea. Then he walked back with even, unhurried paces into the cornfield. He made a pretense of adjusting his sprinkler system—he unscrewed the main valve control—and set his mind on solving the dilemma before him. Absently cleaning the valve with a rag, Patchett forced his premature thoughts through their adolescence and into maturity in a tedious, grinding sequence that made his temples throb. At the same time he tried to cast his will in iron so that he could face the agents calmly, without faltering.

It was during this profound effort that a solution presented itself: fail to provide the agents with a suitable reason to ignore the toolshed. The solution repulsed most of Patchett, but its simplicity disarmed a small fluttering place in his heart. *It wouldn't really be like betraying Berdin*, the flutter said. *It would just be a failure to think quickly enough to save him. Besides, he's asking you to lie for him.*

Patchett frowned and rubbed his forehead with both hands.

Meanwhile, Berdin was talking to Ian. "I've really done it this time, Ian," he whispered as quiet as a breath. "I've put Patchett on the spot and now—I don't know, I'm not sure he can handle the pressure. Help him. Help me. Make me do the right thing. C'mon, you said I'd see you again. Time's up. I can't hide any more. Come on . . ."

Berdin muttered for more than an hour, his ears hyper-sensitive to any noise outside the shed. But the only noises were everyday sounds, and eventually his hunger distracted him enough to turn his attention to the lunch sack. He rummaged through it till he found a cheese danish, which he ate without tasting. He drank his milk and then waited another hour. He talked to Ian again and waited some more. A hideous idea occurred to him: Patchett had made up the story of the search to lure him back into the shed. It made sense, Patchett was scared . . . Berdin's mind rebelled at the insinuation. A man owes it to his friend to believe he'll do right till he proves him wrong. Again, Berdin cursed himself for his nervousness.

"M-morning, agent!" Patchett's voice sounded loud and contrived outside the shed. "What can I do for you?" Berdin's whole body, except for his ears, shut down.

"Are you Greg Patchett, Field Engineer assigned to section R3?" The voice was a male's, powerful but also wheedling. Berdin decided the agent sounded nosey.

"Yeah. Can I help you?"

"I'm Agent Stanicek. We—come here citizen, so I don't have to shout."

"I, I can't. I've got the valve open on the sprinkler system and I've got to . . . manually hold back the water pressure until I reattach the main valve control." It was a lie,

Berdin knew—the sprinkler system wasn't that primitive—
but it was low-risk. The agent had no way of knowing the
truth about the sprinklers.

"Hold on a minute, then," Agent Stanicek said. He
rustled toward Patchett.

"Watch my corn!" Patchett snapped.

"It's *our* corn citizen. You know that." Stanicek spoke
softer because he had moved closer to Patchett, but Berdin's
straining ears took in everything. "And you know why I'm
here. We've got—that is, it has been our community's mis-
fortune" (it sounded as if the agent was reading a proclama-
tion, or reciting a memorized speech) "to condition one of
our citizens to exhibit fatally deviant behavior. Berdin Dwate,
a former Field Engineer recently designated for life-span termination, has refused correctional procedures and has thus
become a fugitive. We have reason to believe the subject . . ."

"Are you coming to the point soon?" It was Patchett's
voice, but Berdin could not believe it. Never before had Berdin
heard Patchett interrupt someone, let alone sarcastically.

"'Intolerance stunts evolution,'" Stanicek replied,
quoting a favorite community slogan. "Try not to be so reactionary, Mr. Patchett. As I was saying, the LEA has every
reason to believe Dwate is hiding—has been hiding—in The
Field for a number of days." He paused. "We've had this
posted by the checkpoints for more than a week, Mr. Patchett."

"That's why I'm wondering . . . why you just read it to
me again." Berdin actually grinned. In spite of himself, he
was enjoying Patchett's character transformation.

"'Free speech conquered censorship,' Patchett.
Frankly, I wasn't sure you Field Engineers could read at all."

"Illiterate discrimination!" Patchett cried. "You're

one of those people who—"

"That's enough, Patchett. Look, I don't like you and you probably don't like me. But I've got a job to do. I've gotta find Dwate. If you know anything—I mean, anything at all—seen a suspicious person or found footprints or anything— tell me. I'm not out to get you. I just want to take care of this deviant. But if they—*we* find out you've been covering for him in any way, you're going to . . . you'll be viewed as a deviant as well. So, what have you seen? Anything?" The agent's voice was more wheedling than before. He did not like being disliked.

"Well,"—Patchett was warming to his new character— "thanks for finally talking straight. Yeah, I've heard rumors but nothing I could trust a hundred percent. Somebody— who was it? Freman? Said he saw a man in the trees on the other side of The Fence. But that was about two weeks ago. And I don't know, he didn't sound, um, convinced about it, like he was sure it happened."

"So this Field Engineer, Freman—"

"No, it wasn't Freman. Who was it? Seems like I just overheard it in the BAE building. Is it important?" Patchett's voice wavered between free-spirited and terse.

"Could be." The agent was responding slowly now, obviously taking notes. "Anything else?"

"I don't think so. No. Everything's been as dull pretty much as ever."

"Uh huh. Mind if I have a look around?"

Long pause. Berdin could almost see Patchett summoning his courage. "Nope," Patchett said, in a strange carefree lilt.

Berdin drew a deep breath and looked at the rake in

the corner. It was the best weapon around.

Agent Stanicek wandered through rows and rows of corn, oblivious to the footprints in the soil and uncertain of what, short of a man, he was looking for. He stopped and stared at the toolshed. "I'll need to look inside your shed. It's routine—we're doing it in every section." He sounded apologetic but unwavering.

"Not in this section."

"What?" Stanicek was hurt. He couldn't believe a man could be so disrespectful to a Law Enforcement agent.

"I said, 'Not in this section.' I lost the key three days ago and the higher-ups still haven't replaced it. So unless you've got a hacksaw with you, you're out of luck. Sorry."

"Oh. I see." Stanicek, oddly, was placated. "Well, thanks for your cooperation, Patchett." Berdin heard boots step on asphalt and stop. Stanicek's voice sounded again, with more authority. "If you discover anything about his location, you are required to contact the LEA immediately."

"Will do." Patchett's voice carried a note of relief. The boots stepped out of earshot on the asphalt road.

Berdin sighed, and the sigh carried words to Ian: "Thank you, thank you, thank you. Now help me make it through three more hours in this shed." He searched his lunch sack again.

The hours in the shed passed slowly, but Patchett finally opened the door and stepped inside. The door swung shut behind him. Berdin stood up and slapped Patchett on the back.

"Great work, Patchett. Great! You're a con artist and neither of us knew it!"

Patchett was smiling nervously, apparently still a little

dazzled by his own performance. He scratched his head behind his right ear.

"You know," Berdin laughed, "you sounded more like *me* than *you* out there. What got into ya?"

"Heh! I don't know." Patchett shook his head. "I— I was feeling nervous and I was trying to make myself not be. And then I blurted out something sarcastic, and it was easier. So I kept doing it."

"Well it sure seemed to work. And saying you lost the key was a stroke of genius. I'd say we fooled 'em. I'd say we got Brophy and her thugs out of our hair for awhile."

But Berdin, as usual, spoke too soon. The next morning Patchett was as grim as thunderclouds, reporting that the agents were at the gate again. Another search seemed inevitable. Berdin was hustled back in the shed with a lavish lunch sack, and Greg was left sweating in the corn. He occupied himself by absently cleaning sprinkler heads and planning sarcastic banter.

Around noon, after Berdin had eaten almost everything in his lunch sack from sheer anxiety, Agent Stanicek reappeared.

"Morning, Patchett." Berdin heard rustling—apparently the agent wasn't waiting for permission to search the corn field. "Anything to report?"

"Just an agent trampling my corn."

"*Our* corn. Look, we know Dwate's out here. Who's hiding him?"

"I don't know. Has anyone checked the International Wilderness?"

"Of course not. If he's out there he's dead." Stanicek sounded moody—probably getting pressure from superiors.

"Wouldn't you want to find the body?"

"What for? And how am I supposed to get into the International Wilderness? It's not like The Fence has a gate."

More rustling. Then a pause. "Patchett?" Berdin froze. Somehow he knew Stanicek had remembered the toolshed. "Did they get you that key yet?"

"What? . . . Oh, bytes no. I'm lucky to get a wheelbarrow at harvest time. It . . . could be weeks." Patchett slipped out of character, uncertain of his last sentence.

Footsteps. Closer and closer—they approached the shed. Berdin's hand edged toward the rake. A burst of adrenaline flushed through his body: Stanicek was rattling the door. Berdin stared helplessly at the polished black boots visible through the crack at the bottom of the door. The boots moved, replaced by a knee—and an eye! Berdin didn't move, didn't blink. He thought of Ian.

"Can't see a hacking thing in there." Stanicek stood up. "We may need to get the BAE brass moving on this lock. You sure you don't have anything else to report?"

Patchett took a long time to answer. "No." Berdin closed his eyes.

"Okay. Hope I won't have to bother you again." The boots thumped away on the asphalt.

Patchett did not unlock the toolshed door that day. Instead, at quitting time he walked behind the shed and spoke in a low voice.

"Berdin, can you hear me?"

"Greg? What's going on?" Berdin wondered if anything would ever happen the way he expected it to again.

"There's still agents in The Field. I could unlock the shed, but then they might snoop around. What do you think?"

Berdin ground his teeth. He hated what he thought. "You're right, Greg—leave it locked. Just . . . bring me a big breakfast tomorrow, okay?"

Patchett hesitated, struck by Berdin's plight. "Sure." He walked away.

The afternoon was long; the night, longer. Everything about Berdin's situation galled him. He liked to make things happen—now he was forced to react. He liked moving—he had to sit. He usually faced his problems—now he ran, and hid. Berdin was beginning to wonder whether his freedom was worth the price of being locked in a shed.

Patchett's arrival the next morning did little to cheer him. The older man unlocked the door and slipped quietly inside, confirming Berdin's fear: the LEA was preparing for yet another search. Patchett looked disgusted.

Berdin was not in the mood to recognize Patchett's distress. He just wanted to complain. "How much longer am I going to be stuck in this LOUSY shed? Why can't those agents realize—"

"How should I know?" Patchett snapped. "It looks like Brophy won't give up." He sighed. "There's at least twice as many agents today. They're intensifying the search instead of losing interest."

"What can we do to make them stop?"

"Nothing. Berdin, we've done everything we can. Just . . . we've got to just hope they never search my shed. What else is there?"

The words opened Berdin's eyes. He looked at Patchett and understood what he saw for the first time that morning. The light in the older man's eyes was dim—his eyes were flat, almost two-dimensional. The fight was wearing on him.

Berdin accepted it, and grew noncommittal to hasten Patchett's exit. Patchett got the message, and locked the door behind him. The gloom settled all around Berdin.

He thought about talking to Ian, but decided he wasn't in the mood to talk aloud with no one listening. Nor did Berdin feel like eating; he meant to ration his food more wisely today. He decided instead to sit around and feel sorry for himself.

Patchett opted for much the same thing. He grumbled most of the morning while he pulled weeds—but, to his credit, he was grumbling at his own unpleasant nature in addition to the uncomfortable circumstances. It was a funny way of talking to Ian, really: Patchett would register a complaint and then chastise himself for his unfaithfulness. In this way he worked himself out of his funk by noon.

But he soon had cause to grumble again. Stanicek came into sight on the old road, flanked by two armored agents. The other agents were carrying something—Patchett squinted: stunguns! Even Stanicek appeared to be armed. Patchett ground his teeth.

"Morning, Mr. Patchett." Stanicek marched officiously into the corn. Patchett almost cried out. Stanicek was carrying something far worse than a stungun. Patchett knew his face registered alarm, but he realized, too, that the time for pretense had passed. He mustered the last of his strength.

"Morning, Stanicek. What's with the bodyguards? And—and why," here Patchett's voice rose to a shout, "are you carrying a hacksaw?"

Berdin's spinal cord shivered with shock and nerve impulses. His ears quivered. He leapt to his feet, grabbed the rake, and faced the door. But the thought of waiting disgusted him, and he clutched at a second option: dropping to his knees, he scrabbled frantically at the escape hole he had begun digging so many weeks ago.

"We've intensified the search. And since the BAE never received a request from you for a new key, I thought I'd facilitate matters." Stanicek took a few steps toward Patchett. "Now, citizen, are you sure you have nothing to report to me?"

"Yes, I'm certain." Patchett didn't hesitate. He glared at Stanicek and his co-workers.

"Remmy, search the section." Stanicek was apparently in charge.

"Look—"

"No, Patchett. Don't talk tough to me. This is the most serious threat society has faced in years, as witnessed by the fact that Our Benevolent Liberator has chosen to involve himself. I'll not be the one to let him down. If that means inconveniencing or even rehabilitating you, so be it. Evolution marches on."

"Why?" Patchett asked in a subdued voice.

"What? Clay, remove the lock from that shed." Stanicek didn't seem interested in a philosophical discussion with Patchett.

"I said, Why?"

"Why what? Patchett, I should think you'd be glad I'm opening your toolshed for you. Unless you're hiding something."

"Aren't I my own boss?" Patchett grumbled in his newly-subdued tone. He felt like a horse that had been ridden too long and too hard.

Berdin simply felt desperate. The sawing noise just

beyond his door seemed to constantly accelerate and his digging was proving futile. With a grimace, he stood up, again grasped his rake, and prepared to go down swinging. He would cure Stanicek's sense of duty once and for all.

"Remmy, get over here! We're almost in!" Stanicek had walked to the toolshed and was looking over Clay's shoulder. Remmy, a stocky woman with puffy wrists, joined them. Patchett sat down.

The saw bit through the metal bar with a snap, and for one breath not much happened. Then Stanicek removed the lock and opened the door—and thirteen seconds of chaos ensued. With a snarl, an unshaven redhead burst from the shed and became a blur of elbows, fists, rake handles, and feet. Agents shouted orders, eyes were blacked and shins were cracked, and then the wild man crashed to the ground, stunned senseless. Berdin's tendency to tackle things head-on had failed him; by flying at the agents he had moved within reach of their stunguns. He had done a little damage, but now he was undone. The world was black and still.

When the world began to move and make noise again, Berdin was conscious of a swaying motion and shouts. As he focused his dissipated thoughts, he realized he was moving at a speedy clip, although he was flat on his back. He didn't have to collect his thoughts to remember he had been captured; he had awakened with the dank taste of failure on his tongue. The thought of opening his eyes actually made him feel nauseous. He knew that from now till the rapidly approaching moment he was terminated, he would not like what he saw. He wiggled his toes and found that his feet were free, but he couldn't move his ankles. He didn't have to try his hands; he could feel the handcuffs biting into his wrists. With a grimace, Berdin chose—as he always did—to face his plight: he opened his eyes.

His eyes were chained too—that is, there was a blanket covering his face and most of his body. The blanket irked him. The LEA wouldn't even allow him the right to see his approaching fate.

He wondered whether there might still be some hope of escape. Could he dupe the agents? Or Brophy? What if he faked his death? No—his death would be verified: Brophy would probably donate his body to CHEW (Cannibals Halting Environmental Waste) to make her vengeance complete. Still, Berdin couldn't convince himself there was no hope left.

The footsteps of the agents carrying Berdin began echoing, signalling that they had entered a building. In moments, a bell rang and doors opened and the agents shuffled and then stood still. An elevator, Berdin guessed. The lurch in his stomach confirmed his theory. He wondered if the elevator was the place for his last stand. He decided it was. He sat up. The blanket fell from his face, he saw six agents carrying him on a stretcher, and then he felt a shock much like the shock he remembered outside the toolshed . . .

Berdin awoke to a sharp pain in his cheek. He opened his eyes, and quickly closed them. Too late. Justice Brophy, purple star and all, was standing over him pinching his face. And she had seen him open his eyes.

"No more games, farmer!" she said, and she slapped him hard.

Berdin steeled himself, and opened his eyes. He was in the Justice Cabinet's chambers, on a cold metal table that had been wheeled into the room. Eleven of the justices were seated, as usual, in their plush chairs facing away from the picture window. But Brophy towered over Berdin, looking sadistic. She also—if such a combination is possible—looked stunning. Her hair was gelled into an unshakably attractive style, and her make-up was as flawless as if she were attending a formal ball.

The twenty video monitors lining the west wall showed a still-frame picture of Berdin, his mouth gaping in defiance. Apparently it was footage from his first appearance before the Justice Cabinet. The room itself was still unlit except for the meager light allowed by the window. The justices blended into their chairs.

"Wh-where am I?" Berdin decided he might buy time by playing stupid.

"In a cold reality." Brophy smiled. She had calmed down after having slapped him, and was now speaking deliberately, savoring her victory. "The stunguns won't scramble your brain more than it's scrambled, Dwate. So you'll be aware of all of this, just as you're aware who's doing it to you." She leaned closer. "I caught you," she whispered. "The LEA, from the Director to his agents, is even more incompetent than you. But you were no match for me. I *knew* you were in The Field—that's where your beloved master found you, isn't it?—and when I learned that only one toolshed in The Field had not been searched and you were still missing . . . it took all my self-control not to accompany the agents the next day to see you arrested myself. I was even a little . . . I thought you might somehow escape the agents, but I knew too you had nowhere to run."

"I suppose you think you've caught me now."

Brophy straightened up. She looked disgusted, like an adult beaten by a child at chess. She seemed to have to catch her breath before she said, "Why shouldn't I think that?"

"Ian will save me. Can't you see who he is? You can—you treat him differently and you know—"

"Ian is gone." Brophy leaned back toward his face and hissed the words. "No one has seen him for forty days. Our Benevolent Liberator—I'm sure of it—has taken care of him. It's time you understood: you're alone, your friend is gone, and you're in . . . my . . . hands."

"Ian said I'd see him again." Berdin was badly frightened, but his stubborn nature had set itself against allowing Brophy to revel in his weakness. He tried to keep his eyes from opening too wide.

"Of course. He probably thinks you'll meet on 'the other side.' That you'll be together in HEAVEN." She deliberately raised her voice for the last word, to shock the other justices with her willingness to speak of concepts from the Close-Minded Age. The word brought a growl to the lips of Bila. Brophy leaned even closer to Berdin. "But by the time you die, you won't care there's a heaven. What I put you through won't be worth it." She straightened up again, turned her back to Berdin, and walked four paces away. Then she turned to him again. "The only thing that . . . concerned me about catching you was—I kept envisioning you in the International Wilderness somehow. I thought—I hated the thought—you had passed even out of my grasp. But of course it was a silly concern. No one can pass The Fence."

"Ian did."

"He DIDN'T!" Brophy's shout echoed through the chamber. By the time it died out she had regained much of her composure and had turned her back to Berdin. She paced until she faced the other justices across their bench.

"During your stungun-induced slumber, the Justice Cabinet reviewed your recent activities and their impact on society, and reached a verdict. Bila, notify this 'man' of our decision."

The growling justice fairly leapt to his feet, and snapped to attention. "The Justice Cabinet of Coastal Community Twelve"—he felt he was talking too fast, and consciously slowed his pace—"has deliberated regarding the charge of social deviance levied against Berdin Dwate, former—"

"The verdict, Bila!"

"Um. Guilty to extremes." Bila looked around and then sat down as quickly as he had stood.

"Boy oh boy, that's a big surprise." Berdin said the words, which he knew would incite Brophy, out of sheer defiance. He was not surprised, then, that she rushed to him and pushed him off his table. It bothered him a little that he landed on his nose.

"Farmer—" Brophy was on her knees hissing in Berdin's ear (his chains kept him from rising)—"You may mock the rest of this Cabinet but you *will not mock me*."

"Why not? What have I got to lose? Chains make men free to rebel, right?"

"I'll show you why not." She stood up, with an unmoving smile on her lips, and kicked him. Hard. In the ribs. The act pleased her and pushed her into a frenzy, so that she kicked him seven more times in the side and stomach. Berdin did his best to roll with the blows, but the damage was extensive. Fire ran up his right side from hip to shoulder, and he was unable to catch his breath. There was still defiance in his gaze, but defiant words died on his lips.

Brophy's frenzy troubled many of the justices, but only

one had the courage to stand. Crashton—the man who strangely resembled a toad—cleared his throat and said, "Excuse me." That was as far as he got.

"Crashton." Brophy's voice and glare as she strode toward the bench silenced him. "I'm sick of you. I'm in control, and I will make the decisions." She stuck her elbows out, directing her hands toward her purple star. "Your name will appear on the LiST tomorrow, and you will be terminated that same day. Your example should set an important precedent for this whole Cabinet."

Crashton wrinkled his brow. "Impossible." He awaited an interruption, and upon finding none, continued: "You . . . are not omnipotent, Chief Justice, much as your overwhelming ego has convinced you . . . The EQL, and the EQL alone . . . generates the life-span termination list, and does not . . . consult you, or any under-evolved species. Perhaps—" he paused. He had begun to say, "Perhaps a visit to Pharmaceutical Counselling would restore your sense of reality," but thought better of it.

The Chief Justice, to everyone's surprise, did not move or shout. She looked somewhat coy, and said simply, "We'll see, won't we?" Then she stepped two steps away from the bench and addressed the entire Cabinet: "For the record I, Chief Justice Jane Brophy, take it upon myself to preside over the documentation of Berdin Dwate's confession. Do not critique my methods. Off the record: interference will be severely punished. Do not stand in my way. Busy yourselves with the meaningless lawsuits filed every day. I will otherwise occupy myself. Justice Bila will serve as Chief Justice until my return."

Brophy turned, looked at Berdin, and then turned back

toward the bench. "Oh—one more thing. Crashton's replacement will not be selected without my permission." She smiled her same unmoving smile, let her hands flutter once more toward her star, and walked toward Berdin. She picked him up roughly and stared at him. "Time to go for a walk."

Berdin's side throbbed. He was furious at Brophy for beating him, but the beating had caused him to become strangely aware that he had a duty to Ian. Berdin had awakened in the Justice Cabinet chambers with the attitude that he would die biting, clawing, talking, and infuriating. Now he realized that he owed Ian more. He was representing his friend to Brophy. As such he must be courageous, just, and merciful. But where to find such qualities in his character? He felt crazy, staring back at Brophy, hating her and at the same time searching himself for ways to favorably impress her. Didn't he know he was going to be tortured to death? A weak part of Berdin begged him to throw himself at her feet and offer heartfelt worship in return for a quick death.

All these emotions rushed through Berdin while Brophy stared, and were shaken into his subconscious when she forcefully began to guide him to the door. With his first step, his bound ankles disrupted his balance and threw him to the floor. Brophy yanked him to his feet again.

"Can't you take off the ankle cuffs?" Berdin tried to sound polite, but seemed to be whining.

"You can make it. I'll give you incentive." When Berdin fell again just before the door, she showed him what she meant—kicking him once in his already-battered side. Then she unlocked and opened the door and dragged Berdin to his feet again. He hopped and shuffle-stepped beside her as best as he could, his ribs moaning their request that he stay on his feet.

They passed through the receiving room without incident; Berdin was so focused on his pain and his balance he forgot to notice the android receptionist. After an elevator ride and a turn through a door unfamiliar to Berdin (and one more fall and one more kick), they emerged in the "square" in the middle of the CPA building. Very few others were out—and those who were walked breezily, aware of their status.

Brophy led Berdin to a door guarded by an armored Law Enforcement agent. When the agent saw Brophy, he hastily unlocked the door and swung it open. Then he swallowed, opened his mouth, paused, and said, "Would you like . . . er, me to escort the prisoner?" He stared at the bloodied clothes and scraggly pained face of the redhead.

Brophy sneered at Berdin. "That won't be necessary." She pushed her prisoner into the room, which turned out to be an elevator. Another armored agent stood near the digital control panel. "Top." Brophy glared at the agent, a pretty woman with cascading black hair. "I thought I told you you were fired."

"I was re-hired." The agent smiled an even, catty smile.

Brophy opened her mouth, and then closed it. The elevator reached the top floor, and Brophy and her prisoner disembarked.

They stepped into a plush, cavernous room. Even as Brophy dragged Berdin forward in his awkward hop-shuffle, he was able to see enough to know he was in the suite of Our Benevolent Liberator. The wall on Berdin's right was a series of windows—progressively larger and then progressively smaller—which overlooked the cirque at the center of the CPA building. The room itself was furnished like a series of rooms, first with stark wooden cabinets and oriental rugs—apparently in the manner of a receiving hall; then with a dining table, straightback chairs, a silver service set, and a chandelier; then a comfortable room of overstuffed chairs and sofas, and a big-screen CWO monitor on the wall opposite the windows; and finally an office/study area complete with desk, bookshelves, reading chair, floor lamp, and Our Benevolent Liberator himself. He was typing on a personal computer on his desk, and frowning at the screen. When he heard Berdin's hopping and clinking of chains, he looked up and frowned at the visitors.

"Brophy!" He said with emphasis, as if he wished to say more.

"It is my honor to be in the presence of Our Benevolent Liberator," Brophy said mechanically. She carried herself more like it was his honor to be in her presence. Berdin realized why she had paid such attention to her appearance.

"No, no, Brophy." Our Benevolent Liberator sounded pleased. "'No one is better than another. We walk our own path.' You know that." He stood up and looked absently at Berdin, who was staring at him. Arthur Aphek's canine teeth were every bit as long in person. "And why is this man in chains? Were not his bars enough?"

"Yeah, I just wanted a little more freedom, that's all." Berdin couldn't choke back his sarcasm. He braced himself for Brophy's attack, feeling her fingernails bite into his shoulder as she tightened her grip on him, but that was all she did. Berdin wondered if she had to restrain herself around the leader of the Globe.

"Ignore him. He's a social deviant who has undermined society in countless ways," Brophy said. "This is Berdin

Dwate, the farm—former Field Engineer who caused the disturbance—along with the man called Ian—at your reception upon your arrival. Remember? The LEA has been tracking him for weeks."

Our Benevolent Liberator looked grim. He drummed his fingertips on his desk. "Ah yes," he said. "Yes. This is the man that so incited the EQL that he placed his name on the LiST one thousand times." He walked from his desk to Berdin, and circled around the prisoner. His long grey-white eyebrows sank and quivered over his deep-set eyes. Berdin was puzzled by Aphek's actions: the man was looking at him like he was a dinosaur. Our Benevolent Liberator stared right in his face, as though Berdin was a being incapable of being offended by improper etiquette. "He looks," Aphek turned to Brophy, "like an average member of our species. Doesn't he? It's remarkable really, to wonder how society could have gone wrong with him."

"Do you really want to know?" Berdin said to Aphek's back, causing him to start. Berdin didn't expect much from Aphek, but he knew what Ian would want him to do in this situation, and he had decided to do it.

Aphek, meanwhile, was staring at him again. "Ignore him," Brophy almost pleaded. "He'll tell you anything. He's beyond rehabilitation. The Justice Cabinet"—her voice gained more command—"has found him guilty to extremes."

"Take his chains off." Our Benevolent Liberator had apparently not been listening to Brophy.

"Arthur, you can't—"

"Take his chains off, take his chains off. Where can he go?" His eyebrows jumped.

"He could hurt or kill us."

"He would do *that*? Hmmm . . ."

"I would *not* do that." Berdin sounded offended. He paused, and then said, "But I would try to escape." Privately, Berdin entertained the thought that he might hurt Brophy just a little.

"Hmmm. Take his ankle bracelets off, leave the handcuffs on. We must allow the man his dignity."

Brophy did as she was told, which shocked Berdin. He realized he might have a small advantage while Our Benevolent Liberator was around.

"Now," Aphek said. "Why don't you,"—he gingerly took Berdin's elbow—"come with me to a more comfortable part of my suite. Brophy—come along." He led Berdin to the sofa in front of the CWO monitor, and then sat next to him.

Brophy remained standing. "What—aren't we going to take him to the EQL? You remember, Arthur, our evolutionary superior wanted to see him as soon as he was captured."

"Yes, yes. Brophy, do sit down. There's plenty of time for that." He ran his hand through his already-ruffled white hair. "Now," he turned to Berdin, "Your name?"

"Berdin Dwate, former Field Engineer assigned to section V5." Berdin was polite and humble, partially because Ian would have wanted him to act that way, and partially because it seemed like it might pay off to impress Our Benevolent Liberator.

"And did you like your occupation?" Aphek was talking slowly, apparently assuming Berdin was less than brilliant.

"My work? Yes. In fact—you may not believe this— I made a deal with a friend to tend his plot as well as mine. I liked bein' outdoors and workin' with my hands."

The Global President stared. "Quite, quite . . . why, now why do you think it is you liked being a Field Engineer? Who made you think this way? Does—does every Field Engineer feel this way?"

"No, I was pretty much the only one that liked workin' so much. And nobody made me or encouraged me to. I just hate bein' cooped up in a unit, you know? I was, well, I was happiest in The Field." Berdin was leaning forward, and his face was expressive. He was trying to help Aphek grasp a concept that was obviously foreign to him.

Aphek kept staring. "I see . . . of course. And . . . what did you do with your leisure time? Before you—terminated your employment?"

"Oh, the usual. Read magazines, watched you on the CWO a little, tried to make sense of the latest procl'mations by the EQL,"—At this point Aphek looked offended and ran his hands through his hair, making it stand up—"you know, standard—*normal*—stuff every citizen does . . . Went to the Gaming Resort, tried Pharmaceutical Counselling . . . even had a girl for a couple years, did the sex therapy thing . . . the usual. None of it . . . *satisfied* me though. Does that make sense?"

Our Benevolent Liberator smiled. "Er, yes—not to my mind, though. A concerned, tolerant community and unlimited freedom should prove most fulfilling—it has to *me* anyway." He showed his teeth, apparently an effort to cajole Berdin. "But, nevertheless, for you it did not. And so, you say, work provided the satisfaction you needed? It was fulfilling for you?"

"It provided more satisfaction than anything I'd yet

experienced. But no, it wasn't completely satisfying—see,"

"Why did you quit? Oh, I'm sorry, permit me to interrupt. But why, if your occupation was even moderately fulfilling, did you walk away and begin associating with . . . deviants?"

Berdin grew more expressive. "That's just the point,
just the point," he said, nodding. He drew a deep breath and
then explained everything about Ian and the significance of
his perspective. He explained, in detail, the first evening they
met. He spoke of silenced androids and fried trout and healed
children and watermelons that tasted like pieces of the sun.
Even Ian's parables recalled themselves to Berdin's tongue,
flowing forth with a strange morse-code-rhythm, punctuated
by "you know"s. Berdin was conscious that his explanation
was not as eloquent as the subject matter dictated, but he made
up for his imperfect words with his enthusiasm. The more
detailed and fervent his explanation became, however, the more
distant Aphek seemed to grow. The world leader would nod
his head and occasionally mutter, "Quite" or "Yes, of course,"
but he also exchanged weighty glances with Brophy. The Chief
Justice responded generally by making a face that involved
scrunching her eyes and sticking her tongue out just a little
between her teeth.

" . . . and so this society, our whole world, is, um,
founded on the wrong principles . . ." Berdin felt his face
growing hot and his scalp start to itch. Our Benevolent Liberator wasn't challenging him. He didn't want to reason to a
better understanding of the truth; he was just humoring Berdin
as an under-evolved member of the species. Berdin got angry: "In other words, Mr. Aphek, your worshipful
uncomprehendingness, the moon is made of grasshoppers and

jellyfish, and you are the most useless excuse for a leader the world has ever seen."

"Yes, quite." Our Benevolent Liberator was looking out the window. Brophy, who had been listening but not seeing, actually smiled at Berdin's outburst. She enjoyed hearing others mocked, even by people she despised.

There was a moment of silence before Aphek realized Berdin had finished his dissertation. Then he ran his hand through his hair once more, smacked his lips, looked at Brophy, looked back at Berdin, and said, "Yes indeed. You, citizen, are definitely deranged. It must—it must be the fault of that robed character. Of course, you showed signs of maladjustment previously—possibly a result of poor leisure education during your adolescence—but the responsibility for most of your deviance lies squarely on the shoulders of that—Ian. I am truly sorry society failed you when you most needed a corrective environment. It's certainly something the EQL must consider. Which, of course, probably explains the fact that the EQL requested that you appear before him. Although, who am I—a mere human—to claim to understand the designs of my evolutionary superior?"

Berdin thought of a sarcastic response, but kept it to himself. Now, more than ever, he was representing Ian. In keeping with this mindset, he decided to keep his mouth closed and concentrate on effecting an escape. No ideas were immediately presenting themselves, but he was heartened by the fact that his feet were free. His chances had increased tenfold.

"Well, why don't we take him to the EQL and find out exactly what it—he—has in 'mind'?" Brophy was mildly sarcastic, knowing her sarcasm would go unheard by the earnest

Global President.

"Yes, we can do that. First—" Aphek's eyes gleamed with an idea—"first, I simply must know what our guest thinks of my sofa."

"What?" Berdin and Brophy spoke the words in unison.

"What do you think of this sofa you're sitting on?"

"Hmmm." Berdin decided to humor Aphek, even while wondering if Our Benevolent Liberator was slipping into senility. "It's nice . . ." It was greyish white, like most sofas in the community, but it was unusually comfortable. "It's . . . one of the best couches I've seen, I guess."

"Why, thank you." Aphek smiled. "The upholstery is human flesh."

With a cry, Berdin leapt from the sofa. "You're sick!" he said, hopping from foot to foot.

"No, citizen, it is you who are sick. Society failed to teach you the most important lesson you can learn: tolerance. Species which are the most tolerant of change and differences are the most pliable, and therefore the most likely to further evolve. Why, think where we would be if society had been intolerant of the idea that Artificial Intelligence would spawn the next species on the grand forward march of evolution! Just think! Some people might even believe man still has . . . but why am I attempting to reason with you? We have settled the matter. Come, it's time to meet your evolutionary superior." Aphek stood and gingerly took Berdin's elbow again.

Brophy led the way to a door in the wall behind Our Benevolent Liberator's desk. She was obviously relishing the grief the EQL might cause Berdin, but she was also anxious to devour him herself.

Her haste provoked Berdin. Forgetting his resolution to be calm, he shouted at her back, "Brophy, you don't buy any of this hocus-pocus this guy's selling either! Tell him! Tell him, you hypocrite!"

She turned and scowled. "I have no problem tolerating a sofa of human flesh. You're deranged." With that, she thrust open the door.

They entered a dimly-lit hallway. At the end stood another door. Brophy reached it by the time Berdin had formulated a retort, and Aphek had begun lecturing him again before he could voice it.

"Try to understand, citizen," Our Benevolent Liberator said gently, "the magnitude of the honor being bestowed upon you. Although you have been found guilty to extremes— that is, although you are a deviant of the most detestable kind— you are allowed the opportunity afforded no other common . . . er, almost no other citizen in society. You will meet your evolutionary superior face to face! You, a former Field Engineer, may converse with the future of our planet!"

"Uh-huh." Berdin was busy scanning the new room they had entered. Filing cabinets lined three of the walls, and a large plastic table stood in the center of the room. The fourth wall was empty, except for a slot near the top, a door, and a speaker in the upper righthand corner. Some papers lay in a bin on the floor. The floor itself was cement, serving to accentuate the stark furnishing of the room.

"Ah!" Aphek sounded pleased. "The Evolutionary Quantum Leap has generated the LiST and dictums for the day." He took the papers from the bin and scanned them. "Very good, very good . . . yes, brilliant as usual." He handed the papers to Brophy. She turned a page, blinked, and picked up a pen from the table. "As I was saying, Dwate," Aphek continued, "you are receiving special treatment, and should act accordingly. You—"

"Hey!" Berdin said. Brophy had just scratched something out on the paper she held. "Who do you think you are? You can't just—"

"I *can*!" Brophy hit him in the face with the back of her hand. She stood for a moment, eyes wild, and then composed herself. "I'm sorry, Arthur. He provokes me so . . . He does not show the proper respect for his superiors."

Our Benevolent Liberator looked away. "'Equal in every way,' I am fond of saying, Justice Brophy. Still . . . between the three of us . . . I understand. Such a deviant, a citizen so detestable to the community, well . . . It can't be helped." He frowned. "Really, Mr. Dwate, you do not deserve to see the EQL."

"Fine by me," Berdin said. "Like I been telling you—"

This time it was Our Benevolent Liberator who struck him. The blow was clumsy—less powerful than Brophy's—but somehow more painful by virtue of its unlikelihood. Berdin gaped at Aphek, who stood panting with his fists clenched and his white hair looking even wilder.

"I, I won't—" Aphek sputtered. Brophy stepped between them, her eyes gleaming. "He's maddening, isn't he?" she said. "Let's get this over with." She put her hand on the doorknob of the door that led to the EQL's lair.

"Wait." Aphek said. "He must understand." He turned to Berdin. "Even . . . Since my arrival, even I have not intruded upon the sanctuary of the Evolutionary Quantum Leap. He is a Being deserving of our utmost reverence. Commune with him accordingly, or suffer the most dire consequences.

Is that clear?"

"Yeah, yeah." Berdin looked at the floor. Silence. He looked at the Global President, whose face was contorted with emotion. "Yeah," Berdin said, his eyes locked with Aphek's.

"Open it."

Brophy swung open the door. Berdin was led in. His eyes acknowledged the massive aquarium-shaped computer, but only subconsciously. His attention was hijacked—his pulse was fired—by an emaciated, noble figure staggering toward him. Ian collapsed in his arms.

Chapter Eleven

"Eternal spirit of the chainless mind!
Brightest in dungeons, Liberty! thou art."
—Lord Byron, "Sonnet on Chillon"

Dazed and uncomprehending, Berdin pressed the elevator button. His friend—the reality he had almost forgotten—leaned heavily on his shoulder. Two cuffs dangled from either of Berdin's wrist, the chain between them inexplicably broken. He had too many questions, and for once he displayed the patience to leave them unanswered at present. Ian was pale and weak, apparently locked in with the EQL for forty days.

"I am sorry she hurt you," Ian said in a hoarse, tired voice. "And I am sorry you were locked in a shed."

"Oh no, no. Ian, look at you. Look . . . what's happened to you." Berdin's throat was tight—whether from rage or sorrow, he did not know.

The day had been strange enough before Ian had appeared; now reality, for Berdin, took on the quality of a dream. When Ian had shuffled toward him, Berdin's hands had separated to receive him as if they had never been bound. Brophy and Aphek, too, had simply fallen away, like mind-phantoms dispelled by the first rays of dawn. No one tried to stop the two men as they moved through doors, the hall, and the suite. The pretty agent in the elevator just stared and pressed the button for the ground floor. Men and women melted before them in their trek through the CPA complex, and the gate to the Zone seemed to cast itself open.

Now, as the men stepped onto the platform, the monorail stopped although no passengers needed to disembark. Berdin did not question these events as they unfolded, but they awed him later. At present, his single-minded purpose drove him toward his unit. Ian needed him.

The same mole-faced conductor bore down on them as soon as they were seated and the monorail began moving. His memory and hunger for information still burned bright.

"Excuse me, excuse me," he began. "I saw who—"

"Get away!" Berdin snarled, as desperate as a treed raccoon.

The smallish, excitable man took a step back, stunned. But Ian silenced Berdin with a whisper, and beckoned the conductor to join them.

"Do you know me?" Ian said, further stunning the mole-man with his searching eyes.

"I, I—yes. You . . . are the teacher that has torn our community in two. I know, I heard—everyone is talking about what you've said and what you've done. I said to myself, I said, I must speak with him, I must know. Because, you see, if everything, if anything—"

"Am I just a curiosity?" Ian's eyes flamed brighter, made even more passionate by contrast to his grey, drawn face.

The conductor was silent for a full two minutes. *Probably the longest he's ever been quiet in his life*, Berdin thought distractedly. *Why is Ian wasting his strength on him?*

"N-no," the mole man finally answered.

"I'll be back," Ian said quietly. "Will you follow me then?"

"Yes." It was plain the conductor would have liked to say more, but he just sat open-mouthed. Ian closed his eyes and slumped against Berdin. The monorail clattered on.

Berdin looked impatient. "Go run the train," he said.

The small conductor rustled away. Ian dozed on Berdin's shoulder. At their stop, Berdin gently lifted his friend in his arms—he was lighter than a child!—and carried him to his unit. With some difficulty, Berdin unlocked his door and set Ian on the sofa.

All around the sofa, a storm raged. Berdin's unit was chaotic—it had been searched and searched again, and finally plundered by agents seeking "clues." Almost nothing of value remained. Some clothes were scattered about, mixed with coffee mugs, salt and pepper shakers, and silverware. Every lottery ticket was gone. The CWO monitor remained, only because every citizen was provided with as many monitors as they requested. In his bedroom, only a bed, one dirty blanket, and a broken chest of drawers were left. Berdin looked in the chest of drawers: some underwear and a mousetrap. He grabbed the underwear and the blanket and stuffed them in the laundry chute. He did the same with the clothes in the living room, until he happened upon the phone. He dialed.

"Hello, Food Prep? What've you got?" He listened in dismay: cabbage, pretzels, frog leg jello from the Evolving Pallet . . . "Listen!" he snapped. "None of that will do! I want—"

The voice at the other end said something about her "right to be selfish," and the line went dead.

Berdin slammed the phone down and paced. He threw more clothes in the laundry chute. He switched on the CWO, caught a glimpse of an enormous red bull goring a bullfighter, and turned it off. Then he dialed the Food Preparation facility again.

"Hello? This is unit A16 here. How many lottery tickets would it take to get a big pot of soup from that Oriental place and a couple—four ham sandwiches on rye? And some orange juice? How much? Make it 300 . . . Come on, I'm a Field Engineer, not some Lieutenant Liberator . . . Okay, okay—but I need it in twenty minutes." He hung up.

It took closer to half and hour for the food to arrive. Berdin killed some of the time borrowing a blanket for Ian from a distant neighbor—he had trouble finding someone who would believe he was no longer a wanted man. Berdin spent the rest of the wait pacing, trying to think of anything that had been "confiscated" that he would miss. It annoyed him that nothing came to mind.

When the food chute beeped, he opened the serving door, wolfed a sandwich, and then gently woke Ian. At first his friend would only sip water, but eventually Ian drank some broth as well. Berdin hovered over him clumsily, feeling powerless to help. He started to ask a question, and then stopped himself.

"Don't worry, my friend, I can talk," Ian said after

finishing his cup of broth.

"How . . . do you want some more soup?"

"Water would be better, I think." Already Ian's cheeks were less hollow, more flesh-colored.

Berdin brought a fresh cup, and sat at the teacher's feet. "Did you have any food at all while you were in there?"

"No. Nor anything to drink."

"I didn't, I didn't think anyone could live that long without food or water."

Ian smiled. "Don't try it."

Berdin thought awhile before asking his next question. "How . . . why were you in there? I mean, I guess I know *why* you were in there, but . . . no I don't."

"Your question has two parts. The first is easily answered: yes, I could have freed myself at any time, but I chose not to until you came to me." Ian paused because Berdin looked startled. "Don't blame yourself—you were supposed to stay away that long. According to plan, I would be freed after forty days, at the same time you were brought to the EQL. As for the second part of your question—why I chose to confront the EQL in such a way—well, not everything is within your understanding. Do not take that the wrong way. Your passion for understanding is an admirable trait, built into your personality in a way that will always serve you well. But such a hunger cannot always be satisfied. I will, if you'll forgive one of my symbolic stories, say this: the farmer cannot appreciate the adversity his crops must overcome until he spends a cold, rainy night in his field. Until freezing drizzle crowns his head and cracks his hair in the blackest dark, he does not know what all his corn or wheat must be saved from. Accept that explanation if you can."

Berdin thought again, his concentration evinced by the single line wrinkled on his forehead. It was true he liked to grasp the reasons behind reality. He tried a different tack: "But why, then, did you bother with us at all? Why not stay in the International Wilderness?"

Ian's jaw stuck out, almost stubbornly. "Because I love you."

"What if I, or nobody loveable, was out here?"

"I love every man."

"Even . . . Arthur Aphek?" Berdin's cheek burned, rekindled by the memory of the blow from Our Benevolent Liberator.

"Yes."

"Will your love change him?"

"No."

"Why—" Berdin hated to ask, but he plunged forward: "Why does your love matter to him then?"

Ian was smiling again, apparently enjoying Berdin's mental effort. "It doesn't."

"Then why bother loving him? It doesn't matter."

"It does matter. It matters to me."

"But—"

"I'm tired, Berdin. Thank you for serving me. Now eat something while I rest."

Berdin didn't mind that suggestion at all. He poured himself a glass of orange juice and ate another sandwich. He still was too hungry to taste it. He tried to savor the third and fourth sandwiches, but his mind wandered. *What had happened? What would happen now?*

At length, his mind turned to the world around him. The artificial ceiling lights had been dimmed quite awhile ago, finally causing him to look for his clock. It was gone. He wondered if he missed it.

He switched on the CWO to get his bearings. Commercials. Channel after channel, commercials. Men and women selling deodorant. Community Home, Auto, and Life advertising pain insurance. SLOTH sloppily and disjointedly asking for donations. The Coastal Infanticide Clinic advertising their method of birth control. Men and women selling breath mints. Pretty women losing weight thanks to Pharmaceutical Counselling. Children solemnly reciting slogans. Winning lottery tickets. Men and women selling plastic surgery.

The inundation of commercials meant it was a few minutes before 11 o'clock—every station was frantically amassing the last lottery ticket of advertising revenue for the day. In moments, Arthur Aphek would deliver his nightly address on every station without interruption. Berdin moved mechanically to turn off the CWO, but stopped. He realized he was finally interested in what the Global President had to say.

"Fellow citizens," Aphek began (as he began every night), "I have not prepared an address for you tonight. My work was . . . interrupted by a distressing series of events, so much so that I feel I must discuss them with you even without adequate preparation. Forgive me if this address lacks some of its typical eloquence . . ." He took a breath, stared off-camera, and continued. "It has come to my attention that some members of our society have forgotten who is in charge. Men and women are not 'a boss unto themselves,' but instead are . . . trying to force their own intolerance and narrow mindset on others—trying to let someone else take the lead. Detest-

able, I know. Unthinkable, I know. But still, it happens, even
in the most highly evolved societies. Every species is bur-
dened with members who will not accept change. Now," he
looked directly at the camera, though his eyes still seemed
distant, "you and I know what happens to such reactionaries
in the evolutionary advance. They are trampled underfoot by
the grand march of nature. It is our job, then—because we
have evolved to the point that we are conscious of our evolution—to speed this process by trampling such misanthropes
ourselves. That is . . . what I mean is, 'Fences and bars make
men free to rebel.' Stand up for your freedom! Shout down—
trample—those who would steal your freedom and cast our
society back into the Close-Minded Age. As a member of the
human species, it is your *right* to discrim—er, trample those
who hinder our progress!"

Our Benevolent Liberator reiterated these themes for
the rest of the hour. Berdin listened attentively, certain that a
direct allusion to Ian or himself would surface; none did. Aphek
was clearly unwilling to specify the problem. Though Berdin
couldn't explain it, he thought that was a good sign. It seemed
to take some of the pressure off. He went to sleep on the
floor beside the couch, feeling optimistic.

He awoke feeling better, though stiff. The artificial
lights were shining with full artificial intensity, signalling that
it was past eight a.m. Ian was in the shower, whistling a tune.
Berdin glanced at the Norvle sisters across the avenue; they
had been staring, but quickly averted their eyes. *Must think
I'm still a dangerous fugitive*, Berdin thought. He picked up
the phone and ordered breakfast.

Ian towelled himself off and donned his robe, which
was apparently none the worse for its ordeal. He looked at

Berdin. "I'm a little hungry this morning." He grinned a mischievous grin cloaked in his tangled new beard.

"No kidding." Berdin laughed. "Then I guess it's a good thing I bribed the Food Preppers again."

Ian became serious. "Reach behind that sofa cushion." He pointed, and Berdin obeyed—finding a huge bundle of lottery tickets.

"Where—"

"Always keep your word." Ian still looked stern. Berdin got the message, and hurried to the Food Prep facilities to deliver his payment. When he returned, he found Ian stuffing clothes in the laundry chute.

"Here, here," Berdin said. "You lie down. Let me handle this. Come on—you're not exactly full strength, you know."

Ian allowed himself to be led to the couch. Berdin brought him breakfast—juice and scrambled eggs and bran muffins and cantaloupe—and ate his own while hustling around the room. Most everything went in the laundry or refuse chute, so that the room was barren when he was done. The only thing remaining on the floor, besides the phone, was this morning's copy of *From the Top*. Berdin picked it up and sat down on the plastic coffee table by the couch. He absently riffled the pages.

"Well?" Ian said.

"More crazy dictums. Listen to this: 'Broken boughs bend brightly beside bedbugs' . . . Oh, and get a load of this: 'The Second Law of Thermodynamics is hereby repealed.' Now why didn't I think of that?"

"Ironic," Ian said. "In a few days that will, in a sense, prove true."

"Huh?"

"Who's on the LiST?"

"Well . . . not me. And not you. And not Brophy, hack it all . . . But—look here—Justice Crashton! Ian, Crashton made the LiST, just like . . . Oh, I forgot to tell you . . ."

"I know. And sadly, Crashton will resign himself to termination, believing he is serving future generations by bowing out of the evolutionary scene. He'll earnestly believe it's a coincidence that Brophy threatened him and his name appeared on the LiST. Tragic." Ian looked a little angry—his jaw was set—"When men cannot recognize truth it always results in tragedy . . . How that hurts . . ."

"Yeah," Berdin said, though he didn't feel hurt much, except in his ribcage. "Well—"

"Count the names on the LiST."

"What?"

Ian looked serious, so Berdin counted. " . . . 198, 199, 200. Five columns of 200 equals one thousand . . . Just like always." He looked at Ian.

"Count them from now on. You'll be surprised."

"If you say so." He sat thinking for a moment. "So what do we—" he stopped.

"—do now? Don't feel bad for asking—I'm doing much better. But I probably should rest for two more days. How are you feeling? Your ribs any better?"

"Oh." Berdin smiled and stretched, hiding the wince he felt in his eyes. "Not too bad. I'll be good as new in a bit."

Ian reached out to Berdin, lifted the other man's shirt, and placed his warm bare hand against his side. "How about now?"

Berdin stretched again, his teeth set to contain the pain. But no pain stabbed him. "Better," he said, the lift in his voice betraying his surprise. "Actually, completely better." He swung his arms. "It doesn't hurt a bit. Thanks."

"You're welcome." Ian stretched out on the couch and closed his eyes.

"Um," Berdin said.

"Yes?"

"One more thing and I'll let ya sleep. I just gotta know. Where's Greg? Is he okay? What's Brophy gonna do to him?"

Ian smiled. "Berdin Dwate thinking of someone else? Unheard of."

"Hey, now, that's not fair. I'm always thinkin' of the other guy. Come on."

"You are *not* always 'thinkin' of the other guy.' But someday you will. In the meantime, as for your question, the hunter afraid of a bear will not shoot her cubs. First he must stalk and kill the greatest bear."

"Huh?"

"Patchett is fine, though deeply worried about you. He curses himself every hour for allowing Stanicek and his agents to take you away."

"But there's nothing he could have done!"

"He thinks he should have fought. So today he works in his same section of The Field, angry at himself and scared for you. His is truly a good heart, Berdin."

"I know, I know. I'm sorry I involved him in this whole mess."

"*You* did not involve him, and anyway you have no cause to be sorry. Patchett will have pain whether he knows me or not, but the pain he faces now is healthy. It will teach him what he's always wanted to learn: courage."

"So what you're sayin' is . . ."

Ian was growing short with Berdin. "You won't see him today. Nor tomorrow. But you'll see him when you should." He closed his eyes.

The thought of waiting did not sit well with Berdin. He rustled around the unit, then remembered the clean laundry chute and removed a bundle of freshly pressed clothes and a blanket. He made his bed, put his clothes in the dresser, and showered. Weeks of caked dirt and sweat went down the drain, replaced by a thin film of soap residue. The hot water soothed Berdin so much he chose to shave in the shower. He watched his red beard hairs swirl in the shower drain with pleasure, glad to be rid of the last vestiges of his exile in The Field.

He could not bring himself to don his clean synthetic clothing, choosing instead his soiled sweatshirt and overalls. *If I'm a social deviant*, he thought, *I might as well dress the part*. Finally he folded the borrowed blanket and set out to return it.

He was stopped by what he saw in the avenue below. A single agent in full uniform stood at the base of the block across the way, unabashedly watching Berdin. The wiry redhead threw open his door and yelled, "Hey agent, I think you're infringing on my right to privacy!"

"You forfeited your rights when you chose to undermine society," the agent responded coolly.

"Yeah?" Berdin said, unconsciously rolling up his sleeves. "What about my right to kick yer butt?"

The agent lifted his stungun so Berdin could see it. "That, too," he said with a grim smile.

Berdin was uncertain about how he should respond, and had he been a different man he would have hesitated. In keeping with his character, however, he slammed his unit door shut and hustled down the stairs, ready for a fight. When he reached the avenue, the agent was gone.

Berdin breathed a small sigh, and then walked to return the blanket. After completing this errand, he found his feet taking him toward Patchett's unit. *No sense waiting and making him suffer*, he thought. But Patchett was still away working in The Field, and Berdin did not have a pen or paper to leave his friend a note. He wondered what to do. At length, he decided to throw his Field Engineer I.D. between the bars of Patchett's unit.

When he returned to his own unit and found Ian still sleeping on his couch, he felt a small pang of guilt. He suppressed this feeling by ordering a healthy lunch of burgers, onion rings, and apple pie.

The rest of the day passed slowly, as did the following day. Ian slept most of the time. Berdin napped more than he liked during the days—it seemed his body needed it. The monotony, for Berdin, was only broken by meals, short visits with Ian, and perusal of the daily newsletter. When Berdin counted the names on the LiST the second day, he found only 999. Ian explained that this meant a name had been omitted by someone other than the EQL. He would not say whose it was. Beyond that, Ian spoke with Berdin only regarding trivial matters. Once or twice he mentioned that his own name would soon appear on the LiST. Berdin downplayed these predictions, comforting himself with the knowledge that the CPA could do nothing to Ian that his friend did not allow them to do.

The community, for its part, seemed to forget the existence of Ian and Berdin. Small groups of followers of Ian still met in various units in the cover of darkness, but the rest of society went about their business and leisure as usual. The only indication that the world was changed by the events that seemed so drastic to Berdin manifested itself in an increased public hostility. Our Benevolent Liberator had coined a new slogan: "Anti-evolutionary forces respond only to force," and citizens had taken it to heart. Men and women berated and beat each other over any complaint—from stealing a lover to talking too loud—while labelling each other as unrepentant anti-evolutionary forces. Minor Justice Department officials, usually unable to maintain even a pretense of activity because 'Fences and bars make men free to rebel,' were now overwhelmed by large caseloads. The citizenry had discovered a standard by which others could be judged, and they were quick to call for judgment (when they lacked the strength or fortitude to apply force themselves). Anger and accusations mounted.

Berdin was blissfully unaware of this when he awoke the morning of the appointed day of action. All he knew was that the spying agent had never dared return, and that Ian had a plan for their day.

He read the daily newsletter to Ian over breakfast. Again, only 999 names appeared on the LiST. Again, neither Ian nor Berdin was listed. Much to Berdin's dismay, however, four other people he knew were on the LiST: two Field Engineers, an old girlfriend, and a schoolchum who had landed an accounting job with the Gaming Resort. Berdin shook his head. "This has been a terrible run of luck for people who know me."

"It is not luck, but design," Ian said. "Do you still not understand? Every person on that LiST, and every person that has appeared on the LiST since the EQL and Arthur Aphek arrived, has been a citizen of Coastal Community Twelve."

"What?" Berdin was surprised and angry. "How do you know—I mean, How can that be? Why?"

"Who else could they terminate?" Ian asked the question as if it were profound, but Berdin thought it nonsensical.

"Citizens in Coastal Community One, Mountain Community Two, Plains Community Three,—"

"How do you know anyone still lives in those communities?"

"Because—well, because where else would they go? They're not all dead, are they? ARE THEY?" The idea dawned dreadful in Berdin's matter-of-fact mind.

"I tried to tell you earlier," Ian said softly. "The EQL and Our Benevolent Liberator chose Coastal Community Twelve as their new headquarters because it's the only functioning community left. Your world's birthrate cannot keep pace with the thousand unnatural deaths planned for it each day. The citizens of Coastal Community Twelve—the men and women inside this dome and in The Field—are the only survivors of a societal suicide. And soon they, too, will see their population dwindle and virtually disappear."

"Unless we stop them?" Berdin looked hopeful.

"Unless things change."

"Well, what about the Benevolent Liberator? He sees what the LiST is doing to our world. Why doesn't he stop it?"

"You know why."

Berdin looked blank. "Won't people put a stop to it

themselves just by resisting termination?" He still looked puzzled.

"That is not an option, as you saw for yourself."

"But . . . but, what about 'Fences and bars making men free to rebel'?"

"What of it? Listen. A man can throw a football sixty yards. Can he choose to throw it thirty?"

Berdin looked, if possible, even more blank. His eyes were glazed and his hands hung limply at his sides.

"Can he?" Ian demanded.

"Of course." Berdin wrinkled his brow, trying to re-mind Ian of his distaste for stories.

"How do you know he can? You've only seen him throw the ball sixty yards. How can you assume he can throw it thirty?"

"This is stupid."

"How can you know?" Ian leaned forward, intense.

"Because—if somebody can do somethin' harder, he can always choose to do somethin' easy."

"Precisely."

There was a long pause. "You know I didn't get that," Berdin said.

"Your mind did not 'get' it. But you also have a soul. Is what we have said true? Truth can speak to a soul as well as a mind. As the soul matures, it can translate truth to the mind. Be patient, my friend. It's not one of your favorite activities, I know. But patience is rooted in courage—some-thing you have in abundance. Be brave enough to persevere."

"I don't know if I'm all as brave as you think," Berdin muttered.

"You are. It takes courage to see your weakness for

what it is, and to hate it." Ian stood, folded his blanket, and set it on the couch. "Time for action," he said.

"Now yer talkin'," Berdin said as he stood. He pushed up his sleeves. "Let's give Brophy some more trouble."

"She has more than she can bear. We're simply going for a walk."

Of course, walks with Ian never proved to be simple. People joined them almost immediately, and soon he was followed by a noisy throng. Ian's figure was a lightning rod; his wild beard and confident stride, his bare feet and his sweeping robe, commanded attention—so much so that men and women jammed the avenue for blocks behind them. When they drew within sight of the CPA wall, in the heart of the Zone, Ian stopped the crowd and ascended the stairs of the nearest block. He addressed the crowd from the second story, while Berdin sat on the steps in a self-appointed watchdog role.

Ian's speech was similar to, and very different from, his previous speeches. The themes played in Berdin's mind like an old, familiar melody, but the stories and exhortations were triumphantly unique. To Berdin it seemed that Ian emphasized the splendor of the International Wilderness and the shortcomings of society more, but such an impression could have resulted from their morning discussion. At any rate, the crowd's reactions to Ian's words were typical. Some stood in raptured silence, some muttered among themselves, and some walked away. No one, however, dared to stop the speech or quell "anti-evolutionary forces" with force. Uniformed Law Enforcement agents stood among the audience, but none tried to halt the proceedings. A few of the most hostile listeners raised objections; these were squelched by direct answers from Ian.

When Ian finished speaking, he descended the staircase and stood by Berdin. The robed man's eyes shone like morning stars, dwarfing the luminosity of the constellations of eyes focused on him. His lips were swollen by the duration of his eloquence. He seemed not to notice Berdin.

"What now?" Berdin said, mostly to remind Ian of his presence. "These people won't just leave you and go home."

Ian still did not look at him. "Now I help those who come to me in the fullness of time." He walked into the crowd, which surged around him, talking and touching. Hundreds of plaintive voices clamored for his ear, for the chance to cast a complaint or a dream into the one well that would not hurl back mocking echoes of their cries. Hundreds of starving people swarmed to be near the man who offered bread and water rather than sugar and syrup. Men and women wept. The Zone became, for one glorious day, a place of joy instead of fear. Berdin reflected on nothing, too enraptured by the events of the day to do anything except experience them. He knew what he watched was too precious to be distracted from by analysis.

Finally—and yet, too soon—the artificial lights dimmed and Ian moved through the crowd back to Berdin. While the men and women in the mob seemed momentarily disoriented, the two friends seized the opportunity and slipped away. Back in Berdin's unit, they discussed the events of the day briefly over dinner and then fell asleep. Ian said they would be busy again in the morning.

In fact, the two men were busy for a number of days, doing much the same thing as in their first day of action. Each morning began with the newsletter over breakfast, and the discovery that the LiST again contained "only" 999 names, some of which Berdin recognized. Then the men would take a walk, and people would crowd after them till they stopped. Sometimes Ian would spend the whole day with the people, and sometimes he just spoke and then slipped away. When speaking, Ian often alluded to the prediction that his name would appear on the LiST. This emphasis unsettled Berdin, but he still had little time for reflection. When a matador fights a bull, he lives the experience and digests the analysis of his actions later (if he is lucky). In the same way, Berdin opened himself to a swirl of emotions, sensations, and impressions, and awaited a less momentous occasion to catalog his experience.

The crowds grew and grew and grew—and then dwindled. Each day of the first two weeks, Berdin would convince himself that the throng could not possibly grow in size, and yet each following day more people joined in. During the second week it became necessary for Ian to climb to the balcony of a block and to speak like thunder to be heard. Men and women packed the balconies and stairways and avenues three blocks deep on every side. But just as Berdin became accustomed to seeing an impossibly larger crowd assemble each morning, the audiences began to shrink. Soon Ian was speaking to the same crowd of about 2,000 people every day.

This bothered Berdin. "What happened to so many of the people that listened to you?" he asked after dinner one night.

Ian waved his hand. "Blown back to worldly commitments and distractions. One has a lover he will not leave. One is preparing a crucial report. Others choose to keep their jobs rather than forsake them for me." He paused. "What I say, Berdin—have you been listening?—is not easy to hear. It troubles many and only arouses curiosity in others. The easy path walks away from my words."

"What about truth?"

"Ah, what about it? You have been built to receive it. You cannot imagine another way. But there is. People are different."

Berdin remembered another question. "What about— hey, this is a different subject an' all, but what about Greg? I've been looking and looking for 'm, an' he's just not there. I've seen that squirrely conductor and the freckled girl with the funny hair, but not him ever. He's . . . okay, right?"

"You're right," Ian sighed. "Patchett isn't there. He's all right, yes—no thanks to the man who threw your I.D. in his unit." Ian looked at Berdin, who was looking at the floor. "That I.D. has caused him much more suffering, which—according to plan—will only teach him a more unyielding form of courage. Today, as he has for more than three weeks, he hides in his section of The Field."

"What? I never—why would he do that?"

"He assumes," Ian continued drily, "as any man in his situation might assume, that your identification was planted in his unit by agents to signal your death and to threaten that he would be the next man punished. He lives by pilfering the lunch sacks of other Field Engineers, and hides in his toolshed all day."

"We've . . . we've got to—"

"You will do nothing. Do you still not understand? You can never act rightly apart from me. But Patchett has been calling for me, and I have heard his entreaties. Word will reach him tomorrow, and he will join us that same day."

Berdin was genuinely ashamed. "I think—I owe Greg a big apology."

"You owe him much more than that."

The words stung Berdin, but he couldn't be silent. "I've got another question."

"Yes?"

"Why does a dumb guy like that conductor recognize the truth and not someone as smart as Brophy?"

"For the same reason you do," said Ian, not unkindly.

"Why are you bein' so hard on me?" Berdin looked at the ground.

"We've already discussed where the easy path leads." Ian looked at Berdin until his friend raised his eyes to meet his sterling gaze. "You've got one more question—let's hear it."

Berdin set his jaw, and half-decided to be stubbornly silent. His friend's eyes, full of uncompromising love, melted his resolve. "What—why do you keep sayin' yer name's gonna appear on the LiST? It's not like the community can do anything to you, right?"

"Can they kill me? That's what you mean. Well—can they?" Ian's eyes blazed with the answer.

"No!"

"Remember that," he said sharply, and then he went to brush his teeth and prepare for bed.

The next day 1,000 names appeared on the LiST. For reasons Berdin did not analyze, his heart sank into his stomach. He looked for Ian's name. It wasn't there—not a single "Ian." He scanned again, and gasped. "Brophy's on the LiST!"

"And there are a thousand names?" Ian asked.

"Yes."

"Well, what does that tell you?"

"Uh—Brophy's responsible for the missing name?"

"And?"

"And . . . and what? Brophy's been tampering with the LiST and so she's gotta be terminated? What else is there?" Berdin's mind was always foggy in the morning.

"Whose name do you suppose she's been removing all these weeks?"

Understanding dawned slowly on Berdin's brow. "Aha . . . wait, though. Didn't Our—Arthur Aphek know she was doin' that? Why didn't he stop her and make her cooperate with evolution like everybody else?"

"Apparently everyone is not 'equal in all things.' Brophy was . . . intriguing to Our Benevolent Liberator for awhile, but today she no longer interests him. So tomorrow she dies." Ian spoke the last sentence softly, with a note of sorrow.

"Yeah, but she doesn't buy all the high-fallutin' 'protecting the int'rests of your species' business either—so won't she fight it?"

"She has fought for many weeks. Now she must run. But she will not be protected, as you were, and so she will be caught and killed."

"Well," Berdin muttered, "I suppose I shouldn't say 'good riddance.'"

"You shouldn't even think it."

That day Ian spoke to the same crowd of roughly 2,000—with one notable exception. Greg Patchett, dirty and weary, stood silently in the middle of the throng, his eyes fixed unswervingly upon Ian. At first Berdin tried to attract the enrapt Field Engineer's gaze, but he soon realized the futility of such actions and turned his concentration to the teaching.

Ian's speech was, as Berdin had come to expect, more powerful and more unsettling than any of his previous talks. Such was the case every day: whatever Ian said seemed, at that moment, the most precious wisdom ever uttered. As a result, the faithful people in the crowd grew more faithful every day. Today they would have torn down the SHELL at a single word from Ian.

But his words, as always, called for much more complex responses: turning away once and for all from greed, thinking constantly of ways to serve your neighbors, humbling yourself even before unjust demands. Would that tearing down the SHELL was all he commanded! If only a concrete task could be assigned—some work that showed definite progress each day. Instead, Ian spoke in complexity and paradox. His words could be comprehended by the heart or the mind, but rarely by both. One command might be grasped intellectually with ease—and yet prove impossible to be translated to the heart. Or more accurately, it would prove impossible in an immediate sense—but a man or woman, hard at work, might begin the translation over a period of weeks or months. The words were never easy. Accepting them was harder. And living always as if you had accepted them was a heart-bursting challenge.

When Ian finished speaking, Berdin immediately dove into the crowd in an effort to find Patchett. He was soon rewarded. Struggling towards him, as politely as possible, was a resolute, gray-haired skeleton. The men walked straight into each other's arms and thumped each other's backs. Patchett's eyes were wet. They shouted greetings over the noise of the crowd, which was dispersing slowly.

"Wait, wait, wait, Greg," Berdin was saying. "Lemme

say this before I lose my nerve: Forgive me. It was me who put my I.D. in your unit an' scared you outta yer home. I blew it, an' I made you suffer. I wish . . . I wish there was a way—"

Patchett cut him short. "Forget it. That's in the past. Look at what Ian's given us—can you believe it? We're to inherit the International Wilderness! To be with him forever!" He was smiling triumphantly. It was obvious that he had already forgotten the ordeal brought upon him by Berdin.

"But—weren't you scared out there?"

"Where? Oh . . . yes, of course scared to death." Patchett smiled again. "And a ridiculous thing to be scared about, wasn't it? Come on, I must see Ian face-to-face."

Ian had been sitting on the stairs talking to Nila (the girl with the dandelion hair), but he arose when he saw the friends approaching. Berdin and Patchett stopped two stairs below Ian, so that he towered over them. Berdin handled the introductions as gracefully as he could while forgetting Nila's name. Patchett stared in awe at Ian's eyes.

"Berdin gave you a bit of a scare, I know," Ian said.

Patchett gulped. "No trouble." He stared.

Ian smiled a ferocious grin. "Ah yes, Greg Patchett. You have found what you should rightly fear. But I tell you, I have come to assuage even that fear. Come home with us."

"Thank you." Patchett shuffled his feet and shifted his battered straw hat from hand to hand in a nervous soft-shoe.

Nila left the three men reluctantly, and then they proceeded back to Berdin's unit. There they ate dinner and tended to an overwhelmed and frightfully skinny Patchett. After a hot shower, plenty of mushroom pizza, and many comforting words from Ian, Patchett grew less terse and seemed to relax.

Berdin added the finishing touches to Patchett's comfort by recounting his adventures with Justice Brophy and Arthur Aphek, and revealing that Brophy was facing termination.

"Good riddance!" Patchett cried.

"You shouldn't say that," Berdin reluctantly rebuked him. Ian grinned.

"So you are the teacher now?" he said.

"I didn't—" Berdin began.

"Then teach what you know. Patchett, you would do well to learn courage from this man. Likewise, Berdin may learn humility and patience from your example. Learn these lessons quickly and well. Tomorrow, already, you will be tried."

"What?" Berdin said. "What do you mean?"

"Tomorrow my name will appear on the LiST."

"What does that mean?" Patchett asked.

But he was drowned out by Berdin. "So what? They can't touch you."

"They can if I let them," Ian said.

"*I* won't let them!" Berdin stood up and clenched his fists.

"Nor will I!" Patchett tried to interject, but his words were swallowed by Ian's sharp response.

"Berdin, you speak again without thinking. When you do that out of loyalty to me it can be endearing, but it is still wrong. Now I tell you, there will be times—quite soon—when you will not find your tongue when you should proclaim loyalty to me."

"Never!" Berdin tucked his neck into his shoulders.

"I speak the truth, as ever."

Berdin slept fitfully that night. He blamed it on the floor—he had insisted Patchett sleep on his bed—but Ian's words caused him to wrestle with his conscience in bouts of fitful sleep. As soon as Berdin heard the slap of the newsletter on his carpet, he was on his feet.

He did not have to scan the LiST too closely. One name stood apart, obvious in its brevity: "Ian." No last name. No distinction. Just "Ian"—the one man who needed no clarification or exposition.

Berdin told his friends as soon as they joined him at the breakfast table. Patchett looked nonplussed, like Berdin had simply told him they lived in Coastal Community Twelve. Ian looked grim—but lately he looked grim quite often.

"What now?" Berdin demanded, surly in his fear.

"We eat, and then go for a walk."

The words were little comfort for Berdin. He only began to feel better when the same crowd of people boiled around them, and Ian mounted the stairs of a block in preparation for another speech. Both Berdin and Patchett stationed themselves at the bottom of the staircase, skinny gargoyles in a silent vigil.

At first Berdin concentrated on the agents in the crowd (were there more of them today?), but soon his mind was awash with the dizzying concepts and commands of Ian's oratory. As always, Ian's speech was unparalleled. His themes and presence were enchanting. To Berdin it seemed he was listening to the master story-teller recounting the most exciting story ever told.

The story lasted hours. For the first time in public speech, Ian's voice sounded hoarse—and even then he continued, till he was little more than croaking. " . . . Stay always on your guard, that you may stand firm when you face me again," he creaked, and then paused.

"But what about the LiST?" A shout came from the crowd. "The EQL has called for your termination!"

The shout made Berdin conscious of the crowd again. He looked up and saw ten armored agents shouldering their way through the throng. They moved resolutely, but slowly—aware that they faced a delicate situation. Berdin and Patchett stood up, their blood pumping furiously in their veins.

Ian remained silent, apparently content to allow the situation to unfold. Soon the agents faced Berdin and Patchett. Berdin's eyes were wide with defiance, so much so that the smallish dark-haired agent wearing the badge marked "Captain, Special Forces" could not look at him. A massive agent, all angles and muscle, beside the Captain shifted his feet impatiently. He looked at his commander, then at Berdin, and back to the dark-haired man again. Finally the big man stepped forward. "Let us pass," he said.

Berdin summoned his courage and hurled himself at the agent. "For Ian!" he yelled, in a vague effort to incite the crowd. He punched the huge agent squarely in his rectangular jaw. In a red haze, he saw the agent buckle and heard a tooth clatter on the metal stairs.

"No!" Ian spoke clearly, his hoarseness mastered. "Let them pass. It is time."

Berdin had already turned with fists raised toward the Captain. He had no intention of stopping, and yet—to his own disbelief, his resolve fell away and his body stopped. His arms dropped to his side. Ian's last three words to him reached his very spirit, and introduced a cold, dark void into his heart. He felt himself, without willing it, reeling backward to allow the agents to pass.

Their boots clanged harshly on the steps. They banged

upward methodically, sounding a scattered rhythm that re-minded Berdin's subconscious of an old, old song. His vision was filled with black boot-soles seen through metal grating above him.

They descended accompanied by a pair of bare feet. Ian walked among them, unrestrained by chains or cuffs or stern grips. He passed by Berdin and Patchett, fixed his reso-lute eyes upon them, and said, "Give no ground to tempta-tion." Then he was swallowed up in the crowd.

Still transfixed, Berdin watched Ian and the agents emerge from the crowd and move down the avenue toward the center of the community. The people dispersed as though in a trance, with only a few following their teacher. Dejected and uncertain, Berdin stooped down to retrieve the tooth on the step below him, and then turned toward the CPA building. He walked unsteadily.

Chapter Twelve

"For what are men better than sheep or goats
That nourish a blind life within the brain,
If, knowing God, they lift not hands of prayer
Both for themselves and those who call them friend?
For so the whole round earth is every way
Bound by gold chains about the feet of God."
—Alfred, Lord Tennyson, "The Passing of Arthur"

Berdin and Patchett sat side by side at the base of the CPA wall. Neither spoke. Neither had spoken since the agents had arrested Ian. Both men felt infinitely alone, trapped on a frozen, endless plain in the midst of a blizzard. No crack or hill appeared on the landscape in their mind, so they sat numb and exposed to the darkness closing in on them. No man was in sight to comfort them. No fire burned in their hearts to melt the snow piling on their shoulders. Just endless greying white, and a desolation so cold it was lulling them to sleep. Alone.

In reality, the men were surrounded by hundreds of people—some concerned, many just nosey—awaiting news of events behind the wall. Since bars had made men free to do anything, people had lost interest in scandal. Now they smelled a drama that might give them something to talk about for as long as a week. Already men and women were wagering lottery tickets, laying odds on Ian's chances of survival. No one that had dared to stay around thought he had much hope.

Berdin was "rescued" from his glum, frozen plain by a light kick from a peevish old woman. "Hey you," she said. "You're the guy that's always with him. Is he gonna make a break for it or not?"

"I don't know what you're talking about," Berdin said after a long pause.

"Yes, you do." Another woman had joined them. "You're the one that hangs around Ian. I've seen you," she said.

Berdin was angry. "I said," he growled, "I don't know him! Can't you old women hear?"

"I—I can hear just fine, you rude little . . . liar," the first woman sputtered. But Berdin was alone again, sunk further in the snowdrift piling on him on the plain. He remained there for hours.

Finally, the CPA gate opened. Four hundred Law Enforcement agents poured out. Ian walked in the midst of them, head bowed. The agents near him poked and struck him almost constantly, but he would not flinch. The smallish leader shouted at the onlookers as he walked, "The time has come for a special termination! See how society deals with anti-evolutionary forces!" Bloodthirsty and harried, the squad of armored agents hustled down the avenue.

Nila dashed out of the gate, and noticed Berdin and Patchett. "Hurry, hurry!" she said, "It's time! Come on!" In an effort to stir the sluggish men, she grabbed Berdin's arm and pulled with all the strength of her 100-pound frame. He shrugged off her grip. "Come on!" she said again. But she couldn't wait. She turned reluctantly and ran after the agents.

A hairy bare-chested man looked at Berdin with disgust. "Why don't you go with her?" he asked. "You followed him, why don't you follow him now?"

"I never followed him!" Berdin spoke the words harshly, to be heard over the blizzard.

"You followed him, all right." The hairy man turned away.

The wind swirled around Patchett and Berdin, driving hard crystals of snow into their eyes. A small voice prodded Berdin's consciousness, reminding him that he must begin moving or freeze to death. He acknowledged the voice and set about searching for his will. It took him two hours to stand.

Once standing, he found it easier to move. With hunched shoulders and eyes staring at the ground, he started walking to his unit. Patchett followed. About halfway, the men found themselves encased in darkness: the ceiling lights had gone out. The strange development did not faze them. They continued on their way, groping along blocks and occasionally tracing unit numbers with their fingertips. All around them footsteps raced, as the more reckless citizens took advantage of the black-out. Once or twice a scream sounded, and sometimes a dark shape would collide with the men. But they reached Berdin's unit unharmed and apathetic to the chaos outside their minds.

Inside Berdin's unit the two men cast themselves on the floor and succumbed to the icy wasteland haunting them. They slept fitfully for the better part of two days.

Nightmares were their only companions. Berdin saw his old lover on the street, and came up behind her and stroked her hair. "Is it my—?" she said, and turned to look at him. Berdin jumped backward; her eyes glowed red like two tiny round coals on her face. "Yes, you are mine," she said, and she stalked him in a forest so thick no sunlight reached the ground. He ran faster and faster, scrambling over logs and crashing through thickets, and she just walked—but he could not escape her. Finally he fell face down in a thornbush. When he looked up, she embraced him like a python.

Patchett played with fire. He juggled burning torches in front of an audience of grey-colored people, stoic in their disinterest. Each time he counted he found himself juggling one more torch than he had thought he juggled, till he was overwhelmed. His fatigue made him grab the wrong end of a torch, so that flames seared his hand. He cried out and dropped the torch. But he found himself irresistibly drawn to catch the next torch on the wrong end, too, till he dropped it in pain. Soon he was juggling all his torches backward—catching each one on its fiery tip. The action tortured him, but he could not stop. He found himself wishing he had more torches. The audience faded away.

Each dream seemed to last hours, possibly days. Yet neither man could summon the resolve to awaken. It was Nila again who brought them back to reality.

"Wake up, wake up!" She was outside, rattling the bars of the door. "What is wrong with you? How can you sleep? Wake up!" She reached in her pocket, found some lipstick, and threw it at Patchett. "Let me in!"

Patchett stood uncertainly and then opened the door. Exhausted by the effort, he sank onto the couch. Nila rushed in and shook Berdin. "Get up! Have you been to Pharmaceutical Counselling or what?   Move around, move around!" She began walking Berdin around his unit. As soon as he was awake, he flopped down next to Patchett. He looked dully at his friend. "I had the worst dreams," he said.

"Me, too."

"It wasn't a dream," Nila began, but she was distracted by the Food Preparation employee answering her call—she had picked up the phone to order a late dinner for the two dishevelled men. She spoke quickly, impatient with the unfriendly employee.

Patchett, in a tired effort to hold onto the reality he had only recently regained, stared at Nila. She was small, and young, and it was true that her wispy blonde hair was sometimes so unruly she looked like a dandelion. Her skin was quite fair—almost a light peach color—and peppered with freckles. How old was she? Patchett couldn't decide. She looked to be only eighteen or nineteen, but she carried herself with more assurance than a teenager. At any rate, she was tiny—perhaps 5'2" and trim. All legs and arms. Her eyes struck Patchett as the most important thing about her: a dusky green, they shone brightly and were always open wide—so that Nila seemed mildly astonished most of the time. Patchett decided he trusted her.

Berdin was also wading back into reality, though in a less pleasant way. He was throwing up in the bathroom. He hated vomiting, of course, but this time it strangely relieved him. When he finished, he was weak but more sane. He washed out his mouth, brushed his teeth, and joined Nila and Patchett.

"Check the food chute," Nila said. "Your lasagna ought to be ready by now." Berdin obeyed, but found nothing.

"Slow Food Preppers," he said.

"How are you feeling?" Patchett asked sleepily.

"Wait," Nila said. "Sit down, Berdin. I need to say this now, before it gets too hard to say. What you saw on Friday wasn't a dream, it really happened."

"We know," Berdin said.

"See . . . oh," she said. "Oh, then why did you just . . . sit there? Why didn't you come with me?"

Berdin shook his head. "I don't know." He bit his lip. Patchett looked at the ground.

Nila brushed her bangs back with her hand and looked at them. Her green eyes opened still wider. She started to speak, stopped herself, and moved to the food chute. She returned with a casserole dish brimming with lasagna, a tossed salad, garlic bread, and bottled water. The food smells unsettled Berdin, but Patchett fell to eating anxiously.

Nila took only a little salad and water for herself. She looked again at the two men, one chewing and one sipping water. "Do you know what happened after I left you?"

The words scared both men. Patchett swallowed and shook his head. "No," Berdin said softly.

Nila brushed back her bangs again. "The agents marched Ian from the CPA building, where he had been found guilty to extremes by the Justice Cabinet—"

"Was Brophy on that Cabinet?" Berdin interrupted.

"Jane Brophy? No, she had been terminated the day before." Nila looked at Berdin to see if he would interrupt her again. When he didn't, she fixed her eyes on the wall behind the two men and continued: "Anyway, the agents led Ian through the streets—beating him constantly—" her eyes grew moist, and she blinked—"to the Perimeter and through the checkpoint into The Field. Many people followed . . . not because they were concerned, just because they were . . . sick, and they cheered as the agents led Ian to The Fence. Then the Captain—" she rubbed a tear out of her eye and gulped— "pulled Ian beside him and said to the crowd something like, 'Is this man an anti-evolutionary force?' and the crowd—it seemed like all the crowd except me—shouted 'yes' and I started to cry out against them and a man . . . slapped me. Then the Captain yelled, 'Should we tolerate this anti-evolutionary force?' and the whole crowd yelled 'no' and I was too busy crying to yell anything . . ." Here Nila paused in an effort to master her emotions. "And all of a sudden these two big men—agents—with long wooden poles and rubber gloves stepped toward Ian . . . and the Captain shouted, 'We don't want you here—go back to your International Wilderness!' and he started cackling . . . and the two big agents started poking . . . Ian toward The Fence . . . and the two agents held him there all tangled and beaten with his hair standing on end and . . . his hands actually smoking, and The Fence electrocuting him." She tried to look at the two men, but her eyes were too full of tears.

Berdin and Patchett had been sitting open-mouthed, staring at Nila throughout her narrative. Now Berdin stirred, and suddenly stood. "You're lying," he said without conviction, still formulating the concept in his mind. "I don't know why you're doing it," he shook his finger at Nila, "but you're lying."

"No," she said. "I wish I was. But I saw him die. It took almost two hours to kill him—the agents holding him were spelled by other agents—and he writhed and cried out till I couldn't bear it. But he finally died and they took down his body and—"

"YOU'RE LYING!" Berdin was furious, and he shook his whole fist at her. "I know now—I'm sure you're lying! Right, Patchett? Ian told us they couldn't kill him. Remember? He told us always to remember it, never forget." Patchett nodded, more from loyalty than remembrance. "Get OUT!" Berdin shouted at Nila. "I will *not* be lied to; GET OUT."

The small, sobbing girl stood clumsily and shuffled to the door. "You can—" she began.

"OUT!!" Berdin's face was red. Nila walked uncertainly out the door, and clanged down the metal steps. Berdin slammed his door behind her. Fists clenched, he turned toward Patchett. "He can't be dead," Berdin pleaded with his friend. "It can't be true. He said they couldn't kill him."

"Why would she lie?" Patchett asked.

"She's crazy. She's gotta be crazy. Maybe he just faked it . . ."

"Why would anyone let themselves be electrocuted for two hours to fake their death? You heard Ian's last speeches. He was preparing us for this." Patchett rubbed his chin and looked at a wall.

"He didn't just come here to die! What are you saying? Don't you think I know? Don't you—"

"I think we both need to be alone right now." Patchett stood up, looked Berdin in the eye, thought better of putting his hand on his friend's shoulder, and walked out. The clang of the door behind Patchett hit Berdin hard, like angry words.

He began pacing.

The dimming of the ceiling lights found Berdin still pacing, nibbling cold lasagna. He would not allow himself to succumb to the icy wasteland again, but he could imagine no other landscape. The thought of sleep scared him. He longed for someone to talk to, haunted by the realization that he had chased away the two people who might understand. What was Greg doing? How was he surviving without Ian? Berdin searched for reasons to continue living.

The search was mostly futile. He thought he might be able to drown his sorrows at the Gaming Resort, but was disgusted by the thought of being recognized. White began to envelop his senses. In desperation, he turned on the CWO.

Channel Ten was airing a talk show which featured a cannibal and an incestual brother and sister who claimed citizens still were intolerant of their lifestyles. Berdin pressed the remote control. Channel 12 showed randomly-generated music videos, which featured naked men and women writhing randomly. Berdin gaped for a moment and then changed channels. The next section had programmed a rerun: an old episode of "Graphic Gang Wars." He switched channels again and again. Finally, Berdin found something to distract him without being too offensive: Channel 37 was airing children's cartoons which mostly involved blood-sucking aliens and lasers.

The cartoons staved off the desperate swelling in Berdin's heart till Our Benevolent Liberator made his nightly appearance, wearing his predatory smile. Berdin became suddenly attentive at the sound of Aphek's first words.

"A great victory has been won today, global citizens," Aphek said. "The man who would have reversed evolution and cast us head-long into the Close-Minded Age has been terminated." Our Benevolent Liberator looked straight at the camera and smiled his same empty smile. "'Fences and bars make men free to rebel,' as you know, but this man wanted people only to follow, like docile mindless sheep. The man—known as 'Ian'—claimed to be from the International Wilderness and attracted some social deviants with his hopelessly reactionary message. Thus, it became necessary for him to be terminated, a fact which the EQL was the first to recognize. As always, our evolutionary superior was looking out for the best interests of our own humble species. Today, he squelched a man both socially irredeemable and physically dangerous. Roll the tape, please." Aphek looked slightly off-camera, and his image was replaced by a video tape of Ian and the agents by The Fence. Berdin stared.

"As you can see," Aphek narrated, "the man called Ian put up quite a fight before he was subdued by our progressive and helpful Law Enforcement agents." The screen showed only the footage of the agent hitting Ian into The Fence. Berdin cried out but then controlled himself, unwilling to miss any of the footage or narrative. Images of Ian's electrocution flashed cruelly on the screen.

Aphek droned on: "He was put to—ah, terminated in this rather unorthodox way out of necessity, because he would not submit gracefully to the Evolutionary Quantum Leap's plan. We regret employing such measures, naturally. It could not be helped. Needless to say, the man's death was virtually instantaneous." Here the tape skipped and showed Ian's body falling from The Fence in a heap. Berdin felt hot tears melting from his eyes. He muttered angry threats.

"Doctors confirmed the success of the termination, and

the body has been donated to science." The video tape ended; Aphek reappeared on the screen. He wore a puzzled look which he seemed to think indicated regret. "One must always pause at times like these to evaluate the cause of such a tragedy. How could one man stray so far from the evolutionary path? Why would world citizens encourage his mental illness by professing to follow him, forsaking the freedom to follow their own whims? How can we avoid producing such an undeveloped being again? The answers are not easy. But as always, the EQL has provided them. Only two days ago he declared, 'Chop first, grow second.' His mandate to us is clear . . ."

Our Benevolent Liberator's speech grew murkier. Berdin's mind swam, anchored only by the small comfort that Nila had not lied. What to do? He did not want to return to the wasteland; he did not want to sleep; he did not want to think or feel. He wrestled toward a catatonic state. His mind did not re-surface until Aphek's closing statement.

" . . . danger is not entirely behind us," he was saying. "Citizens poisoned by the words of Ian still bind us to his memory. We must remain firm in our commitment to progress and freedom. We must actively discourage reactionary, close-minded rhetoric. To this end, the Evolutionary Quantum Leap has indicated that such poisoned social deviants will receive top priority in the formulation of the LiST. We *will* counter anti-evolutionary forces with force!" He showed his teeth. "We will overcome!"

CHAPTER THIRTEEN

"When sorrows like sea billows roll . . ."
—H.G. Spafford, "It Is Well with My Soul"

An early morning mist dampened Berdin's clothes and hair. The sky was gloomy with low clouds, but they were more white than grey. It looked, at least, like the weather would not worsen. Perhaps when the sun reached its peak the fogginess would burn off. Berdin opened his long-unopened, toolshed and searched for a gunnysack.

At 5 a.m. that morning he had awakened Patchett to retrieve his Field Engineer identification card. He had tried (rather weakly) to convince Patchett to return to The Field with him, but Greg had sleepily indicated that he needed more time to think. Berdin was impressed by his friend's words; the last thing he wanted was to be forced to think. He left Patchett somewhat abruptly—he didn't like to remember.

Once back in The Field, Berdin felt better. The mist

had not daunted him; indeed, he thought it appropriate. He had trudged to Bureau of Agricultural Engineering building #4 and clocked in (astounded that the higher-ups had never re-assigned his plot or revoked his ID number), and there encountered Willis. The young loafer had been complaining to another Engineer about the weather, but interrupted himself when he noticed Berdin. He greeted Berdin warmly, acting as though the truant Field Engineer was simply returning from vacation or a prolonged illness. No word was said about Ian. Willis made it clear that he'd be glad to spend time with Berdin, should the opportunity arise. Berdin left the BAE building shaking his head.

Now he was engaged in a familiar task: pulling weeds. His section had again fallen into disarray, a state of affairs which set him to grumbling in the satisfied way that fussy people with too much time on their hands like to grumble. In his heart, Berdin was relieved to see the amount of effort his section would require. Cataloging and planning his care for his plot crowded all reflection from his mind. He stuffed weeds in his gunny sack and mentally noted the steps that would have to be taken before harvest-time.

The mist thickened. Water saturated Berdin's sweatshirt and made it stick to his skin. The knees of his overalls were blackened with mud, and his red hair lay plastered on his head. Clouds had settled over the treetops, enclosing The Field within a larger dome—a strangely silent one. The whole world seemed to have closed down to the size of The Field ringed by The Fence and trees. Berdin felt profoundly alone. Drops of water clung to his eyelashes, making it difficult to see. His world appeared all greyish-white and wet green. Nothing moved except the mist. He didn't care.

"What are you doing here?" The words frightened Berdin, for many reasons beside the fact that he had not heard anyone approach. He looked for their source. He saw a tall man in a white robe standing not ten feet away.

"What—" Berdin stuttered. "Have I gone crazy?"

"That's what I'm asking you." Ian moved closer. "Have you gone crazy? Why are you here when there is so much work to do?" Ian loomed over Berdin, who was on his knees. The whiteness of Ian's robe made the clouds seem black by comparison. A real sorrow was etched on his brow. He was speaking rather sharply to Berdin.

"Is—it . . . Is it you?" Berdin reached out to Ian's robe.

Ian took a step back. "Berdin Dwate, do you love me?"

Frozen with surprise, Berdin could barely answer. "Of course."

"Then why have you abandoned my teachings? I tell you, though your courage is great, it served you poorly. Do you love me?" Ian's brow was uncreasing. His eyes—those eyes with depths and heights unmeasurable—showed a glimmer.

Berdin's natural impatience asserted itself in indignation. "'Course I love you. But you told me you wouldn't die."

The glow in Ian's eyes brightened. He lifted his arms in a shrug. "Am I dead?"

Berdin was beginning to believe his eyes. He stood and took two uncertain steps toward Ian, like a man stalking a ghost. But Ian signalled him to stop.

"You must tell me first," Ian said, with a smile playing

on the corners of his mouth, "do you love me? Do you love me more than this?" He held up the gunnysack full of weeds.

"You know I do! Search me, you know my heart." Berdin looked at his friend stubbornly.

Ian smiled. "I can tell you, then, that you are not crazy. At least no crazier than before." The two men embraced. Berdin cried uncontrolled, like a child.

"I didn't know what to believe, I'm sorry," he said.

Ian looked at him. "Now you know beyond doubt. Cling to it."

Berdin wiped his eyes and straightened his spine in an effort to look like a man prepared for such a task. He had hundreds of questions, but he stifled them. Better to take his time interrogating Ian. Unanswered questions would serve to ensure that they would have more time together.

Ian allowed Berdin to pull himself together emotionally. When the barefoot man spoke again, he was walking. "Follow me."

"Where—" Berdin began, and then remembered with whom he was speaking. He hurried to Ian's side.

"I—I saw you die with my own eyes," Berdin said.

"You shouldn't believe everything you see on the CWO." Ian paused. "But in this case, the CWO was showing real footage. Nila did not lie, as you should have known."

"You told me they couldn't kill you!"

Ian raised his arms in a second shrug. The two men drew near The Fence, and stopped.

"This is where they electrocuted me."

Berdin hung his head. "I'm sorry, Ian. You know I'm sorry. I should've—I don't know, I'm so weak . . ."

"That's past. Put your hand here, on the wire." Ian

pointed to a strand shoulder-high on The Fence.

"I don't,"

"Of course you don't want to. Now is the time for courage."

The two men looked at each other. Ian's eyes glowed brighter than Berdin had ever seen, with an expression of fiery anticipation. His gaze played a strange trick on Berdin's subconscious, reminding him of a boy he had befriended four years ago who had once presented him with a crudely-wrapped gift. The boy's eyes had glowed, too, with a certainty that Berdin would treasure the hand-made clay jar in the package. He had been right.

These murky memories further muddied Berdin's already-overwhelmed mind, so that he reached out to the wire without weighing all the possibilities. The wire stung him, but only with cold. He was grasping a piece of The Fence, between the barbs, and felt no jolt of electricity! He looked again at Ian, who was smiling broadly and rubbing his hands together.

"You didn't . . . die," Berdin said slowly, trying to solve an equation with too many variables. "But you didn't fake your death . . . or near-death or—why on earth isn't this Fence electrified?"

"The Fence *is* electrified, everywhere except here— where I died. Do not try to understand everything now, my friend. But understand this: the International Wilderness is your inheritance, as well as the inheritance of all who follow me. Someday you will climb this Fence and join me."

"Someday?"

"You have much more work to do."

"But—not in The Field?"

"Not in The Field, no. Listen. Jane Brophy is gone. That does not mean all danger is gone, but it does mean you will face only persecution, and not death for a time. In that time you, and all who follow me, must bring the news of this gateway to the Wilderness to every person designated for termination. Each morning you will read the LiST, so that you may spend the rest of the day telling those on the LiST about this place."

Berdin nodded, looking serious because Ian looked serious. "And people like Greg will help me tell people?"

"Yes. Greg already knows, as does Nila. So do others. I've not given you more work than you can handle."

"Oh no, no. I wasn't worried about that. I—hey, what if somebody doesn't believe us, or thinks they should obey the EQL and be terminated? Should we drag 'em to The Fence and make 'em hop it?" Berdin clenched his fists.

Ian looked sad. "Of course not. The International Wilderness would seem a terrible place to them—it's wild and irrefutable, you know—and they would try to return to the community over The Fence. People cannot have truth forced upon them. It would choke and sometimes kill them. Just present the opportunity to them plainly and *humbly*. People have trouble listening to know-it-alls, even when they are right."

"How will I know who to trust? I mean, how can I know which followers will help spread the word?"

"Judge their actions. Anyone can say the right words. But not everyone works to please me."

"Uh huh." Berdin shuffled his feet and looked at the ground, trying to formulate another question. He was too late. In a continuous motion so graceful that it flaunted grav-

ity, Ian climbed The Fence and alighted on the other side. He
looked at Berdin.

"Where'r you going?" Berdin's voice was whiny, like
the mole-faced conductor's.

"Home." The soft-spoken word bundled Berdin's mind
in profound emotion and noble sentiment.

The men still looked at each other.

"I mean," Berdin, almost overcome, pressed on:
"where'll you be?"

"Far away and very close." Ian threw his right arm
back, and then drew it forward in an arc toward Berdin. The
smaller man held his breath, expecting more and unwilling to
break the spell.

"We still have much to say to each other, I know," Ian
said. "But we will have plenty of time to say it later. Yes,
we'll see each other again. The day will come when we will
never be separated. But before then you'll face many trials
and some pain." His eyes penetrated Berdin. His gaze seemed
to originate across an awful gulf, reaching Berdin from an
unfathomable distance away. Oddly, the sensation comforted
Berdin. He drew strength from Ian's boundless vision, his
lower jaw jutting out.

"I'll face whatever I have ta. They can't stop me from
doin' what you say."

A faint grin showed in the wrinkles by Ian's eyes.
"Brave . . ." he said.

Berdin was smitten by Ian's affirmation, reminded of
his recent failings. He broke off eye contact with Ian and said,
"At least, they can't stop me with yer help. That is—ah, I
should just shut up and let my actions do the talkin', like you
said." Color rose in his cheeks.

Ian smiled. "Better than brave. Wise. You are learning, Berdin. I'll teach you more. Follow me." He turned and walked into the forest, melting quickly behind the rough trunks of pine.

The wiry redhead stood staring into the International Wilderness a full minute after Ian disappeared. He tried to convince himself that Ian's final words meant he should follow over The Fence, but he knew he deceived himself. Tears filled his eyes and dazed him. He turned around.

The Field sparkled with rainwater on the corn leaves and tomato vines and stalks of grain. A gentle breeze moved the green and gold. The rain had stopped; soon it would be time to harvest.

**FINALLY, CHRISTIAN FICTION
WITH SOME GUTS.**